It Rained

in

Bora Bora

By

Sylvie Short

New Generation Publishing

About the Author –

Sylvie Short

After many years in the teaching profession, Sylvie retired to East Anglia where she now concentrates on writing full time. Her other books to date are:

Novels:

The Bubble	-	published in 2009
Home to Roost	-	published in 2011
Starting Out	-	published in 2013

History:

Two Churches Together	–	a history of the small Cambridgeshire village where Sylvie grew up - published in 2013

Other books:

Short Cuts	–	a book of short stories, published in 2013, nine of which have been published by Cambridgeshire County Life.
Short Steps Along the Way	–	a book of reflections published in 2014
Short 'n' Savoury	–	a book of reflections and short stories published in 2015

Sylvie has also given several talks to various clubs and groups in East Anglia including The Cambridge Writers' Group, Probus Clubs, Village Groups and Women's Institutes. Two years ago she was the guest speaker at The Isle of Ely Federation's Literary Lunch. She recorded eight of her 'Reflections' for Radio Cambridgeshire.

For Dave ('Freddie') my travelling companion

Many thanks to Bev Housden and Lewis Bennett for their help with proof-reading and presentation

Best wishes,

(Signe)

Preface

The television flickered as I pushed the iron steadily back and forward across the never ending pile of shirts, sheets and pillow-cases. The camera panned slowly across a bay taking in the beauty of a perfect beach surrounded by a patchwork of green fields nestling beneath smoky hills. Ribbons of yellow, orange and red unfurled beneath the setting sun, gently touching the ruffled surface of the sea and the presenter continued his commentary against a background of oars being lifted and lowered rhythmically in and out of the water. Suddenly he stopped, struck by the beauty of the scene before him and, script momentarily abandoned, he let out a long sigh,

"My goodness…look at that…stunning… absolutely stunning! If that was Portugal or Spain, we'd all be raving about it, wouldn't we? But it's just Dorset….

Introduction

2.20 a.m. and lights pierce the darkness, crisp and clear; everything's still – a strange, echoing stillness as if the world has stopped turning and hangs suspended beneath those lights, waiting…waiting.

"I think I'll be happier if we go outside now," she whispers, but why is she whispering? The world is asleep. Freddie drags six cases out onto the driveway, every scratch and scrape ringing through the air, magnified in this strange world where nothing else moves.

"Open the gate." Still whispering Stella turns but nothing happens and she notices that the red lights which should operate the tall, iron gate are not glowing as they should. The taxi, due in ten minutes, will already be speeding through the darkness towards the little cottage, its driver fervently wishing he was at home asleep in his warm bed. For a moment, a very long moment, Stella is convinced that their long-awaited world cruise is about to be sabotaged by an electric gate that won't open. The whole scene flashes before her eyes with great clarity – the taxi-driver looking sympathetic and shrugging his shoulders as he climbs back into his vehicle then disappears into the night. Shame, but what can he do? And there they are, stuck securely behind their new iron gates, surrounded by cases, while he and the rest of the world are on the other side. That's how it's supposed to work, but not when there's a ship waiting to take them off for the trip of a life-time.

Stella holds her breath, says a prayer and looks in desperation towards Freddie. She is beyond words, but not quite ready for tears.

"Damn…I've switched off the electricity supply to the gate."

He dashes back into the house. Stella still can't breathe. It's going to break down…this is the unforeseen disaster…the one thing their careful planning couldn't avert.

The lights glow…the gate clicks open and together they walk slowly out into the silent street on their way to see the world.

CHAPTER ONE

Loudspeakers crackled and Rod Stewart's husky growl –
'We Are Sailin'' – blared out across the deck amid a
frenzy of arm-waving as the entertainment crew attempted
to whip up reluctant passengers into celebration mode.

"Come on people…let's go BALLISTIC…"

Tommy leapt around the edges of the swimming pool,
gyrating like a gorilla on speed, while the others jumped
down, weaving their way through the anorak-clad brigade
on the deck, smiling and pulling them up to dance.

Edie's tiny, beady eyes were everywhere. She patted a
jet black helmet of hair and pulled the bright yellow
jumper down over her large bosom as she spotted one of
the entertainers coming towards her – good looking…dark
eyes…black pony tail. That'll do me. Springing up out of
the wheel chair she thrust her walking stick at her husband,

"'ere, Stanley, 'old on ter this. I'm goin' ter dance."

She grabbed the man's hand and pulled him onto the
edge of the pool where she jigged about, waving and
grinning.

When the music stopped she pushed her way back
through the crowd, flopping into a chair, legs spread, large
chest heaving.

"I pulled, Stan, did yer see? I pulled!"

"Yes, love,"

"Eee, I'm goin' ter enjoy every minute of this creewse.
Come on Stanley, let's goo find our cabin."

Walking stick thrust out in front she cleared the way as
Stanley pushed her through the crowd.

Stella and Freddie, impressed by the enthusiasm of the
young, dynamic entertainers, did a little waving of arms
from the safety of their seats then, when the music
stopped, they turned and looked over a choppy, grey sea to
watch the shores of England disappear into the distance.
The coast line was dotted with the few remaining folk who
had lingered to watch the great ship depart and were now

shrinking to tiny specks. Stella smiled at her husband as they went below to find their cabin.

Up on deck 8 Jeannie took a swig of gin and threw the last remaining clothes into the wardrobe.

"I can't close the bloody door."

She kicked it, but it swung open again. She turned and shouted,

"Donald! I can't close this bloody wardrobe door!"

Donald, her partner for the past eighteen years, stubbed out his cigarette, pushed the clothes into the bulging wardrobe and leaned against the door. Gingerly he moved away and for a few seconds it stayed shut before swinging slowly open again. He gave up.

"You'll just have to take some of the stuff out again, that's all."

He glared angrily at Jeannie and she glared back,

"Oh yes, of course – and put it where exactly?"

She flopped down onto one of the twin beds and took another swig of gin.

"What a crappy bloody cabin,"

Donald sat on the opposite bed.

"Look, I know it's probably not as glamorous as 'The Princess Royal,' but we are getting three months and going all the way round the world for a really good price."

He tried not to sound as exasperated as he felt; the trouble was he agreed with her. What the hell were they going to do stuck on this boat for three months? There'd better be some bloody good entertainment that's for sure.

Jeannie walked out onto the tiny balcony and looked over onto the private deck below – the one designated for the people in the larger cabins with French doors and sitting rooms. She lit a cigarette and took an angry puff. 'We Are Sailin'' What was that all about? She snorted. Huh catch her dancing about with all those plebs and hugging everyone nearby. No thanks. She had grabbed Donald and got off that deck as quickly as she could. She looked at the sea, tiny grey waves flecked with white – oh well there'd be bars aplenty on those so called 'tropical paradise islands' they were visiting. She shivered, hugging her cardigan around her; at least it would be warmer than this.

"I'll 'ave some tea – no not that stuff in't pot, I'll 'ave Eeerl Greey and some 'ot water – oh yes and I'll 'ave a cheese and 'am omelette as well…with two pieces of toast."

The raucous voice demanding breakfast in a broad northern accent belonged to Gracie ('named after Gracie Fields yer know…me mam loved 'er') and startled Stella out of her reverie. She had been staring at the sea, still iron grey and choppy, while contemplating with some excitement the voyage that lay ahead. Now her attention was caught by the woman opposite – stocky, almost square, grey spiky hair and a round, puffy face with loose, coarse features. Stella smiled at her,

"It's a lovely ship, isn't it?"

The woman stared at her,

"S'alright, I've bin on better…much better."

Her mouth was wide, loose lips forming a sort of letter box shape. Stella wasn't sure how to reply, so the woman continued, warming to her theme,

"Oh yes, I were on 'The Regent Princess' last year, beautiful boat…beautiful. And in 2005 I were on the 'Queen Mary' – now that's what I call a ship – luxury…real luxury."

She paused, but failed to acknowledge the waiter by so much as a glance as he placed her tea, toast and omelette before her then, picking up her fork, she jabbed the eggs, waving her other hand in the general direction of the rest of the dining room.

"This ship is supposed to have had a refurb…well," She glanced quickly round, "I don't see a refurb…I mean…call this a refurb?"

She made a sound somewhere between a snort and a sneer, at the same time stuffing a large piece of omelette into her mouth and chewing on it sulkily, her lips occasionally parting to reveal the masticated contents within. Somewhat taken aback, Stella looked around at the gold-covered chairs, the red carpet with gold flecks – obviously brand new – and the red and gold drapes at the windows swathed in loops and tied back with gold cords finished off with rich, shining tassels. She smiled again at her companion then turned back towards the sea, sipping her tea and waiting for Freddie.

"Ladies and gentlemen…welcome to The Club…it's …SHOWTIME!!!"

Denny, the Assistant Cruise Director leapt into the centre of the small stage, all large white teeth and dark hair – spiky with blond tips and beautifully styled.

"Ladies and gentlemen have we got a show for you tonight!" With ever widening 'cheeky-chappie' grin, he told jokes while introducing the dancers and singers who strutted their stuff around the stage for the next hour.

Edie had got herself to the front of the queue for first seating at dinner then, after a few strategic jabs at the waiters with her stick and pleading delicate digestion, had insisted on being served first and was now in the centre front seat of the audience, a position she was determined to occupy for the entire cruise. She clapped loudly, 'ooooing' and 'aaahing' at the ever increasing glamorous display of sequins, glitz and feathers that passed before her.

"Eee Stanley, in't it lovely,"

Then, quite carried away with it all, she turned to the person sitting next to her,

"In't it lovely. Don't the dancers look pretty – all them sequins and stuff."

Gracie's lip curled upwards,

S'alright…the stage on 'The Regent Princess' were much bigger…."

But Edie wasn't listening; her attention had been caught by Antonio, the dancer she had 'pulled' at the sail away party. She raised her arms in the air and clapped even more loudly as he whirled his beautiful blond partner, Irma, round the stage.

"Go on, love...eee, don't 'e dance lovely..." She jabbed Stanley in the ribs with her elbow, then sat back and sighed, dreaming of dances ahead in Antonio's arms.

At the back of The Club Jeannie and Donald sat with a bottle of whisky on the table between them. It was one they had brought with them from the cut price store at home in Glasgow and they were now halfway through it using glasses they had carried out from the dining room, impervious to the disapproving looks they'd got from the Maitre d'. Being seasoned cruisers, they had all this down to a fine art, determined never to pay the bar prices, but to stock up in cut price shops at all the ports along the way.

"What a load of bloody rubbish," Jeannie leaned towards Donald, her words slurred and her head flopping onto his shoulder. He looked at his wife,

"C'mon let's go to the cabin."

He got up, grabbed the half full bottle, and then helped Jeannie to her feet, holding her elbow so she didn't fall.

"Aye... then we can have another little drinkie...and a ciggie...and drop the ash onto the snobs on the deck below."

Also at the back of The Club Freddie and Stella were sitting with their table companions from second seating, Denise, Adam, Sheila and Bernard, They were relieved to be getting on so well as they would eat dinner together for the next three months. They were also pleasantly surprised at how much they were enjoying the show until a half-drunk Scots woman trod heavily on Adam's foot as she staggered past. He moved his large bulk further back in his seat,

"Watch it, love,"

He raised his dark eyes and glared at Jeannie who glared back and the two fingers she put up wobbled perilously near his face. She tottered away and he turned to Sheila,

"Did you see that?...Did you see that Sheila? Cor, she's 'ad a skin full and no mistake. One to avoid I'd say wouldn't you? Eh…eh?"

He nudged his new friend playfully and she giggled, flushing slightly.

"Five times is equal to a mile," shouted the leader in red "T" shirt, with a turn of the head and encouraging smile. Stella and Denise walked briskly in single file with the others, trainers thudding on the deck and arms swinging as they pounded round, watching the sea and trying to get used to the still unfamiliar motion of the ship. They braced themselves against the biting wind that tore into them as they struggled around the bow before heading back towards the stern.

Adam stretched out on his bed, hands behind his head, and looked through the tiny porthole at the iron grey sea. He was longing for the days when he could bask outside on a lounger, soaking up the warming rays of the sun.

In their quite nicely appointed cabin, Sheila and Bernard were arguing. Well, Sheila was arguing, Bernard was quietly resigned to his fate.

"Bernard, you are going to come with me to bridge; you promised you would and you know you need the practice. It's embarrassing playing with our chums at the villa in France when you are constantly so appallingly bad."

Sheila had been folding a cashmere sweater that she then put carefully in a drawer. Snapping it shut, she turned to her husband,

"Well?"

"Yes, yes, of course I'll come…it…it should be fun,"

Bernard knew when he was beaten. He looked out at the grey sky above a grey sea. Would it ever turn blue? That at least would be something; and relaxing in the sunshine would be good for his legs which seemed to be getting worse. The pain was unbearable at times. He looked at Sheila, now busy with more tidying, and wondered if he would be allowed to relax in the sunshine. He watched as she embarked on yet another drawer and also wondered when they would be going up to one of the bars for a lovely hot cup of coffee. He sat down in one of the chairs to wait.

CHAPTER TWO

"Ladies and gentlemen...welcome to the beautiful island of Gibraltar."

In a clipped, clearly articulated voice, Judy Thomas, the Cruise Director, announced the arrival of 'The Matisse' at her first port of call.

Stella and Freddie clattered down the rickety steps with the others and climbed onto the waiting coach, off to see St. Michael's Cave and stop at The Apes' Den on the way back. Edie and Stanley were already ensconced on the front seat – not behind the driver, the one with the clear view – and Jeannie quickly pushed Donald onto a seat as near to the front as she could get, having told the driver they wanted to be dropped at the supermarket she had already spotted from the quay. Jeannie's first impression of this rock in the Atlantic Ocean was not favourable. She had actually made an effort and looked at the guide book where it was described as 'the gateway to the Mediterranean and one of the Pillars of Hercules.'

"So much for that," she muttered, staring out at a lump of grey rock rising from a dark, grey sea into a cloudy, grey sky. There was some mist as well – a Levanter or something, Donald had said. Never mind – supermarket here we come...all those lovely bottles of booze. No looking at boring caves or smelly apes for me.

Stella gazed in awe around the cave, part of a system of limestone caverns running like a honeycomb through the rock; and there, set amidst the shining stalagmites and stalactites, was a theatre with acoustics good enough for occasional use as a concert venue.

"They're not Apes at all, they are actually Macaque Monkeys..."the guide at the front of the coach gave his passengers information about Gibraltar after they'd left the cave and sped around the tiny island. The coach had now stopped at the Apes' Den so they could watch the antics of these monkeys, preening each other and protecting their young, sharp eyes ever alert for danger.

"They were probably introduced by British sailors and tradition says that if they die out British sovereignty of the Rock will end. Not only did Winston Churchill order that they should be well fed during World War Two, he also, apparently, introduced more!"

"Good old Winnie," whispered Freddie. He looked again at his chunky little guide book, "It says here that there were two referendums, one in 1985 then another in 2002 and both resulted in the people of Gibraltar voting overwhelmingly in favour of staying British. Ain't it good to be popular?"

But Stella was only half listening, her attention drawn to a large monkey carefully picking at the coat of the tiny, bright-eyed baby nestling against its chest.

"They seem OK, don't they...our table companions?" Stella twisted and turned in front of the small mirror in the bathroom...white trousers, black top, white jacket...suitable for informal, as opposed to casual or formal, dining. In the little cabin Freddie tucked his shirt into his trousers,

"Yes, I think we've been lucky. I was surprised when Adam told us he's an architect; I thought he looked more like the owner of a large construction company. He certainly loves his food."

Stella slipped on dangly black earrings, necklace, rings and bracelet, then back in the cabin reached into the wardrobe for her shoes. She glanced around. The cabin was small but perfectly adequate for their needs and, though in her heart of hearts she would have loved one of the larger ones with a sitting room, she was perfectly content, thrilled to be able to see the world and determined to enjoy everything that was on offer. She watched Freddie tying his tie,

"I don't think Bernard is as keen on Bridge as Sheila,"

"That, my darling, is a masterly understatement," Freddie grinned, "bit hen-pecked if you ask me. Still I think the six of us will rub along just fine. Denise is lovely and a good foil for Adam's exuberance." Freddie pulled on his shoes, "He certainly has a terrific sense of humour, couldn't stop laughing when you told us all about 'Gracie the Grimmie' and her 'call that a refurb?' comment. Honestly. What a sourpuss."

A little later at dinner they were all discussing the amazing caves when Adam suddenly raised huge bear paws in the air, silencing everyone. His dark eyes darted quickly round the table

"Cave?" He tutted in mock disgust "Call that a cave!!?" The ensuing laughter attracted the attention of several neighbouring groups of diners.

"Do you mind if we join you?" The question was delivered in a whispered growl and came from the taller of two elderly gentlemen who hovered over Stella and Freddie.

"No, of course not," Stella whispered, motioning them to sit down. The quiz had already started and they were playing for Sailaways sewing kits. This was serious stuff!

"Okay ladies and gentlemen, question number two…are you all ready now?" Tommy paused and looked round for dramatic effect.

"What are the colours of the Danish flag?"

"Ooooh, I don't know that one. What do you think?" The tall, distinguished looking gentleman turned towards Freddie.

"What was that…? What was the question?" The other man, short and quite round with very little hair and tiny pointed teeth was leaning across the table. Stella repeated the question, but he still didn't hear, while Freddie wrote down three colours.

"And the next question, ladies and gentlemen…what do you call a collection – or group – of dolphins?"

"A group of what?" The short man peered across the table, squinting through steel-rimmed spectacles.

"I'm not sure about that...I think the third colour is green, not yellow," said the tall man in a stage whisper that echoed around the Mermaid Tavern. He was pointing at the answer to the previous question. One or two people smiled and looked in their direction.

"...And question number four. Who wrote 'The Glass Menagerie?'"

"John Osborne! It was John Osborne!" Growled the tall man with a triumphant smile, pointing to where he wanted Freddie to write the answer.

"No," Stella whispered, "it was Tennessee Williams."

"Are you sure? How do know?"

"Because I was in it at College."

"Oh...OK. Better write that down then," The tall man twinkled.

"What was that? What was the question?"

The shorter man leaned in again and his friend explained, while Stella and Freddie struggled to hear the next question and missed the one after that altogether as Stella couldn't stop giggling. There were still ten questions left, so she did try to persuade them to move on and not linger so long over each answer, or at least keep their voices down, all of which added to the amusement of the people at the neighbouring tables.

At the end of the quiz, which they didn't win, they discovered that the taller of the two men, a seventy year old called Jack, had his own home in Herefordshire; while the other one, Jim, a little older at seventy five, lived in sheltered accommodation on the Welsh border.

"So, have you been friends for long?" Stella asked, the obvious rapport between them leading her to assume that they must have known each other for most of their lives.

"No," Jim grinned, "We'd never met until we got on the ship. Now we're sharing a cabin."

Jack laughed too when he saw Stella's expression then he leaned towards her,

"Yes, you see I contacted Sailaways saying that I wanted to book a world cruise but couldn't afford to pay the single occupancy supplement, so the Company set about finding a cabin mate for me. They contacted me a few weeks later with Jim's address, so we wrote to each other and sent photos, but only actually met the day the ship sailed."

"But we're determined to make it work," chuckled Jim with a throaty laugh that showed his row of tiny pointed teeth and made his cheeky round face look more impish than ever. Jack smiled and nodded.

CHAPTER THREE

"There's one missing."

The guide counted again and frowned,

"It's Kieran. I think he went to the shop. Shall I goo an' ge' 'im?"

Nancy looked at the guide who nodded, her lips drawn into a thin line and her face an inscrutable mask, hiding the irritation she felt towards the one member of the party who had failed to obey the strict instruction to return to the meeting point by 12.30. She had made it quite clear there were other places to see and time was limited. Nancy hurried off towards a distant shop, the only one in the area, and it was in the opposite direction from where the coach was waiting. Everyone's eyes followed her and Freddie stamped his feet impatiently, muttering,

"All those who can't tell the time…stay on the ship."

Stella watched Nancy disappear into the shop. She had seen her around the ship and knew that she was from South Shields and had come on the trip alone. She was a friendly, attractive young woman with bright eyes and long, dark hair, and Stella had a bet with Freddie that she wouldn't be on her own for long. Kieran had already managed to sit with her at tea time and Wayne Bradley, a singer with the professional entertainers, had gazed at her while crooning a love song into the microphone. The answering sparkle from her eyes as she gazed back was caught in the lights from the stage. Stella thought he was rather wet looking with a pasty-face, and she didn't think much of his voice either.

Inside the shop, Kieran was lost in the description he had found of Domus Romana, the museum they had just visited:

'…a fine town house built within the Roman city of Melitae circa 200 BC…'

He took off his dark-rimmed spectacles and gazed upwards, picturing again the exquisite mosaics he had seen in several of the rooms…so delicate, an effect achieved with the use of miniature tesserae. Maybe he could try that in his studio back home in Ireland…would they sell…?

"Kieran, you'd better come, love, everyone's waiting on you."

The clanging of the shop door and Nancy's voice had the effect of jolting Kieran out of his reverie. He jumped and the book he was holding dropped to the floor. Nancy picked it up and replaced it on the shelf just as the shop-keeper appeared. She smiled at him, at the same time dragging Kieran towards the door by his sleeve. He quickly replaced his glasses and followed her out, giving a little wave and stammering his thanks to the man in the shop.

"Did you lose track of time, love? Come on we'd better hurry…everyone's waiting and the guide's not best pleased. Malta's nice, isn't it? We're off to a silent city now…I can't imagine that, can you…being silent all the time?"

Nancy rattled on not waiting for a response, and Kieran followed. He could have told her that it didn't mean they couldn't speak while they were there, but the words just wouldn't come. He ran his hands through his mop of thick, dark hair and watched Nancy's hips swaying from side to side in front of him. She turned occasionally to make sure he was keeping up before hurrying on, and Kieran thought he'd never seen anyone so lovely in all his life.

"Not even one word of apology. So that's an example of Irish manners is it?"

Freddie looked in disgust towards the mop of wild hair sticking up above the back of the seat where Kieran was sitting with Nancy beside him.

"Never mind that now, we're here. Look…Mdina. Come on, Freddie, let's go."

Stella followed him out of the coach and they stood gazing up at the archway above the city gate where, among the intricate decorations carved in soft, golden stone, stood statues of St. Paul, Publius, a Roman Governor and St. Agatha, an early martyr. The guide pointed'

"...and the Apostle Paul healed Publius who was so impressed by this that he converted to Christianity."

They all followed as she click-clacked into the silent city, so called because no motor vehicle traversed the ancient cobbled streets, their tranquillity broken only by groups of pedestrians and the clip-clopping of pretty horse-drawn carts. They walked along the narrow pedestrian roadways winding between beautiful, cream-coloured stone buildings and Stella was reminded of a set from a Shakespearian play. She looked up at the dark green, wrought iron balconies, some of them entwined with geraniums in terracotta pots, and half expected Juliet to appear at any moment.

There were some shops selling lace and one with an abundance of fruit spilling out onto the cobbles in pale wicker baskets. Edie, who had been pushed around the museum by the ever-patient Stanley, had relented at the sight of the cobbles and was 'struggling along' with the aid of her stick. Freddie noted that the expression on her face clearly showed that she believed her effigy would one day grace the archway with the other martyr, though that place should, of course, rightfully be claimed by Stanley. She had stopped and was handling the fruit,

"Ooooh, Stanley, let's buy some of these. I do love a nice juicy pear."

Freddie managed to turn his bark of laughter into a cough before nodding towards Edie's large, top heavy mass, nudging Stella and whispering,

"I think Stanley does too!"

"What about that Mosta Church...Eh?,,, Eh?" Adam leaned towards Sheila, "What did you think of that then?"

"Oh, absolutely beautiful." She replied in a voice Stella had already decided was classic girls' boarding-school. "I loved all the pale blue, cream and gold – it was dedicated to the Virgin Mary, you know, the colours are in her honour."

"Yes, but what about that bomb, Sheila? Did you read the story about the bomb?" Adam leaned back on the small gold and red chair which creaked ominously. He looked round the table waiting until he had everyone's attention.

"On 9th April 1942 a bomb dropped through that elaborately decorated ceiling, fell onto the floor..." Pause for dramatic effect "...But didn't detonate! This was a miracle." He leaned forward, "because there was a service taking place at the time and if it had – exploded that is – several hundred people would have been killed. But what it did do was S-L-I-D-E" – he zoomed one of his large bear paws above the table to indicate sliding – "across the floor before coming to rest, and no-one was even injured! You can still see the place where the bomb pierced the dome."

Bernard looked up and said quietly,

"If you go into the Sacristy, there's a photograph of it – and even a replica of the original bomb."

But Adam wasn't listening; he was signalling to the waiter,

"Miguel...is there any more of that pangasi? It's beauooootiful!"

CHAPTER FOUR

Having completed a couple of laps round the deck to fill his lungs with sea air, Freddie was sitting quietly by himself enjoying an early morning cup of coffee and trying to imagine it was, at last, getting a little warmer. He had helped himself to his drink which was always provided for the 'early birds' out on deck. He could have had tea instead as there was a large, shallow rectangular tray full of good quality tea bags and, of course, a machine that dispensed boiling water.

He was quite alone on the deck and partially hidden from the drinks area by some steps when he suddenly noticed a furtive movement out of the corner of his eye. Remaining perfectly still, he watched through the slats of the steps as a strange-looking man in steel-rimmed glasses and a flowered hat with a small, floppy brim sauntered towards the coffee machine. He was glancing surreptitiously around then when he reached the machine he stood for a moment before, still looking from side to side, he suddenly whipped a plastic bag out of his pocket and, believing he was unobserved, began stuffing it with a large quantity of tea bags. A member of staff appeared and started to sweep the deck at which point the thief hastily knotted the bag and scuttled away. Freddie grinned as he could already imagine Adam's loud laughter as this was relayed at dinner that evening.

"Good morning, ladies and gentlemen...can you all hear me?"

"We can hear you...it's seeing you that's the problem," muttered Freddie as he and Stella, together with a room full of other passengers, all craned their necks towards the front of The Club where Isobel, the diminutive port lecturer, was half hidden behind a large microphone. Lively, but watery, blue eyes looked out from where soft skin and wrinkles still held traces of a once pretty face. Her back had a permanent stoop and she was now bent over the microphone tapping it fiercely and only stopped when the assembled company assured her they could hear her perfectly. This little pantomime was to be the pre-curser to all her lectures.

"What do you reckon…77…78…?"

Stella nodded, agreeing with Freddie's estimate of her age.

Isobel smiled and pushed back a curl of white hair from above her right eye.

"Ladies and gentlemen, I would like to liven up the rather dull stuff by starting with a little joke…if I may." She paused, looked round and cleared her throat,

"A man's canary dies and he misses it dreadfully as it was a terrific singer and cheered him up all day long with its beautiful song. He went along to a pet-shop and asked to buy another one, stressing that it must be a good singer. The shop-keeper duly obliged and sold him a bird with a fantastic voice. However, when the man got outside he noticed that the bird only had one leg, so he went back into the shop and complained. 'Make up your mind,' said the shop-keeper, 'do you want a singer or a dancer?'"

Everyone laughed and clapped, Stella and Freddie agreeing that this not particularly brilliant joke was only funny because it had been told by such a serious, modest little lady. The lecture, all about Cairo, far from being 'dull stuff' was very interesting. Cairo itself was to be a shock to the system.

In the front seat of the coach Edie wriggled and squirmed, turning this way and that,

"'ow much longer are we goin' ter be drivin' through this desert…? And what on earth are all them lorries doin' up on them poles? Stanley, ask the guide why there's lorries up on poles at the side of the road."

Obediently Stanley looked round for the guide, but she was further down the coach attending to some of the other passengers. It didn't matter; by the time he'd turned and faced the front again Edie had forgotten all about lorries on poles. She looked across the aisle to where the armed guard was sitting directly behind the driver, then peered again out of the front window. As she was in the front seat of the first coach in the convoy of six she had a clear view of the police car escorting them to the city.

"What a palaver, eh Stanley escorted through Port Said like that with all the traffic held up in them side roads until we'd passed," she nudged her husband, "Eee, now I know what the Beckhams feel like." She looked out of the window again, "'Ow much longer in this flamin' desert?"

"Now my pharaohs, you must all call me 'Mama' as, for today, you are very special…my special children, and I'm going to look after you as though you were my very own precious infants."

The guide, an attractive, fleshy and fairly flamboyant lady, her dark hair wrapped in a long white scarf and wearing some heavy, gold jewellery with white tunic and trousers, flashed a huge smile down the coach. Jim smiled back showing his row of little pointy teeth and Jack, sitting next to him, growled,

"I'm a bit long in the tooth to be anyone's precious infant."

"She's nice, though, isn't she," Jim took off his little steel-rimmed glasses, polished them and put them back on, hoping that would give him a clearer view of Mama. But Jack's attention was elsewhere. They'd been on the ship for ten days now and for the last five of those he'd been noticing one particular lady among the passengers. He'd found out that her name was Chrissie and he was certain she was travelling alone, though she seemed to be making friends quite quickly – not surprising really; although she was quite elderly, probably late sixties he thought, she was vivacious and bubbly. Tall, elegant and well-dressed, she stood out from the crowd, but there was nothing stand-offish about her. Every evening he watched her at the pre-dinner dance sessions waltzing around and laughing with the other passengers, male and female, as they were partnered by the entertainment staff.

He could see her now, sitting just across the aisle from him next to a rather odd lady who also joined in with the dancing sessions, but stubbornly refused to do any steps other than line dancing. Whatever the music, it could all be 'achy-breaky heart,' as far as Margie was concerned as, hands on hips, she skipped out her line dancing steps. And skipping it was, as she didn't press down through her feet to give the steps the weight they needed. She usually had a small group of spectators watching this 'performance' but seemed oblivious to everyone around her, often dancing quite alone in the middle of the stage, trying to fit her hops and skips to totally inappropriate music.

"My dancing is my life," Jack had heard her say to Chrissie, in a lugubrious voice with an unmistakeably Cornish accent. They were queuing for tea and he had managed to manoeuvre himself in close behind them, "I just want to have fun," She continued, "I'm a fun person, me. Everyone knows that."

The dry desert, bare and devoid of life apart from a few tufts of grass and sparse bushes, gradually gave way to a city street, and Stella couldn't believe what she was seeing. Shabby cars, nose to tail and all vying for position, were weaving in and out, sounding their horns to warn other road users they were coming through regardless. She watched with open mouth as they somehow managed to avoid pedestrians wandering across the road as though protected from harm by an invisible barrier. Feet, knees and arms hung out of battered old camper vans, and she stared in further disbelief at one vehicle with people all standing on the outside of it, clinging on as it careered precariously through the traffic.

"Look at all that rubbish...and the piles of rubble...oh, and those buildings! Could they be any uglier?"

Freddie turned to look with her at the houses, square at the base then built up into cuboids of red brick with metal rods sticking out where the roof should be as though the top had been knocked off. He felt Mama brush past him,

"What's the story with the houses?"

She leaned over him, all warm flesh and exotic perfume.

"They are unfinished; quite often a family will start to build a house then run out of money and be forced to stop until they have more funds. You will notice, too, that many of them are without windows. This is because no tax has to be paid until windows are added."

She smiled and swept on down the bus in a scented cloud. Stella continued to stare out of the window at the strange array of houses; she touched Freddie's arm,

"Look...look! How on earth do they even manage to get to them? There doesn't seem to be a plan, they are all just plonked anywhere, crammed in on top of each other,"

She twisted around in her seat, craning her neck to see if there was any access – a road or even just a path – to some of the buildings squeezed together in a totally arbitrary fashion, but she couldn't see any.

Chrissie stood and gazed at Tutankhamen's famous blue and gold death mask. She was blown away.

"The quality of this piece of work is absolutely staggering isn't it? Much brighter and more exquisitely fashioned than can ever be shown in any of the photographs or reproductions."

"Yes, it's very nice," said Margie, fanning herself with her straw hat and wishing the museum had air conditioning. She felt quite disgruntled. You wait for the weather to warm up and when it does it's too flipping hot. She trailed after Chrissie who was now staring at something called 'treasures.' They had been found in the tomb, dull gold objects and strange dog-like creatures, that didn't look at all like treasure to Margie. She leaned forward, screwing up her eyes as she looked at some old, grainy black and white pictures of a man called Howard Carter standing at the mouth of the tomb surrounded by some of these objects. It said he had discovered and retrieved these things from the tomb in 1922. Chrissie pointed at the collection,

"What an amazing number and variety of treasures and jewels they unearthed from the final resting place of this young, relatively minor King." She paused, "One can only wonder what must have lain alongside the greater Pharaohs before their tombs were robbed."

Margie nodded,

"Can we go outside now, I'd love an ice-cream – even though it won't be as good as the ones we have in Cornwall."

The buffet lunch was very good, eaten in the vast dining room of a five star hotel within sight of the Pyramids at Giza. Stella took in the palatial surroundings: red and gold wallpaper, a thick red carpet and everything bathed in the glow from very large, exquisite chandeliers, heavy with huge crystal drops – 'and somehow,' she thought, 'incongruous…at odds…with the poverty in the streets outside. Let's just hope that by being here we're helping the country's economy.'

All six coach loads of passengers from 'The Matisse' were seated at round tables and still the huge room didn't look crowded. Red-coated waiters moved swiftly and silently between tables looking after everyone's needs, and more waiters stood behind the long tables laden with food, ensuring all the guests got exactly what they wanted.

Adam and Denise were sitting with people they hadn't met before, most of whom seemed pleasant and were happily chatting about everything they'd seen. A contented smile spread slowly across Adam's face as he contemplated his large plate, overflowing with food. Chewing happily, he looked up and noticed the woman opposite him pushing the food around her plate with an expression on her face like a slapped bottom. Her equally miserable-looking companion, possibly husband he surmised, was eating a little more than her but both kept their heads down and didn't speak to anyone. At the end of the meal they all got up to leave and Adam stared as the man stuffed four bread rolls into his pockets; the woman put two oranges and two bananas into her handbag and they both helped themselves to one each of the spare bottles of water on the table. Adam leaned across towards them,

"Expecting to get a bit peckish on the way back, are you?" He said with a smile, curious to know what the rationale could be for such odd behaviour. The man scowled and grunted,

"Yeah…well, it's a long time till dinner, ain't it mate?"

Adam waited until they'd gone then looked at Denise who had also been watching this little pantomime.

"Pigs," he snorted in disgust, at the same relishing the thought of relaying the incident at the dinner table that evening.

Edie trudged across the uneven ground, jabbing her stick down into the sandy tufts and leaning heavily on Stanley, who was looking up at the great pyramid of Kheops and trying, like everyone else who had ever stood there, to work out just how it had been made. In his free hand, the one that hadn't been commandeered by Edie, he was holding the guide book:

"…. Two million 2½ ton blocks were, in all likelihood, tugged along mudbrick ramps on sledge-like rockers…"

Nope! Stare as he might, he just didn't get it. Next to him Edie was counting:

"…..seven…eight…nine. Nine. I can see nine pyramids altogether, Stanley."

"You ride…you ride…you buy post cards."

Suddenly they were surrounded by the pyramid mafia, pushing and jostling, pestering them to buy post cards or go for a camel ride out into the desert. Edie looked at the beast nearest to her, snorting and baring its teeth, and suddenly made up her mind,

"Stanley, I want ter goo on a camel ride. Come on."

Stick forgotten, she marched up to the very swarthy-looking man holding the camel's rope and shouted,

"'Ow much?"

His white teeth gleamed,

"Twenty dollar…only twenty dollar for lovely lady like you."

Edie turned back to her husband,

"Well that's worth it to show everyone back 'ome. 'Ere, give us twenty dollars, Stanley… and when I'm oop there make sure you take me picture."

The man was bustling around her, hand held out for her money and a huge, smarmy grin on his face, at the same time persuading the camel to kneel. Just as Edie was about to heave her vast bulk onto the waiting animal, assisted still by the obsequious, over attentive minder, Mama came rushing up. She grabbed the camel rope with one hand and Edie's arm with the other, separating the two, then she turned to the man who was glaring at her, his face like thunder. They jabbered away furiously in their own language, shouting and gesticulating at each other, while Edie stood looking like a child who's had a treat whipped cruelly away.

"Did you give him any money?" Mama asked her.

"Well…no, not yet."

"Good."

She turned back to the man and dismissed him by clapping and flapping her hands, then watched as he stomped sulkily away. Edie took a deep breath and addressed Mama,

"Why were I not allowed ter goo on t'camel?" She demanded, poking the guide on the arm. "You've infringed me 'uman rights!"

Mama was still cross.

"I told you all as we left the hotel on no account to get on the camels. They charge you one price here, then take you out into the desert and refuse to bring you back until you give them more money." She turned to the rest of the group, who had all gathered round to see what the fuss was about, and clapped her hands again,

"Come now. We go to the Great Sphinx," and with that she led the way to where poor old 'no nose' was nestling quite close to the Great Pyramid. It was with some difficulty that Stanley persuaded Edie not to go straight back to the coach.

They all stood staring at the giant sandy sculpture, familiar since childhood from the pictures in history books, but awesome in reality, the facial disfigurement lending pathos in its imperfection to an otherwise grandiose work rising from the desert sand.

Jack had managed to edge his way through the crowd until he was standing very close to Chrissie. He risked a quick glance sideways and saw that she was enraptured at the sight, breathing gently, her lips a little parted. She moved slightly and he became aware of her perfume, not the overpowering scent that had wafted over him as Mama passed by in the coach that morning, but a subtler, flowery fragrance that he found utterly enchanting. He cleared his throat,

"Amazing isn't it?"

She turned and smiled,

"Oh yes, absolutely amazing."

Seizing his advantage Jack continued,

"It was sculpted in the image of Pharaoh Khephren to guard his tomb, but was hidden from sight for thousands of years…the desert sands had drifted over it…"

He stopped and looked down, afraid that he may be sounding like one of those boring old know-it-alls, but as he glanced up again Chrissie was looking at him and she seemed interested, the warmth of her smile encouraging him to continue.

"Thutmose IV had the sand cleared away to reveal the huge beast because he had been told in a dream that he would only become Pharaoh if he did so."

"Oh really…I must have missed that bit in the guide book," Chrissie grabbed the chunky little volume from her bag and flipped through the pages,

"But look, this is interesting…it's about how he lost his nose…it says that three thousand years later the Mameluke Turks shattered the statue's nose by using it for target practice. Honestly, can you imagine? They wouldn't get away with that today."

"No indeed."

Mama was beckoning so they all started to follow her back towards the coach. There were crowds of other tourists as well as their own party, but Jack managed to stay close to Chrissie. Suddenly she stopped,

"Oh look…it's like…like a film set,"

She was laughing and pointing as a line of five camels, topped by their colourful cloths and riders, suddenly ran across in front of them. With the sun, pyramids and Sphinx behind and the crowds jostling all around, Jack could see exactly what she meant.

"Yes…maybe a clapperboard will suddenly appear and we'll hear a director barking orders…"

"…come on crowds…more jostling please. Fifth camel keep up with the rest…" She finished off and they both laughed.

A little way behind Margie was telling Jim all about herself. She had already covered the childhood in Cornwall, her job in local government, (which meant she worked in the town hall near where she had lived all her adult life – still in Cornwall, of course), and had now reached the part where Raymond had asked her to marry him.

"…And we bin married now for nearly forty years. We get on well enough, but he likes to stay at home…has his model railway, see…he loves his model railway. Always buying and building new bits for it and now we got a little grandson, well he says it's for him, of course, but me and my daughter know differently. Still…keeps him happy, and he don't mind me coming away like this…I'm a fun person see, everyone knows that, and I love me line dancing…you probably seen me doing it in the evenings. Nothing keeps me from me dancing."

By the time they reached the coach steps Jim could see exactly why Raymond chose to stay at home with his model trains.

Back on the coach safely ensconced next to Stanley in her accustomed seat at the front, Edie felt tired. She stretched her stumpy little legs out as far as she could and sighed then looked out again at that blessed desert they had to cross before they reached 'The Matisse.' She closed her eyes and thought about the cool comfort of her air-conditioned cabin – and then dinner. She was hungry; it had been a long time since lunch in that fancy hotel and, although mollified to some extent by the visit to the bazaar where she had bought some nice little souvenirs – mainly for herself – she was still smarting from her treatment by that guide over the missed camel ride. Honestly, what a fuss. That foreign man had been really nice. Edie opened her eyes as she had a sudden thought. 'That guide (Edie refused to call her 'Mama') was probably jealous, yes that was it. Done up like a dog's dinner in all that white gear she didn't like it because I was getting all the attention. I think I might go and complain when we get back.'

With that thought in her head she glanced at Stanley, nodding beside her. He probably wouldn't let her complain – he could be really bossy at times – well she would see about that. With one final glance at the offending desert and a quick check to be sure the armed guard and police escort were still in place, Edie closed her eyes and dozed.

It was an irresistible, attention-grabbing, opening gambit and Adam waited until everyone was quietly seated before leaning over,

"Teh…What?? Call that a pyramid???"

He threw back his head and roared with laughter; the rest joined in.

"Seriously though, guys…what did you think? Wasn't it a fantastic day eh…eh?"

He leaned his large body towards Sheila.

"What did you think, Sheila? What about that Sphinx eh? And the lunch…beauoooootiful!!"

It was just as he was finishing the huge steak on his plate, a blissful look on his face and a large forkful nearing his mouth, that he remembered the incident at lunch time and entertained them all with the tale of the disappearing bread rolls and fruit.

"Pigs! – Honestly can you believe such behaviour?"

Miguel cleared away the plates and Stella smiled as she listened to Adam ordering a double portion of cheese and biscuits to follow his ice-cream.

They had all been discussing the terrible hassling they had experienced at the pyramids and, placing a morsel of cheese onto his carefully buttered biscuit, Bernard looked thoughtful before saying quietly,

"You know, I couldn't help thinking that if those men were properly organised they could make a fortune. Someone should take the trouble to explain that we English just don't respond to such 'in your face' poking and prodding, that we won't be bullied into parting with our money and they would do well. After all we've got money to spend, they know that, and many of us would love to ride a camel and be photographed doing so with the pyramids in the background, but not at the risk of being robbed."

They all agreed.

Later that night in his cabin Jack could hear Jim gently snoring in the adjacent twin bed while he tossed and turned, trying to sleep, but the memory of a warm fragrant scent, soft, clear skin, pale blue eyes and a merry laugh kept him awake well into the night.

CHAPTER FIVE

Stretched out on the sun lounger with her eyes closed, Chrissie was feeling very relaxed and contented. Her long, white hair was twisted up into a casual top-knot and hidden by the huge, black straw hat that also shaded her face, the brim balanced over large sun glasses. Every so often she lifted the hat to enjoy the scenery as they drifted along through the Suez Canal. On this side it was Egypt and, earlier on, she had stood by the ship's rail on the other side where, she had been informed by the guide book, the landscape was Sinai. How fascinating. After they had left Port Said and entered the Canal they had passed through the Small Bitter Lake and then into the Great Bitter Lake where they had anchored for six hours to await the passing of the Northbound convoy which, apparently, always took priority.

Margie had been with her but, bored by all the hanging about and feeling 'too flippin' hot,' had gone back to her cabin for a while. Chrissie had to admit she was relieved, grateful for the respite. She sighed. Oh dear, she didn't want to hurt Margie, but was already beginning to feel quite worn down by her dour monologues, all centred on her model-train-mad husband, Raymond, daughter, Elizabeth, ('but we call her Lizzie – always have done, ever since she was a toddler,') and, of course, the adored grandson, Kevin. The trouble was Chrissie was a good listener and Margie had latched on to this, not really pausing to wonder why her glamorous new friend didn't say much about her own life.

Chrissie had no desire to talk about her past; in fact she had come away precisely to avoid dwelling on the circumstances that had led up to her nursing Maurice for the last three and a half years of his life even though he had left her six years before. She closed her eyes again, remembering that awful day when, after thirty five years of happy – (or so she thought) – marriage, Maurice had dropped the bombshell. It was classic – '…bored…in a

31

rut…I am so very sorry…it's just that Shelley and I have to be together…so sorry…' and then the fillip in the finale – '…I just don't love you any more.' She had put her hands over her ears and shouted for him to stop as he'd gone on, falteringly trying to explain – '…well, it's not that I don't love you, darling…it's just that I'm 'in love' with Shelley…'

'Shut up…stop…stop…' Chrissie didn't want to know. It didn't matter. He was going, he was leaving, deserting her, Amber and Sarah and going off with Shelley who, of course, was much younger and very beautiful. The girls were a great comfort and, along with Chrissie, could see exactly what had happened '– honestly if you wrote it for a woman's mag, they wouldn't print it it's such a cliché – aging bloke worried he's losing his looks, very flattered by the attention of younger, very attractive woman, can't believe he's pulled – does she really love him? – Male menopause. Capturing lost youth etc…etc..'

Amber had stormed about the kitchen, running her fingers through her thick red hair, furious with her dad for his behaviour while Sarah had sat quietly with Chrissie, an arm around her mum's shoulders.

"He's a cliché…a walking bloody cliché!"

Then she had flung herself down on the sofa, the other side of Chrissie, and burst into tears.

Chrissie had hugged her younger, fierier daughter and then tried – yes, she had actually tried – to excuse his behaviour. They'd had a good life together as a family and, in spite of everything, she didn't want him to lose his daughters. Amber was up on her feet again,

"You must be bloody joking. I'm not seeing him – and I'm definitely not seeing HER!"

And then when Maurice had been diagnosed with cancer and the doctors had said there was nothing they could do, Shelly had tearfully declared that she couldn't cope. It was Chrissie who had found him alone in the tiny flat in town and brought him home, Chrissie who said she would look after him and Chrissie who had told Amber, very firmly, of her decision,

"We had thirty five good years together, I'm going to see it through, Amber. Please try and understand."

And to her surprise Amber had taken her into her arms and hugged her then, instead of objecting, had said quietly,

"OK mum. And I'll be here for you when things get tough."

Which, of course, they did; but Chrissie was there at the end holding Maurice's hand when he died. She told him she loved him, because the truth was, she had never stopped loving him. His vitality and zest for life had given her the happiest years she had ever known.

But now it was all over and when she had told Amber and Sarah that she was going off round the world they had given her their blessing.

Up on deck 8 Jeannie was furiously scrubbing her smalls in the tiny bathroom sink.

"I'm buggered if I'm paying those laundry prices, I'll manage just fine in here," She'd told Donald earlier.

Knowing that she would 'manage fine,' but also knowing that the effort would bring on a spate of very bad temper, Donald had made for the door.

"I'll just go down for a swim in the wee pool,"

Jeannie snorted,

"Rather you than me. It's not a pool, it's a pathetic excuse for a pool."

"Well, anyway…will I see you for a drink in the Sky Bar afterwards? They've got a Happy Hour there."

He knew that would please her, and she liked the Sky Bar as it was the only place on 'this God-forsaken ship' where they could smoke.

"OK then. As long as you don't expect me to stand and gawp at the muddy canal we're going through."

"Oh no. I'll see you then."

"Aye."

Squeezing out the last pair of pants, Jeannie rummaged at the top of a tiny cupboard, cursing as several things fell out onto her head, until she found what she was looking for. She fixed her scanty panties and small bras onto the circular dryer with some tiny pegs and dangled it over the balcony, then throwing her cigarettes into her bag she went to join Donald in the Sky Bar, glad the chores were over for the day.

On the private deck below, Colin, a retired CEO of a large company, was sun-bathing in one of the superior loungers supplied exclusively for that area. His wife, Venetia, was in the sitting room keeping cool. They were a pleasant couple, already christened 'Indiana Jones and his wife' by Adam on account of the expensive-looking, but impressively battered, hat that Colin often wore. Colin's eyes were closed when he felt the first drop of what he thought must be rain, then something brushed past his cheek. He opened his eyes to see Jeannie's smalls circling in front of him.

Waking from a doze in her sun-lounger on the main deck, Chrissie became aware of a voice nearby:

"...and it extends for 117 miles from Port Said to Port Suez, reducing the route from Western Europe to India by almost 5000 miles. It's 507 feet wide and can admit vessels with a draught of up to 53 feet. It takes a ship 15 hours to pass through..."

Nancy, listening as Kieran read out this information from the guide book with earnest expression and furrowed brow, was beginning to think it must surely be much longer. She saw Chrissie looking at them and made a face, crossing her eyes and stretching her mouth up at one corner and down at the other. Chrissie smiled while Kieran, unaware of this exchange, cleared his throat and continued,

"...You know, this is really interesting. It says, 'the construction of an earlier canal, begun by Ramses 11 from 1298 to 1235 BC was said to have killed some 120,000 men. The canal in its present form was begun in 1859 by the French Engineer, Ferdinand de Lesseps and inaugurated ten years later by Empress Eugenie of France. In 1956 it was nationalised then closed from 1967 to 1975 because of Egyptian-Israeli hostilities."

He took off his glasses and looked up. Nancy was asleep.

Chrissie smiled to herself. Oh dear, the poor smitten young man was going to have to try a different tack if he wanted to win the heart of our lass from South Shields. She had chatted to Nancy a couple of times and found her very pleasant, but not the sharpest knife in the drawer. Now if he'd regaled her with the tale Isobel had told during her lecture about the Suez Canal he might have fared better. Apparently de Lesseps' Suez Canal project succeeded when all the previous ones had failed owing to his discovery that Egypt's ruler, Said Pasha, had a passion for spaghetti. This had developed when he was a boy, but he was forbidden by his father, Mohammed Ali, to eat it. Ferdinand became a firm favourite with the Egyptian ruler by inviting him to clandestine pasta binges, so while Said grew fat on pasta, de Lesseps got his shares in the Suez Canal.

CHAPTER SIX

Out of the Suez Canal, through the Gulf of Suez during the night then, at 8 o'clock the following morning, 'The Matisse' docked at Sharm El Sheikh on the Southern tip of the Sinai Peninsular.

Stella and Freddie were up on deck, leaning side by side against the rail in the blazing sunshine to watch as, one by one, a flotilla of small, white boats, moored in a nearby semi-circular bay, made their way out to sea.

"Most probably taking guests from the smart hotels out for a day of water sports."

Stella looked round to see that Jack had joined them at the rail and, shading his eyes with the guide book, was pointing towards the departing boats. He took the book away from his forehead and looked down at it.

"It says here that until 1967 this place was merely a small outpost used by customs men to watch for smugglers, but its potential as a holiday resort was recognised and developed so that today it has an airport, hotels and facilities to enable tourists to take full advantage of the beaches and underwater delights. It's probably the best known beach resort on the Gulf of Aqaba."

Stella smiled, delighted to feel the warm sun against her back and excited about the day ahead.

"Freddie and I are off on a 'glass-bottomed boat experience.' What are you and Jim up to?"

"The same. We'll probably see you there. I wouldn't imagine the boats are very big."

The nearby resort of Na'ama Bay was described as "…an idyllic setting with clear turquoise sea lapping the sandy, picturesque coves against the glorious backdrop of the Sinai Mountains," but Stella was finding it hard to fit this description to the uninviting scene before her. She picked her way carefully across hot sand packed with people in various states of undress, some wandering about and others looking bored as they tried to find shelter from the intense heat. Children cried, threw sand and licked ice-creams; while the shallow water provided a cool, temporary refuge for bodies baked by the sun.

Pleased that they were not expected to linger here, Stella and Freddie, with the rest of the group, followed their guide straight out along a strange walkway made from what looked like empty, blue plastic water containers and onto a boat. They all sat around the glass bottom, leaning against a rail provided for that purpose, and waited for the trip to begin. Stella watched a few bright yellow and blue fish swimming in desultory fashion below her and pointed them out to Freddie, but didn't get over excited as she realised that the real delights were still to come.

They were off, speeding along the coast, blue water churning below and the noise of the engine quite deafening. Then it stopped, suddenly silent, the boat rocking to a standstill at what must be a place known to the skipper as a good one for spotting fish to delight the eyes of tourists. And it was. The boat swayed gently while the water cleared and everyone stared down through the glass as the space below gradually became filled with a fascinating array of many-coloured fish, swimming about like bright jewels in a corralled landscape. Yellow, blue, black, multi-coloured, striped – they dived down towards the sea-bed or stared up at them, mouths slowly opening and closing, goggle-eyes swivelling. There were many different shapes and sizes, some the length of an arm while the smallest measured less than a finger; and their movements varied accordingly. Stella watched, mesmerised, as the tiniest of them jerked and juddered along, flicking their tails; while the largest meandered through the water with little apparent effort.

"You can swim if you like," a smiling, brown-bodied boy announced from the cabin doorway, but this was greeted with a general groan of disappointment as they hadn't been told it would be an option. Only Jack stood up and followed the lad, smiling at everyone as he went. He had been sitting with Jim on the side of the square around the glass bottom to the right of Stella and Freddie. Looking to her left Stella noticed Chrissie and Margie sitting directly opposite the two elderly men. Chrissie's eyes followed Jack's progress towards the door, but she quickly looked down as he turned to smile at her. Margie whispered something in Chrissie's ear and, getting up, made her way around the square to Jack's empty space next to Jim.

Stella looked down through the clear water and saw Jack, in snazzy blue trunks and equipped with mask and snorkel, swim in leisurely fashion into the space directly below them. He was immediately engulfed by a shoal of fearless fish that seemed to think he may have been food. Discovering he wasn't, they dispersed and Jack looked up, treading water and waving. Glancing to her left Stella noticed that Chrissie's hand had shot to her mouth in alarm at the appearance of the fish, but she was now waving and smiling to the figure below. Freddie laughed, still watching Jack,

"Came prepared – that's his army training."

"Well what about you, ex-military man?" Stella teased, "You didn't bring your trunks – or mask and snorkel,"

"No…well, I'm really in holiday mode now. Can't be thinking as well as relaxing. Besides, I don't need to impress you, do I? Not after nearly forty years."

The both looked down to where Jack was tumbling in the water watched by a smiling Chrissie.

Stella nudged her husband in the ribs,

"Oh I don't know, it wouldn't go amiss."

Jack disappeared from view and there was a lull on the boat as everyone waited for the return journey along the coast to begin. To their right Stella and Freddie became aware of a monotonous droning and caught the odd word or two of Margie's monologue "…Oh Kevin would have loved all them coloured fishes, he would…often take him out, we do....loves his nanny and granddad ...only five and reading already...really clever his teacher says..."

Freddie looked at Jim's face,

"I hope the Skipper starts the engine soon; I think Jim's about to throw himself overboard."

Back at the beach the sand was burning beneath their feet and it was more crowded than ever. The guide decided it was too hot even to visit the few shops at the side of the road, so she shepherded everyone quickly back onto the air-conditioned coach.

"This is the most mind-numbingly boring boat I've ever been on!"

Donald flipped his cigarette packet over and over on the table in front of him and stared in disbelief at the woman sitting opposite. Bright, attractive, not particularly young but wearing well for her age, obviously a bit naïve and not worldly wise or well-travelled. He had seen her around the ship, always laughing – the sort who joins in with everything. She had actually asked him if he was enjoying the cruise in a voice that implied she was loving every minute.

Stella looked back at the man. He was grey. His hair was grey and greasy, his face grey and lined, particularly around the mouth where the creases appeared to follow the down-turn of his lips. It was also wide and puffy with dry, flaking skin on his forehead and cheek bones. With elbows on the table and his thick shoulders hunched forward, he was staring at Stella as though she had just asked him the most stupid question he had ever heard. She was intrigued, morbidly fascinated by the spectre before her then, knowing she was going to regret it, but unable to prevent herself, she ploughed on, lemming-like, towards the cliff-edge,

"So what's wrong with it then? The cruise...and the boat?"

Donald stopped 'flipping' and stared. Was she serious? OK,

"What's wrong with this boat?" He repeated the question slowly, only it wasn't really a question, then proceeded to list all the faults in a thick, Scottish accent, his eyes drooping with the misery of it all.

"Why wasn't the swimming pool filled the day before yesterday? I wanted a swim and couldn't get one…"

(Well we were in the Suez Canal – did you really want them to fill it with that polluted water?)

"…And why was there no entertainment around the pool the previous evening…?"

Again Stella thought, but refrained from saying, that there was plenty of entertainment in The Club which he and his wife hadn't bothered to attend. Well into his stride, he continued,

"There aren't nearly enough games…"

"There's Monopoly," his listener ventured tentatively.

"Monopoly?? – Oh, c'mon – please!!"

"The lectures."

"Can't be bothered with those…and as for that trip out yesterday in Sharm El Sheikh – well, I'm going straight down to the desk after breakfast to cancel all the rest of the excursions I've booked."

Still keeping her voice bland and, apparently, sympathetic, Stella asked what had been wrong with it.

"We went on the 'city tour,' and I don't call that place a city – crummy little town, steaming hot with nothing much to see at all."

Stella struggled to keep a straight face remembering the old lady in 'Fawlty Towers' objecting to the scenery out of her window because it was just Torquay – she'd asked for a view, was that the best Basil Fawlty could do? Then came the crux of the matter,

"Oh yes, from now on Jeannie and I will be organising our own excursions – we can do it much cheaper ourselves."

Like 'Gracie the Grimmie' on the first day, Donald then sang the praises of the bigger, more luxurious ships he'd been on, one of which, by the end of breakfast, Stella heartily wished he'd chosen again. Never one to give up easily, she tried for one last time,

"It is still a wonderful experience, though, isn't it? Going round the world. And you can always use the time for reading."

Donald gave her a withering look and announced that he was already on his fifth book, his tone suggesting that the reading of these had given him as little pleasure, and was as great a burden, as everything else, then he got up and shambled out of the dining-room.

Back in the cabin Stella flopped onto her bed. She was cross and disgusted with the man, thinking of all the lovely, hard-working people she knew who would relish an opportunity such as they were enjoying and might never be able to afford it. She also thought about his remark regarding the expense of the excursions. She and Freddie had decided at the outset that they would book an excursion at every port of call. As they would only be at each destination for such a relatively short period of time, it would be better to be taken to the most interesting places by the people who knew, rather than risk failing to see anything because of their lack of local knowledge.

"What's up? Breakfast not agree with you?"

Freddie put his laptop on the little desk and sat down opposite his wife. He had breakfasted early in order to go to the Computer Club, something that didn't interest Stella at all.

"There was nothing wrong with the food, it was the company. Come on I'll tell you about it while we walk. The port lecture starts in fifteen minutes."

CHAPTER SEVEN

"Ladies and gentlemen, I'm sorry to interrupt your meal for those of you on second seating, but this is too exciting an opportunity to miss. The Captain has just informed me that in approximately an hour and a half we will be passing an erupting volcano."

The loudspeakers crackled, talking stopped and cutlery clattered to a standstill while everyone waited for the message to continue.

"If you go to the bow of the ship, short pause – that's the pointy end – you will get a good view."

"Wow! Well, thanks Judy for the message and for reminding us which bit of the ship is the bow – cheeky mare – but hey, what about that gang?! Let's finish our dinner and go."

For the rest of the meal Adam concentrated on his plate, determined not to miss a morsel, then everyone did a quick dash back to their cabins for scarves, shawls and cameras before making their way up to the 'pointy end.'

The wind was warm and very strong; people clung to the ship's rail staring out to sea at a cascade of red, molten lava being thrown out of a dark land mass, clearly visible against the moonlit sky. They watched, mesmerised, as the sparking mixture of liquid and gas billowed out, ebbing and flowing as if from some giant cauldron being swung back and forward, its lethal contents leaping and spilling over the sides then trickling down into the sea. In spite of being buffeted by the wind, most people persevered with cameras desperate to capture the momentous spectacle. The Captain took the ship as close as he dared, two nautical miles from the volcano, then swung round so that everyone could get an even better view.

"What an amazing sight," Stella shouted in Freddie's ear, her words torn away by the wind, as he struggled to keep the camera steady.

They learned afterwards that the tiny volcanic island was called Jazirat At Tair and the evening's enjoyment was somewhat tainted when it became known that nine people had died during the eruption.

There was a dull thud followed by a grunt of pain. Stella turned and was horrified to see Chrissie sprawled forward, her face, upper body and arms spread out on the ground, her legs and lower body submerged, hidden by the hole into which she had just fallen.

"What the…?"

Freddie was immediately there at her side, trying to give her some space to breathe, while the three coach loads from 'The Matisse' continued to plod slowly up the incline towards Job's tomb. Those nearest stopped to see what had happened and Stella shouted for Irma, their excursion leader for the day.

"I don't know…honestly…one minute she was there walking beside me, the next she's fallen down a big 'ole."

Margie, upset and confused, was persuaded to sit down on a nearby grassy bank while Irma and Freddie gently lifted Chrissie out of the hole and manoeuvred her onto the bank next to Margie. Chrissie's shins toes and fingers were bleeding; she was white and very shaken, winded by the fall, and near to fainting. Freddie held her head down between her legs while Irma extracted water and bandages from the first aid bag. Stella looked round, trying to establish what had happened and saw a fat Arab quickly replacing a thick slab of glass over the hole. She strode up to him,

"Why did you remove the glass?" She asked angrily, "Look what you've done."

She pointed to Chrissie then glared back at the man waiting for an answer. He shrugged,

"To see foot print of Job…there you see…" He lifted the glass again, "you cannot see footprint with glass on."

Stella peered into the muddy hole but couldn't see anything remotely resembling a footprint – the marks down there could have been anything. What she did see, though, was a smattering of Chrissie's blood.

"Put the glass back and only remove it when there are a few people around to look into the hole, not armies of us milling about unprepared for the ground to open up at our feet."

The man looked at the hot, angry woman in front of him and shrugged his shoulders again before slowly replacing the glass.

She returned to the group on the bank where they had now been joined by Jack and Jim. Jack's face was nearly as white as Chrissie's and he was holding her hand, while she rocked gently back and forward looking dazed and confused. Irma took charge,

"She must sit here quietly until she is ready to move; I will clean and dress the wounds. Jack, you stay and Freddie," she smiled apologetically, "would you mind…?"

"No, of course I'll stay."

She turned to Jim and Margie,

"Thank-you both, but there's really nothing more you can do; go and enjoy the tomb and we will see you back on the coach."

Margie was indignant,

"Oh, but I gotta stay…she's my friend. She'll want me here…"

Chrissie smiled weakly,

"No, dear, you go; I don't want to spoil your day. I'm being well looked after…"

Margie opened her mouth to protest again, but before she could Jim insisted,

"I'll stay; I can help get her to the coach…makes sense…"

A pleading look over their heads from Irma, and Stella stepped forward putting one arm gently round Margie's shoulders and, with the other under Jim's elbow, she manoeuvred them both back to join the crowd still plodding steadily up towards the tomb.

"I'll see you later," she mouthed to Freddie while firmly steering her two elderly companions carefully past the sheet of glass.

44

"Well this is a rum do and no mistake," Margie wrinkled her nose as the pungent incense crept into her nostrils, "bit weird if you ask me. I mean what's them cloths doin' over that big mound in the floor?"

"I think that's the tomb," Jim's rasping whisper echoed round the whitewashed walls of the tiny room.

"I know, but they're all fancy with silk and embroidery and that. He were a religious man, weren't he? Wouldn't have all that...falderal." She paused and looked up,

"And what on earth is that doin' 'ere?"

She was pointing indignantly to the large and very splendid chandelier suspended from the ceiling directly above the elaborately dressed tomb. Everyone shuffling round stopped and followed her pointing finger. There were a few gasps and giggles, and for once Stella found herself in complete agreement with Margie.

Halfway down the hill between the tomb and the coach, Stella stood in the sunshine enjoying the beauty of the bright, fuchsia-pink bougainvillea flowers growing in profusion on nearby bushes. Beyond them, a heat haze hovered over scrubby desert and the distant hills of Oman. Unable to endure Margie's twittering and Jim's growled concerns for a moment longer, she had said she was sure it would be alright for them to return to the coach to see how Chrissie and Jack were faring. And she hoped it would be, as she really felt she'd done her bit.

She turned to go and almost bumped into Freddie; he put his arm round her and she smiled,

"How is she?"

"It's not as bad as it looked at first. Irma's cleaned her up a treat and, although there was a lot of blood, it was mostly from grazes. One or two of the nails on both her toes and fingers will need some attention from the ship's doctor. I don't think she'll be doing much dancing for a while."

They started back down towards the coach,

"So how was the tomb?"

Stella laughed,

"You really didn't miss much. I'll tell you about it as we go along."

The coach stopped and everyone stepped out into the baking heat of the Souk where they wandered around admiring brightly coloured cloths, souvenirs and bottles of perfume in a variety of shapes and sizes.

"Oh my goodness, it's like standing inside an oven."

Freddie was concerned as Stella looked quite distressed; he took her arm,

"Come on, let's take refuge in here for a few minutes."

They went into a shop filled with all manner of gold jewellery along with other quite expensive gifts. While making her way slowly round, Stella suddenly became aware of a young woman glaring at her. She was covered from head to toe in a birkar with only her eyes showing and savagely ripped lengths off a roll of masking tape, resentment…dislike – or was it hatred even? – emanating from every pore. Stella was puzzled as to why she should feel like this and could only assume it had something to do with her relative lack of freedom, even to dress as she pleased.

Back on the coach to visit a nearby museum where Irma discovered they were experiencing a power cut and, before she could decide whether to take everyone in to try and peer through the gloom, those in charge closed the doors. Thinking on her feet, Irma directed the driver to another Souk, a little more up-market than the first, and once again people wandered around in the sunshine. But, back on the coach, Stella noticed that a few people had not taken advantage of this second shopping opportunity, apparently preferring to stay in their seats; she also noticed that the expressions on their faces did not radiate a spirit of joie de vivre.

"That was interesting," she said brightly, smiling broadly at a large lady with gingery-red hair and coloured wooden elephant earrings who she knew had stayed on the coach. The woman gave Stella a sour look.

"No it wasn't. We're not 'appy!"

And she and her friend, equally large with tobacco-coloured curls, stared straight ahead.

Keeping her ears open Stella picked up enough moans and groans from around the coach to realise that some people were annoyed about not being able to visit the museum, though she was at a loss to know what Irma could have done – kick down the doors, perhaps? The power-cut was no-one's fault and Stella made a mental note to tell Judy how impressed she was with the dancer's handling of the situation, particularly as she was sure there would be a mini stampede of complainers!

As they travelled back to the ship which was waiting for them at Salalah, she was fascinated to see camels roaming freely by the side of the road and then, further along, they passed miles and miles of perfect, but deserted, sandy beaches.

CHAPTER EIGHT

"Come on...stretch and twist...stretch and twist...swing those arms...work that waist..." Bryony bullied and the passengers grunted, trying to emulate the lithe movements of one of the ship's company dancers.

'Shape and define those wobbly areas at 'Bums and Tums' – the Stretch Class with The Entertainers.'

So said the blurb in 'Cruise News,' and, as it was raining with still an hour to go before lunch, Stella had decided to give it a try. She twisted again and caught sight of two friendly faces, their grins getting broader each time she turned round. The man, small, wiry and quite bow-legged, had a wide smile that stretched across his already tanned face showing a row of very white teeth as he exercised with some vigour. The woman, plump and jolly-looking with a light brown curly perm and throaty, infectious laugh, was twisting, turning and bending with the others, her handbag clutched securely to her chest!

Chatting to them after class, Stella was immediately drawn to this unpretentious couple – Ray and Vera, from Essex and having a lovely time. She knew Freddie would like them and they arranged to meet for a drink in the bar before dinner.

"So, what about Cochin, then? Bit of a farce all round really. Denise and I didn't get visas while we were still in England as we would have had to travel to London and wait in line for goodness knows how long at The Indian High Commission without any guarantee of both getting one."

Adam leaned back and took a large gulp of his drink.

"Yes, and at thirty pounds each, the cost was far higher than those required for Australia which we got over the internet. And then hardly anyone went ashore anyway."

Freddie looked at his wife. He knew Stella wasn't too disappointed not to have visited Cochin, her attitude being that if she was going to offer some help in such a poverty-stricken country that would be a different matter. As it turned out, all the shore excursions had been cancelled owing to political unrest and a strike in the part of India they were due to visit. As they approached Cochin harbour they were told that, for safety reasons, the harbour tour had also been cancelled; then, when 'Cruisenews' was pushed under their cabin door, Freddie gave a bark of laughter as he read:

'The British Government have advised that major disruption to services, including transport, can be expected. They strongly recommend that individuals avoid any of the numerous, potentially volatile, political rallies and demonstrations that are taking place. We have been further advised by our agent that independent travel in Cochin and surrounding areas is strongly discouraged during the strike period. It should also be noted that shops, restaurants and all public services are expected to be closed.'

He lowered the paper, "Welcome to India."

Stella had hung over the side of the ship and watched their slow progress into Cochin harbour. The weather was hot, humid and cloudy; the sea extremely dirty and a few black crows flapped lazily around the ship, occasionally perching on parts of it to escort them in. The sea was thick with clumps of foliage as they approached the quay, and the shore on each side looked green and fertile with attractive, red-roofed houses just visible over the tree-tops. The harbour was shabby and smelled of petrol. After a quiet day spent sending emails and writing post cards, Stella had watched again in the evening as the ship left the quayside, pulled out through the weed by a tug until it could safely turn and head out to sea.

"Well, as you know, I did venture into Old Cochin and was very glad I did so, even though Bernard couldn't be bothered to accompany me."

Sheila helped herself to some vegetables, at the same time directing a withering look towards her husband. Stella wondered if Bernard ever managed to get anything right and Adam, sensing a change of subject might be a good idea, turned towards her,

"Ray and Vera are good company, yep...I like them. They're going to join us for a drink again tomorrow. Good idea of yours, Stella."

Stella smiled at the memory of Adam and Ray walking into the dining room – the 'Little and Large' of the Matisse.

Round the corner and they were there. At midday, two hours ahead of schedule, 'The Matisse' docked at the capital city of Colombo on the island of Sri Lanka, just off the tip of Southern India.

Freddie and Stella joined the group on deck gathered to watch the docking procedure, and were fascinated as always by the manoeuvres needed to bring the large vessel safely alongside the quay.

"It's just like 'Toad' but on a much larger scale," Freddie said, referring to their small narrow boat moored on a river back home.

As usual, one of the crew stood poised ready to throw out a small ball, attached to which was string tied to one of the massive ropes that would secure the craft to the bollard. He waited for an opportune moment and hurled it towards the quay where another man stood waiting to catch it. To his mortification, it fell short and landed in the water. The watching crowd cheered, but Stella and Freddie sympathised as they knew that most of the time, when there were fewer people watching, the aim was spot on and the ball easily retrieved by the catcher on the shore. It made them think again of their own efforts on "Toad" where perfect manoeuvres were carried out at solitary locks, while mistakes always had an audience waiting for just such entertainment.

Keen to learn something about Sri Lanka, Stella had looked it up in the guide book where it was referred to as: 'a resplendent land shaped like a pearl dropped from the sub-continent of India with seas rich in fish, superb beaches and cool highlands.' These didn't feature on the hair-raising tour undertaken during the afternoon, and she was beginning to discover that guide-book speak and people's own romanticised notions of these places were often a far cry from the reality of just another part of the planet where people of a different culture were trying to eek out a living the best way they knew how.

She was interested in the few delightful pieces of folklore that she learned had grown up around the island. It is said that here, on a misty peak, Adam rested and repented after his expulsion from Eden. Apparently his footprint (what is it with these footprints!?) is still there to prove it, though Buddhists have claimed it as Buddha's mark, while the Hindus believe that it is the place where the god, Siva's, foot struck the ground during the great dance of creation.

Although at only 25,000 square miles Sri Lanka is smaller than Ireland, but has a population of twenty million people. There are two national languages, Sinhala and Tamil, and four main ethnic groups: Buddhist Sinhalese, Hindu Tamils, Muslims and Burghers. For many years Western powers fought for control of the island and traces of British colonisation can still be found in the ceiling fans used to cool old hotels and ancient Morris Minors used as taxis.

Stella was also fascinated by the origin of the name. Apparently the Sinhalese have always known their country as 'Lanka,' but Arab traders called it 'Serendib' from which came the word, serendipity – 'discovering pleasant or valuable things by accident.' The Portuguese corrupted the Indian name 'Sielediva' into 'Ceilao' which was then changed to 'Ceilon' by the Dutch and 'Ceylon' by the British. In 1972 the 'new' name of Sri Lanka was officially adopted, but it was really just the original one with the added 'Sri' meaning 'resplendent' or 'favoured by fortune.'

Stella and Freddie were to discover that anyone taking to the streets of Colombo certainly needed to be favoured by fortune! Their organised excursion was an evening one, so in the afternoon they shared a taxi with Ray and Vera for what turned out to be a roller coaster ride through the city. On the way to the port gate to find a taxi they passed an array of multi-coloured goodies: – trinkets, jewellery, wooden carvings, scarves and kaftans – all spilling temptingly out onto the quayside from simple, shed-like stalls erected by the locals in the hope of enticing a ship full of retail-starved passengers to buy their wares. They were covered on three sides and open at the front where coffee-coloured vendors with smiling white teeth waved handfuls of bright materials. Vera and Stella looked at each other,

"On the way back!" They said in unison and laughed.

They had all been told by Isobel to negotiate a fare as they would find plenty of taxi-drivers willing to take them anywhere they liked; what she didn't tell them about was the state of the vehicles. Not one of the waiting taxis looked road-worthy but, up for an adventure, they negotiated a deal with the friendliest-looking driver they could see who offered to take them anywhere they liked for two hours at a cost of fifty dollars. As that worked out at about three pounds fifty an hour each, they were happy to climb aboard.

What an experience! The taxi itself was so shabby they expected something to fall off at any moment. Stella clung on to a side-strap, laughing,

"Well, I thought the driving in Cairo was bad…but this is beyond belief!"

Buffeted about, they looked out at the total chaos around them as battered vehicles of all types just careered ahead, weaving in and out of each other with horns constantly blaring.

"Look at this," Vera gave her throaty laugh and pointed to a small fan suspended from the roof of the taxi. She pulled a piece of string which started it going, and then they laughed even more when the driver, with a wide grin, touched another switch which made the fan move from side to side – luxury!

Helpless with laughter, they continued to peer out of the windows until Ray covered his eyes and shouted above the rattles,

"It's a wonder we don't 'it something…there's bound to be a crash."

And there was! Turning a corner they ran – or were shunted, no-one could remember which – into the back of a bus. Rocking back and forward with laughter, they waited to see what would happen. But the driver just continued to smile and they moved forward again with the rest of the traffic. Documents? It was probably a case of 'what documents?' No-one was hurt and the state of both bus and taxi was such that another dent or scratch was neither here nor there.

They visited a beautiful Buddhist Temple and were then taken by the ever obliging driver to quite a smart shop before being driven once again through the chaotic streets and back to the quay. Along with the rest of the traffic, Stella noticed a prevalence of fascinating little vehicles called Took-Tooks. They are tiny, smaller than a mini, with three wheels and powered by a motor cycle engine. Many of them are used as taxis and their owners individualise them by painting them a variety of bright colours, sometimes even covering them in swirls and different patterns. She thought they looked fun, but even more perilous than the taxi they were in.

Back at the quay-side they paid the driver then added a ten dollar tip on top of the negotiated fare as they felt he had been very pleasant and had looked after them well, in spite of the crash, which had really just added to the entertainment. A little shopping at the stalls then back on board to get ready for the evening excursion.

Called 'Colombo by Night,' this proved to be spectacular. Stella and Freddie entered the large room set aside for the party and smiled at each other as they noticed the usual jostling for first place. Handbags and shawls were draped across seats at what people thought were the best tables; Indiana Jones and his wife commandeered a table right at the front, then he stood up and, with a lot of elaborate arm-waving and beckoning, ensured that the occupants of the other up-market suites joined them. Edie glared round, then pointed her stick towards the other table near the stage and ordered Stanley to head for it, her frown only turning to a smile when the very front places had been secured. She didn't care a jot who occupied the remaining seats. As it happened, Stella and Freddie sat in two of them. None of their new friends had opted for this trip, so they were not bothered where they sat, but these actually turned out to be pretty good for seeing the show, scheduled for after the meal.

The food was excellent and the dancing that followed quite enchanting, with women executing exquisitely delicate hand movements, and men striding and leaping around the stage with great strength. Then came a fire-eater, a real show man, who got wilder and wilder until everyone's gasps of amazement turned to cries of horror when one of the batons flew out of his hand, landing right at Edie's feet.

"Eee, watch it sunshine," she barked, jumping out of her chair and stepping smartly to one side. The fire-eater leapt down, retrieved his baton and was back on the stage in one fluid movement, his well-oiled skin glistening under the lights. Edie sat huffily back in her seat, arms folded in front of her and mouth turned down, reminiscent of the female character created by Les Dawson.

Freddie stifled a laugh and observed, as many of the other passengers already had, that Edie could certainly move fast when she wanted to. Her transformation from invalid to dancer was becoming a standing joke during the evening pre-dinner sessions when, as soon as Antonio appeared, she was up and plodding purposefully down to the small dance-floor, ready to trip the light fantastic, and oblivious to the muffled cries of,

"It's a miracle...halleluiah...praise the Lord...she's cured."

After the show there was a little time to spare before the coach arrived, so Stella and Freddie explored the hotel, noting the old colonial touches – plenty of dark wood, potted plants and huge ceiling fans. They wandered outside to where the waves were crashing onto the beach, a scene Stella was sure would have been enhanced by moonlight, but it was cloudy and the patio was still wet with the earlier rain that had prevented them from enjoying the whole evening outside as had been advertised.

Stripped of all vestiges of day-time occupation, the streets from the coach windows on their return to the ship looked forlorn and shabby. Tin skeletons of market stalls, devoid of their bright wares, seemed incapable of standing independently and were kept upright only by leaning on each other. Stray dogs scavenged in piles of rubbish and old men sat drinking on the de-roofed upper storey of a house as though it were a balcony.

CHAPTER NINE

"Calling all actors and actresses wishing to take part in our forth-coming performance of Aladdin, please meet Denny at 11.15 in the Nautical Bar."

This two line announcement in 'Cruisenews' was sandwiched between a call to join 'The Money Man' for his seventh lecture – this one dealing with the paper money of Thailand – and the pre-lunch quiz with the possibility of winning a pack of Sailaways playing cards.

Denny had already taken some names of potentially interested people and Stella let slip that she had, in a previous life, been a Drama Teacher, not really thinking he would take much notice of this, being a professional himself. He had, however, latched onto it.

"…Oh that's great, darlin', you can give me a hand with the directing…." ignoring her spluttering protests that it was a long time ago and she really wasn't sure….

"…OK, guys, look out for the announcement in Cruisenews…we'll get togever…sort it all out… have a great time…"

And here it was. But did she want to go? She frowned,

"Freddie, what do you think about taking part in this Pantomime?"

Freddie picked up his laptop ready for the morning session,

"Well, as you know, I'm happy to come and support. I may even be of some use back stage, but as for getting up onto the stage – no way. I'd rather have each finger nail removed one by one without the aid of an anaesthetic."

Stella shuddered at the grisly image,

"OK. Let's go along, but I'm not at all sure about this."

Freddie disappeared, whistling, with his laptop under his arm and Stella set off in the direction of the Mermaid Tavern for an hour's card making.

"Where do you get your ideas?"

Sharon sat back and thought for a moment,

"I don't know…I suppose it must be all the years of make-do-and-mend, not to mention costume-making at Christmas time."

Stella was particularly drawn to Sharon. Plump, down to earth and practical, she nevertheless displayed a surprising creative ability which meant her cards always had an original twist, eagerly copied by the rest of the class. She had brought up five children and now, like Stella, was making the most of her round the world cruise, something she never thought she would be able to experience.

"We're so lucky aren't we, Stella? I mean to be able to do this…sit back and see the world, everything done for us…everything provided, marvellous food, friendly staff – and so much to do, all day and every day. There's no excuse for being bored, even for a minute."

Stella smiled as she agreed, glad to have found another kindred spirit, and was pleased to see Sharon in The Nautical Bar at 11.15.

Stella sat quietly next to Freddie, reminding herself that this was a holiday and if she didn't want to take part it was OK. Denny was at the front flashing his cheeky-chappie grin at everyone who came in. One or two seemed to know each other from the previous trip and had been in the pantomime then, with Denny directing. She felt like an intruder.

"Good evening, peasants. What's this? Twelve o'clock and still no Dick?"

Stella turned to see a tall, dark-haired man standing in the doorway. With heavily rimmed glasses and a small moustache, he had delivered the line in a loud, stagy voice, simultaneously slapping his thigh then, when he saw he had everyone's attention, he made a low bow and sauntered into the room. Several people laughed but Stella heard Freddie groan, not being a fan of extreme, extrovert behaviour. They recognised him as Desmond an expat, professional quiz master living in Majorca.

"OK, ladies and gentlemen, let's make a start. Thank-you all for coming. Now who wants to 'ave a go at a big part?...It don't matter if you don't...we can find something for everyone...but don't be shy..."

Denny threw several thick wads of paper, which turned out to be scripts, onto the table and proceeded to go through the parts, handing them out to anyone who was interested. Stella sat in silence, feeling totally alienated by this way of working, and didn't think she had anything to contribute. She kept her head down and when all the parts had been allocated whispered to Freddie,

"Come on, let's go."

"Are you sure?"

"Yes."

But just at that moment Denny turned towards her,

"Oh yeah...and this is Stella...she's gonna help me with directin', aren't you darlin'? Cool. Can you stay behind? OK...thanks everyone. Look out for rehearsal times in Cruisenews. It's gonna be great."

Several people glanced in her direction, obviously wondering why she had been singled out in this way, then drifted off in small groups.

By the time she left the Nautical Bar that morning Stella had agreed to help with the directing and also to come up with some ideas for a warm-up session, "...you know, just to get everyone togever like...know what I mean?"

She had no trouble understanding what Denny meant but, when she had carried the large wad of script back to her cabin and started to read, her heart sank further and further into her boots with every page.

"Ooo, you poor thing. Honest to God, I felt that sorry when I heard. I says to Kieran what a dreadful thing to happen – falling down the hole like that. How are you feeling now?"

Nancy sat down next to Chrissie who closed the book she was enjoying and moved her sunglasses up onto her head.

"Oh, not too bad. It could have been so much worse and the doctor's fixed me up extremely well. Everything's healing nicely, though I am still rather stiff. With a bit of luck, though, I should be able to do some dancing again very soon."

"Oh that'll be nice."

Nancy glanced over to where Jack had just appeared and was trying to hide his disappointment on seeing that Chrissie was not alone.

"So, will he be giving you a whirl around the dance floor then?" Nancy motioned towards Jack with her thumb, "I've noticed he's been looking after you pretty well."

Chrissie felt herself blush,

"Oh…I don't know about that…"

Nancy started to get up,

"Had I better go? He looks as though he wants to come over?"

"No…no, please stay."

Chrissie spoke quickly and held Nancy's wrist until she sat back down again. Changing the subject she asked,

"What about you and Kieran? He seems very keen."

"Oh, I know." She leaned forward, relieved to have someone to talk to about her problem, "he's been following me about like a pet lamb, but…well…he's not really my type and the thing is there's Sean at home."

She slumped in the lounger, swinging her sunglasses between two fingers and looked so perplexed that Chrissie felt obliged to ask,

"So who's Sean?"

"Sean's my boyfriend who wants to be my fiancé. I've known him since we were both at primary school and I think I do love him but…there's just something…I don't know. He's so good and kind. I mean…I just rashly blurted out one day, 'I can't marry you…I haven't seen anything of the world yet.' And next thing I know he's bought me this ticket to go round the world. He's hoping that when I get back I'll have got it all out of my system and I'll settle down with him." She paused looking really unhappy, "The trouble is the further we go, the further away I feel from him."

She sighed. Chrissie waited for a moment and then said,

"And is there anyone else?"

Nancy looked up,

"You mean Wayne, don't you?"

"Well, I can't help noticing the way he looks at you while he's singing one of his romantic songs."

Nancy giggled,

"I know, it's dead romantic, in't it. Honest, my tummy turns over when he does that. I love it, but I don't know where it will lead. I mean he must have had so many girls on these ships." She paused, "He has asked me to have a drink with him after the show tomorrow night and I'm going to go. Do you think I'm doing right?"

Chrissie wasn't sure how to respond, but realised at the end of the day it didn't really matter what she said. Nancy was young and would do as she pleased, making her own mistakes along the way.

"Well, one drink can't do any harm and may help you to sort out how you feel."

Nancy looked pleased to have her thoughts clarified for her and Chrissie wished she could get her own problem sorted out as easily as she seemed to be able to help others.

CHAPTER TEN

"Wow, just look at them go!"

Freddie gave a bark of laughter as he watched the 'front seat grabbers' heading for the tender boat. Edie knew she had competition in this particular race and was not happy. 'Central eating,' so christened by Adam as he had only one tooth in his mouth, right at the centre of his upper jaw, was closely followed by his wife, 'two sticks,' moving faster with the aid of two walking canes than most able bodied passengers. Coming up on the inside lane and making good progress were 'Nina and Frederick,' a Danish couple, again christened by Adam, who was amused by the exaggerated public displays of affection as 'Frederick' constantly fussed over his wife who, with blond tresses snaking down her back, was trying too hard to look much younger than she obviously was.

'The Matisse' was anchored off-shore near the island of Phuket and many of the passengers were making their way to the tender boat that would take them onto the island for the day's excursions. Travelling on these little boats, designed for use in emergencies and therefore not models of style and comfort, became yet another arena for the display of the best and worst in human nature. Entry and departure could have been eased considerably if people had done what they were asked instead of constantly trying to manoeuvre themselves into the best positions to be first on and first off.

"Move right round please, ladies and gentlemen." The ever patient Sailaways staff were trying their best, but those who had pushed their way to the front had no intention of losing this advantage on arrival at the quayside, so stubbornly plonked themselves near the doorway, forcing everyone else to step over them and glaring in extreme displeasure if their feet got trodden on. Which they did – and not always by accident. Stella hid a smile as she saw Freddie 'apologising' to Edie and

'Frederick' for stepping on their toes – quite unintentionally, of course.

The little boat swayed and Stella sat reflecting on the guidebook description of Phuket as 'The Pearl of Thailand.' Regularly voted one of the world's top holiday destinations, it did indeed look inviting; a lush green and pale, sandy coast line dotted about with small, red-roofed bungalows peeping above the tree tops. She had noticed several derelict buildings, wrecked – completely gutted – and guessed they were relics of the tsunami that had devastated this part of the world on Boxing Day in 2004. The little boat started to move and, as they bounced about on the waves, she looked forward to the day ahead.

Edie stood staring at the great grey creatures with some fear and trepidation but, having been denied her camel ride, she was determined to get the most out of the elephant safari.

"But 'ow do I get oop onto its back?"

She stood in line, not at the front this time as she wanted to see how it was done, and wasn't feeling at all confident.

"'E'll show you love. Look, he's 'elpin' everyone."

Stanley tried to reassure his wife, but she stood clutching her handbag in front of her as she moved slowly towards the front of the queue, her mouth turning further down at the corners with every shuffled step.

"Oh my goodness, now I've seen everything."

Safely mounted in a double seat next to Stella on the back of one of the elephants, Freddie was watching Edie's antics with undisguised amusement. She had managed to struggle up onto the elephant's back and, with her handbag still clutched against her chest with one arm like a plastic security blanket, she was hanging on to Stanley with the other. The animal lumbered forward and she gave an almighty shriek, clinging even more desperately to her husband,

"I'm gooin' ter fall off, Stanley…"

"No, love, yer alright. Don't fret. These elephants know what they're doin'"

But Edie did fret and for once Stella felt some sympathy for her. The elephants plodded slowly over boggy ground and into lots of muddy puddles, making slurping, sloshing sounds. Edie's shrieks were frequent and even Stella gasped several times as the elephant plunged down dips so steep they were almost vertical. She did feel a little nervous and, trying not to think about accident statistics, (sometimes it's better not to know), she just hoped the elephant was sure-footed.

Perched nonchalantly in front of the passengers on each elephant's neck was a young boy, a mahout, effortlessly controlling the animal by doing something to its ear with his big toe. They all exuded confidence and kept up a strange, chant-like singing, occasionally laughing and calling out to each other in their own language. Stella had a feeling they were making insulting, or perhaps just teasing, remarks about their English passengers.

Stella felt sorry for these huge, docile elephants forced to traverse the same route day in day out with excited tourists on their backs. She had been told that only females are used for this as the males tend to be very aggressive – something to do with a hole in their temples that secretes fluid. She noticed strange orange spots and patches around their ears denoting age and thought it was probably similar to humans going grey. The day was hot and very humid; a few birds flew or hopped around the swampy mud and there was a warm, pungent smell rising from the damp ground.

"I don't like that, do you?"

Sharon had crept up quietly to where, following the ride, Freddie and Stella were standing watching the baby elephant show. The little creatures were made to pirouette, playing tiny harmonicas on the ends of their trunks and begging for bananas, thanking the assembled crowd for giving them in a sickeningly, cutesy way.

"No, I don't," Stella whispered, "I don't like to see animals performing silly tricks like that; they seem to lose all their natural dignity."

"And that's even worse!"

Sharon was pointing to a pen nearby where the young elephants were kept chained by a back leg between performances. One of them was showing signs of stress by continuously swinging its body from side to side. Stella felt even more of a bond with Sharon as she agreed wholeheartedly that it was a distressing sight. They both tried to take some consolation from being told by a nearby keeper that if it were not for these activities the animals would die out altogether, but they were not entirely convinced.

The jeeps bumped and bounced along a muddy track between fields from which water buffalo stared and pure white egrets skimmed across the uneven, tufts of grass. Then a short walk through the jungle to a clearing where mats, looking very like large, crude versions of the slip mats used in baths at home, were hanging out on fences to dry. There was an unpleasant smell around these, rather like sour milk; the air was stifling and very heavy, and a few stray dogs scratched and lazed in the dusty ground. Margie fanned herself with her straw hat,

"Pooh, what a stink…and it's too flippin' 'ot."

"Go and stand over there in the shade. It's further away from the rubber so it won't smell as bad."

Jack tried not to sound cross, but his patience really was being stretched to the limit. Chrissie was not yet well enough for an excursion that involved an elephant ride and a jungle trek, so Margie had latched on to him and Jim. She turned to Jim with what she hoped was a winning smile,

"Come over there with me, Jim."

"No…I'll stay here. I want to hear all about rubber growing."

Even if he didn't, he would have stayed put as anything was better than listening to even more exploits of the wonderful Kevin. Margie trudged sulkily over to the edge of the clearing where she stood, shoulders drooping, with one arm across her chest and the other still fanning her face in an attempt to move a little of the stagnant air.

Noom, the guide, smiled, teeth pearl-white against olive skin, and he began to explain the rubber production process in Thailand. The group, listening intently, were surprised to learn that it was begun a hundred years before when a man walked from Malaysia to Thailand with a rubber tree seed hidden in his naval. He had to walk at night to avoid detection as removing rubber seeds from Malaysia was illegal owing to the fact that they did not want competition in this market. He pointed out that the rubber trees are planted in rows to make it easier for the farmer to see which ones he has tapped, and pineapples are planted in between because it's not possible to get latex from the rubber tree for the first seven years. Pineapples, which only take ten months to grow, provide the farmer with income until he can start obtaining rubber.

After seven years, when the rubber trees are fully grown, their foliage blocks the light to the pineapples so production of these stops and the rubber takes over. Tapping the trees for rubber takes place early in the morning as the sap runs out faster when the air is cooler. A hooked knife, with a blade on the inside, is used for the tapping process and a cut is made in the tree bark downwards from right to left. Only one tap is made in a tree in one day as the amount of latex obtained is the same regardless of the number of cuts. The white, milky latex is collected in a cup made of plastic, clay or coconut, depending on the region in which it's being harvested, and is left for about three hours before the farmer returns to collect it. During this time one tree produces about 40cc of latex which is then taken to a factory where it's turned into solid rubber sheets. This process is accelerated by the addition of a solidifying agent, usually formic acid.

Freddie, with camera held steady, was filming Noom's talk. He pressed the pause button and asked,

"How long can a tree go on producing latex?"

"For about eighteen years, from age seven until it's twenty five. If it rains in the night the effect on the latex is so bad that the farmer loses a day's income as the tree cannot be tapped. After twenty five years the tree is chopped down and the wood, undamaged because its smell is repellent to insects, is sent to factories to be made into furniture."

"Well I shouldn't want any of that, probably stink your house out."

Margie had crept back to join Jack and Jim and was giving the assembled group her opinion in a loud whisper that travelled round the small clearing. They all turned to follow Noom back to the coach and Jack, catching Stella's eye rolled his own to heaven. She smiled as she heard him muttering to Jim,

"I swear I'll swing for that bloody woman."

Back on the coach they headed for a cashew nut factory and Noom kept up his commentary, in perfect English, all about Thailand in general and Phuket in particular.

"…and I want to tell you now about the Thai greeting – 'Sawati-ka' if you are a woman; 'Sawati-krup' for a man. Only be very careful with the second one."

He smiled and everyone laughed – everyone except Margie who tapped Jim on the shoulder,

"What's he mean? What's that about?"

"Think about it!" Said Jim, and Margie sat back frowning, deep in thought.

Stella found it very humbling to hear this lovely young man not only able to speak a foreign language with such competence, but to understand and be able to use innuendo as well.

The cashew nut factory was clean and modern. Everyone gathered round to watch a woman calmly and systematically removing the nuts from their outer shells then separating the whole and broken ones into different pots. Noom told them that her wage for this monotonous task, carried out eight hours a day for six days a week, is very meagre. The nuts are harvested between February and May then washed and laid out in the sun to dry, after which they are roasted to make it easier to break them out of their skins. This is quite a long process which is why these particular nuts are so expensive.

Edie was in her element. Greedily scoffing the free samples, she went from counter to counter and was then even more delighted when a pretty, young assistant greeted her with a wide smile and offered to be her personal shopper for the afternoon. She carried the basket while Stanley took charge of the stick and Edie selected her packets of nuts from the thirteen different flavours on offer.

"…and I'll 'ave some of them chilli ones…Ooo and look, Stanley, butter and garlic…better 'ave some of them…"

By the time she reached the checkout the basket was over flowing and the assistant's smile even wider.

"It's amazing how far benefits will stretch these days," Freddie chortled.

"Oh, you cynic." Stella slapped him playfully on the arm, but couldn't help thinking he'd hit the nail right on the head.

CHAPTER ELEVEN

Waking early after a good night's sleep, Stella looked across to the adjacent bed and, seeing it was empty, knew that Freddie was already up on deck for his pre-breakfast morning coffee. She pushed the hair out of her eyes and picked up the chunky guide book. Penang…Malaysia. They were due to arrive at 11 o'clock that morning and would be anchoring off-shore from the capital, Georgetown. She looked out of the window and reflected on the joy of being able to eat, drink and be entertained then, after a good night's sleep, arrive at yet another exotic destination. No fuss, no airports, just open your eyes and you're there, with all the work and worry taken care of by someone else while you were asleep. It was like that TV programme she used to watch with her son when he was small. A man in a bowler hat walked through the back of a shop and found himself in a new, colourful destination each time. She looked back at the guide book and turned to the page about Penang,

'Here you have Asia in an Oystershell: a holiday island so compact you can circle it in half a day, yet big enough to encompass a colourful microcosm of Malay, Chinese, Indian and Thai cultures – a fitting gateway to the East.'

So said the book, going on to talk about '…jungle-clad hills…' '…palm-studded, golden beaches…' and '…Eastern scents of frangipane, cloves and nutmeg perfuming the soft air…'

Stella smiled. Yes, it looked interesting and she was keen to explore, but she was beginning to realise that these exaggerated claims for the places they visited were probably part of the cause of so much disappointment among the discontented few. No-where could live up to these descriptions; there's always a serpent in paradise in the form of bad weather, sharp coral, over-zealous vendors, bad smells in the jungle or venomous, unpleasant creatures. Much better to travel embracing the realities rather than believing the impossibly glowing pictures painted by the travel brochures, then the places can be enjoyed and appreciated for what they are.

She got up, had breakfast and by 11 0'clock was standing at the ship's rail with Freddie, eager to get their first sight of Georgetown. It was bustling with freighters, junks and ferries, but Stella had learned that only fishermen and pirates were living in Penang in 1786 when Captain Francis Light landed there and founded a British trading post. Lying just off the West Malaysian coast in the Straights of Malacca, Penang flourished in the early nineteenth century as Britain's easternmost trading centre. It was then upstaged by Singapore, but Georgetown is still one of Malaysia's leading ports.

"Did you put your insect repellent on?"

Stella nudged Freddie as she asked the question.

"No, I forgot."

"So did I."

She rummaged in her bag thinking that now would be a good time. Everyone was already on the tender boat waiting to go ashore, but there seemed to be a short delay and they rocked gently on the waves waiting for the engine to start. She found the spray and applied a little to her legs before passing the can to Freddie. As he sprayed it liberally on his arms and legs, Stella became aware of people around them starting to cough. The coughing was joined by spluttering, both of which spread and rose to a crescendo. There were gasps, handkerchiefs appeared followed by inhalers and somebody tried to open a window. Edie covered her face with her hands as she rocked back and forward,

"I can't breathe…Stanley…I'm fightin' fer me life…"

Fingers were pointed as the victims gradually worked out who was responsible for polluting the air,

"It was her…yes…it was them…"

Stella was mortified and started to mouth 'sorry' to all and sundry. Faces turned red, eyes watered and still she apologised, finally standing up so they could all clearly see she really meant it and was accepting full responsibility. As she sat down again she saw 'Central Eating' take his inhaler from 'Two Sticks' and start sucking on it, his eyes streaming.

"I'm very sorry," Stella said, once again, looking straight at him. He removed the inhaler from his mouth and she waited for him to tell her exactly what he thought of their inconsiderate behaviour. Instead his watery eyes held hers and he tried to smile,

"It's alright…you weren't to know," he wheezed, forgiveness written all over his face, which only made Stella feel worse. The coughing gradually subsided and they set off for land.

"You were a bit quiet," Stella muttered to Freddie, her tone indicating that, as the most enthusiastic sprayer of the noxious substance, he should have done his share of the apologising.

"Flaming drama queens!" He growled, and she knew to some extent he was right.

"Now there's a marriage made in Heaven!"

Freddie was looking over to where Edie and Stanley had been joined by Margie, and Stella turned in time to see Gracie the Grimmie sidle up to them. She stifled a giggle and whispered,

"Now it's a full set."

"Not quite – no 'Crankies.'"

They both laughed and realised that, of course, there wouldn't be since the Scottish couple, christened 'The Crankies' by Adam, had decided to save money by 'doing their own thing' since Sharm El Sheikh.

A little further away from this group, Jack and Jim were standing protectively one each side of Chrissie who, although having to lean heavily on two sticks, had managed to venture out on this excursion. Adam, Denise, Ray, Vera, Sheila and Bernard were standing with Stella and Freddie, and they, along with the entire party from 'The Matisse,' stared up to where Pit Vipers were hanging from the rafters of the Snake Temple they were visiting. Adam pointed to the altar,

"Look…they're even coiled around that!"

Bernard started to read from the guide book, informing the group that the Temple was built in 1850 and the local belief is that the snakes are the disciples of the deity Chor Soo Kong.

"Be quiet, Bernard,"

Sheila hissed at her husband as the commentary was continued by an official guide who assured them that, although the snakes they were seeing were the most deadly of the local species, they are not dangerous as they are kept sedated by incense oil; and anyway most of them have had their fangs removed. Adam gave a bark of laughter,

"Most!! Well, we can only hope the fanged ones have had an extra dose of happy oil…"

"…Yes…or that they are having a day off," added Freddie as they all made their way to another room where, to Stella's horror, they were offered a photo opportunity – with the snakes!

She shuddered and stood well back as she watched Freddie and Adam having Malaysian Pythons coiled around their necks and yellow and green Pit Vipers placed on their heads where they slithered about, hissing and flicking forked tongues out of their mouths.

Adam was in his element as he posed for the photos, holding the snakes out on his arms. Sheila glared at Bernard, daring him not to go anywhere near the revolting creatures; and Stanley suffered the same fate, plodding obediently after Edie and her two new friends as they stomped out of the building.

"I'm not gooin' ter risk me life by having snakes crawlin' all over me," Edie declared. Gracie and Margie agreed.

"Well…just look at that!"

The same three ladies stood gazing in horror at the scene before them. The coach had stopped at a village,

"…not what I call a village…I've never seen a village like this in me life…" Gracie had muttered as she stepped out into the dust and heat. The crudely built shacks by the side of the road were raised on stilts, and squatting underneath one of them was a thin, bony old woman skewering pieces of chicken onto sticks to make satay for the evening meal. With only ragged cloths wound round her head and body, she turned and smiled at the unexpected visitors, revealing her few remaining teeth and causing even more lines to appear in a face already creased, weathered and very brown. Her only companions were the flies that swarmed over the food, until a young woman, now aware of their arrival, came out of one of the huts and sat on the steps. She was hugging a small child whose yawning and stretching indicated that he had been woken for the purpose of charming the group, and he looked far from happy about it.

Stella wondered why until their guide explained that the mother was hoping they would take photographs and give her a little money for this, which most of them did. More brown-skinned children came out to greet them and, as they were polite and flashed huge, white smiles from shiny brown faces, the group didn't mind parting with some more money. The heat was becoming unbearable; scrawny chickens with long gangly legs scratching in the dust around the loosely grouped shacks suddenly scattered as Edie's voice boomed out,

"Typical…just typical!"

She pointed in disgust to where, underneath one of the huts, a young man was fast asleep in a hammock.

The other two joined in,

"The poor old woman doing all the work while that lazy young beggar sleeps the day away. Typical.!" Snorted Gracie

"Just typical!" Echoed Margie, "she wants to go and tip him out. If that were my Raymond, he wouldn't 'alf get what for. I'll bet he wakes up in time to eat some of that food, though. Mind you, I don't think I'd want it after all them flies have been on it."

"No, nor me." Edie declared and led the way back to the coach followed by Gracie and Margie. Stanley brought up the rear carrying stick, bags and cardigans, but said nothing.

"What an absolutely fabulous place,"

Chrissie breathed, and Stella agreed. They were standing side by side in a batik factory watching brightly coloured inks being skilfully applied to fabric in flowery swirls, creating glorious patterns. Freddie, Jack and Jim stood a little way off, chatting and glancing occasionally at what was going on. They could appreciate the skill involved in what they were seeing but it was not, for them, the highlight of the day.

"The finished lengths of cloth are stunning, aren't they?" Stella pointed to where examples were hanging,

"Oh yes...and look how quickly the women work, applying the colours so casually with never a mistake...and aren't they beautiful, such lovely skin?"

"I wonder how they manage to stay so calm."

Listening carefully to the guide's explanation, both ladies were fascinated to learn that there are two ways of making batik, one where the pattern is drawn by hand and for the other a block printing technique is used. The latter process is begun by dipping a large metal block into the hot wax then stamping it onto cotton, silk or rayon – which is usually white – creating the outline of a design in wax. The material is then dyed and printed for a second time followed by a second dyeing. Light colours are applied first and finally all the wax is washed away with boiling water revealing the pattern.

For the other process, hand-drawn designs are first pencilled onto the fabric by the artist, then the lines are covered in wax using a janting tool. The pattern is easily visible against the white material as it is turned to a golden colour by adding paraffin and pine resin to the hot wax. The rest of the colours are painted on by hand using wide brushes dipped in dye and applied liberally with great confidence, the wax preventing the colours from running into each other. When the painting is finished, the design is fixed using sodium silicate before the fabric is washed to remove all the wax.

"What do you think?"

Chrissie turned sideways, leaning on one of her sticks and holding a wrap, which they learned was called a pareo, up against her slim figure."

"Beautiful," enthused Stella hoping, not for the first time, that she would look as elegant as Chrissie at her age. She chose a pretty silk top for herself and, as she followed Chrissie to the checkout, realised that she had not only gained a lovely item of clothing to remind her of this visit, but had made another friend.

In the evening a group called The Creative Dance Company was invited on board ship and treated the passengers to a wonderful, colourful display of Malaysian dancing. The costumes were stunning and the movements accompanied by the most exquisitely delicate hand gestures.

"Ooo, goo on Stanley…goo an' 'ave a goo."

From her vantage point in the middle of the front row, Edie nudged her husband, at the same time waving towards the stage to where a smiling dancer was inviting members of the audience to join him. Not to dance, but to try and burst a balloon with a blow-pipe dart. He had just demonstrated that it could be done and, for once, Stanley was being encouraged by his wife to be the star of the show. Looking confused, he ambled up onto the stage where, to everyone's amazement – most of all his – he managed to burst the balloon with his first dart. While the audience erupted in whoops and cheers, Edie, pink with pleasure, poked Gracie and Margie,

"That's my Stanley, that is."

CHAPTER TWELVE

"Oh, Stella darlin,' I'm glad I've seen you...tomorrow's the last day at sea before we arrive in Singapore...we're gonna get 'em togever...'ave a bit of a warm up session. Know what I mean? Can you come up wiv some ideas...your experience an' all that...you know...help me run the session..."

Denny put up a thumb, flashed his cheeky-chappie grin and was gone, down the stairs and away to a rehearsal for one of the professional shows. Stella continued up the stairs to her cabin where she looked in Cruisenews and sure enough there was the advertisement calling all guests who had been cast for Aladdin to meet Denny at 10.15 the following morning in The Club. She'd had a feeling that notice for this would be short, so had already sat on her bed in the cabin a few days before racking her brains, digging back into the past and trying to remember what had worked really well in her Drama classes.

She had managed to come up with some activities she thought would be suitable, but it was with some trepidation that she sat next to Denny the following morning and watched everyone file into The Club. Would they accept her? After all, she was just another passenger, maybe they would resent her. What if she'd lost the knack and ended up making a fool of herself? And then there was the problem of that script...

"OK everyone, thanks very much for coming...now Stella's gonna do some stuff wiv you and then we'll see how we go...OK...over to you Stella."

She stood up and just went for it with a big smile, trying to radiate a level of confidence she didn't feel, hoping it would work – and it did. To her surprise she realised she was enjoying herself and so was everybody else. At the end of the session the ice was well and truly broken and people were profuse in their thanks...but what about that script?

They all sat down smiling and chatting, then someone plucked up courage,

"Denny, how on earth are we going to do a full scale pantomime with singing, dancing and costumes in the time we've got? We can't…"

"Yeah we can; no sweat. We done it before and it was great, wasn't it Glenda?" He turned to one of the cast who'd been on the ship previously and she nodded.

"Oh yeah, we done it alright," agreed Margie while the rest of the group looked blank. Stella noticed for the first time that Desmond wasn't there and realised she must have been very nervous not to have missed his overpowering presence. She learned later that his absence was due to the fact that he had taken one look at the script, pronounced it unworkable and himself out.

Then Denny dropped his bombshell.

"Yeah, you'll be alright. I know it's a good show, cos it's the one I'm going to be in at Christmas…back in Norwich!"

Stella was stunned, her mind turning over very slowly. So if Denny was in a panto in Norwich at Christmas, how could he be on 'The Matisse' as Deputy Cruise Director and working with them…? Somebody stated the obvious,

"So, you won't be here."

"No, but you'll be fine. Stella will do a great job."

Oh no! That wasn't the deal at all. Stella was furious, but didn't say anything until all the others had left, considerably more subdued than when they had arrived. She turned to Denny and didn't think it was her imagination that the grin was more sheepish than cheeky-chappie. She took a deep breath,

"Look, Denny, I'm not at all sure about this. I'm on holiday and to be frank many of us are concerned about the logistics of the whole thing. The panto is just too huge to manage with the time and facilities at our disposal…people are really freaked. And I'm not doing it on my own!"

"It's OK, Stella, you won't be on your own, I promise, cos we got another bloke comin' to take over from me. So, you got any ideas then, darlin,' about how we can make it better?"

"I think I may have," she told him and they arranged a time to meet so she could show him what she had in mind.

She went back to the cabin where she was pleased to find that Freddie had gone up to take part in the pre-lunch quiz. Sitting on the edge of the bed, she started to write, surprised and relieved to discover that the ideas flowed quite easily if she stayed focused on the people she had to work with and the needs of an audience at Christmas time.

By the following morning "The Spirit of Christmas" was ready for Denny to see. But first there was Singapore.

CHAPTER THIRTEEN

Singapore and civilisation! Tower blocks, clean streets and a mooring at a very efficient quayside; no tender boats this time but a walkway to exit the ship instead of the usual totter down a rickety metal stair-case.

"Singapore is a fascinating place," Freddie muttered, reading from the guide book: '...there is a splendidly dynamic feel about this island republic, strategically located between the Indian Ocean and the South China Sea where East merges with West. The temperatures are high all year round and there is an impressively prosperous atmosphere about the place...' He peered out of the coach window trying to marry up what he was seeing with what he could remember from being stationed there. He smiled at Stella,

"We have to go to The Raffles Hotel; you know why, don't you?"

"Yes...so that you can once again have a glass of Tiger beer, just like you did all those years ago, but that will come later...look, we're here."

The coach had stopped and everyone climbed down the steps then clambered onto a bumboat for a ride down the Singapore River. These boats had been used since the nineteenth century to shuttle goods between trading ships and the river quaysides, but now provided the ideal mode of transport for showing tourists the sights. They glided past the restaurants and gracious buildings of the old waterfront set against the towering skyline of the modern business district; then paused to admire, and photograph, the strange white statue of the Merlion – half fish and half lion – spouting water and apparently 'guarding' the mouth of the river. It was an impressive sight.

Back on land, Stella shuffled round a quiet, dimly lit Asian Civilisation Museum, full of exhibits giving visitors a taste of the rich cultures that make up Singapore's multi-ethnic society.

"Oh look, there's a gallery telling the story of the immigrants who lived and worked on the Singapore River. Do let's go and see."

Chrissie, now managing to walk without the aid of a stick, gently touched Jack's arm and together they turned and made for the gallery. Watching them, Stella thought she had seldom seen such an attractive elderly couple. Jack, tall and distinguished-looking with a shock of white hair and straight back; Chrissie, almost as tall, stylish and elegant, her white hair piled up in a loose top-knot. They were both smiling as they passed Stella, but didn't notice her as Chrissie was speaking and Jack, stooping slightly, had his head inclined towards her to hear what she was saying. They stopped and stood side by side, completely absorbed in the artefacts and the story, apparently oblivious to everything but what they were seeing – and each other.

'Mmmm…I wonder,' Stella turned and made her way back out into the sunshine.

"This is the oldest Church in Singapore, you know. It's Armenian and was built in 1835 by G.D. Coleman shortly after the founding of the city, but it's not now needed for worship as there are no longer Armenians living here. It's very interesting, though, isn't it?"

Father John stopped speaking and treated Freddie and Stella to his twinkling smile. They smiled back and Stella thought, not for the first time, that if you made him up you would be accused of stereotyping. Bright, watery blue eyes looked out from his little round face and a fringe of sparse white hair encircled a bald spot. His rotund body meant he had to lean back when he walked, and Stella had watched every Sunday since joining the ship as, clad in his long white robe, he moved quietly back and forward, preparing for the morning service on 'The Matisse,' his arms all the while making small paddling movements by his sides.

Father John adjusted his tiny, steel-rimmed spectacles and peered out from the simple, white interior of the

Church they were visiting to the garden, where several statues were clearly visible.

"Those are worth a look, you know. There are several depicting Christ's journey to Calvary carrying his own cross and falling under the weight of it. I'll catch up with you both later."

And he toddled off leaving Freddie and Stella to follow at their own pace, which they did, admiring the statues and also finding the tombstones of the Sarkie brothers who founded The Raffles Hotel.

"And so. Ladies and gentleman, to the highlight of today's tour – the legendary Raffles Hotel, first opened in 1887 and named after Sir Thomas Stamford Raffles who founded the city in 1819. It is a must for every first time visitor to Singapore. You will see that the elegant white building retains a wonderful colonial atmosphere providing a tranquil oasis of charm and old world dignity set right in the heart of the modern, bustling city which has grown up around it."

Following his well-rehearsed little speech, and proud to be able to present such a phenomenon to a group of tourists, the guide opened the door of the coach and indicated with a flourish that the passengers could alight.

They walked past peaceful gardens and stone fountains to a courtyard where Freddie suddenly stopped, a broad grin spreading slowly across his face,

"This is it!" He said, and Stella was sure she saw him smack his lips as he made his way over to where a dark-skinned bar tender was calmly serving beer.

"I'll see you later," she laughed, and set off to explore.

The small tropical gardens were overflowing with lush green foliage and bird-song filled the air; across another courtyard she noticed a row of boutiques and, entering one, then another, discovered that these fiercely air-conditioned outlets for expensive merchandise were identical to those in every top class hotel anywhere in the world. She suddenly found herself walking past the Ritz or along the Burlington Arcade and had no desire to buy anything.

"Look, I've got meself some jewellery and a Raffles bag."

It was Edie, in wheelchair mode this time, being pushed along by the ever-patient Stanley. Stella had seen her earlier in the day walking around in the sunshine eating an ice-cream, then cavorting about with Margie and Gracie – all having their photos taken next to the statue of Sir Thomas Raffles. She opened the bag and took out a necklace along with a pair of matching earrings.

"It's one o' them what gooes up and down."

She proudly demonstrated the movement of the pendant on the chain and Stella made suitably admiring noises before going to find Freddie.

"So did the Tiger beer live up to expectations?" She asked.

"Well, yes it did…but the price was ridiculous. Took away some of the pleasure really."

Stella made suitably sympathetic noises as they walked back to the coach.

They returned to the cruise terminal which they discovered was joined to a shopping Mall called Vivo, something they hadn't noticed earlier, and decided to have a look round before returning to the ship. It reminded them of home with many of the shops that could be found in the High Street of any town in England. They wandered half-heartedly up and down the busy precinct where they saw several fellow passengers shopping with great enthusiasm.

Chatting in the bar that evening, they were amazed to find that the splendour of The Raffles Hotel and other delights of Singapore were all but eclipsed by the joy of finding 'proper shops at last!'

"Why on earth do they want the same shops as we have at home?" whispered Stella,

"I don't know, beats me," growled Freddie, equally mystified.

"I mean...I know I can shop for England – when I'm in England – but I came away for 'different' and 'different' is what I want."

"I agree, love, you don't have to convince me."

The determined hunt for local supermarkets by guests 'doing their own thing' at their ports of call was a constant mystery to Stella and Freddie. With all their food provided in five meal opportunities a day, what could they possibly want to buy? The question was answered by the clinking of bottles in some very heavy looking bags accompanied by mutterings of, 'they needn't think we're paying those bar prices' or 'we like to have a couple of drinks in our cabin before we come down.'

Of their growing group of friends, Ray was the one who raised this to an art form. His bar bill was zero yet his glass of red wine always full. He and Vera sat having a pre-dinner drink with the group on many an evening and the mystery of how the glass went from empty to full was never solved, proving to be the source of much amusement and teasing. His grin became broader and white teeth flashed in his mischievous, tanned face as he enjoyed their bafflement.

Stella smiled as she recalled standing at the ship's rail with Adam one morning, looking out at a sea which they were hoping wouldn't be too rough for the tender boats, when all of a sudden he pointed towards the shore.

"Look...look, there, can you see...?

She followed his finger which was indicating a small boat and lone oarsman, bobbing up and down on the waves as he tried to reach land.

"Can you see him? It's Ray heading for the grog shop."

He threw back his head and roared with laughter.

CHAPTER FOURTEEN

Two sea days to Bali and Cruisenews was full, as always, of things the passengers could do to amuse themselves. Some lounged about in the sunshine with their books, swam or played table tennis and deck quoits; while others took refuge in the air-conditioned interior of the ship where there were quizzes, jig-saw puzzles, games of scrabble, dominoes, darts and chess. They could watch a film in the cinema, or on the television in their cabins, socialise with a drink and chat, sit and watch the sea – or just sit and moan.

The moaners were in the minority but, like all minority groups, seemed to be able to make their voices heard. Stella, Freddie and their friends were constantly amazed that they could find things to moan about, floating along as they were in a bubble where every need was met and food appeared in plenty, served with a smile, all day long.

Guests were invited to 'walk a mile and exercise with the entertainers' or take part in a 'pool aerobic class.' And, of course, there were the usual clubs and classes. Stella enjoyed card-making in the mornings then, after a light lunch, climbed up on to deck eight for the Art Class. Freddie went down below to the Computer Workshop where Gareth and Gwyneth were explaining hardware, while Sheila dragged a reluctant Bernard off to play bridge. Adam, happily sun-bathing with Denise on what he called the poop deck at the bow of the ship, watched them go.

"Poor old Bernard," he chortled, "he reminds me of Hyacinth Bookay's husband in that sitcom."

Cruisenews also advised that a masseuse had come on board in Singapore offering 'a vast range of massage and beauty treatments;' in which bars there were 'happy hours;' and that the duty free shop had a special two day gift clearance. Making her way down from the Art Class to The Club for tea, Stella decided to have a look at those 'bargains,' and found a familiar array of picture frames, jewellery and trinket boxes among the hats, scarves and toiletries – '…and all at 50% off!!' She smiled. Weren't they told last time these items were dragged out of a cupboard that it would be for one day only and positively the last opportunity for guests to avail themselves of such bargains – yet there they were again.

Although appreciative of just about everything on board 'The Matisse,' Stella did regard the ship's shop as a sad saga of lost opportunity. It was the only retail outlet for a captive group of shopping junkies deprived of their regular fix. It was impossible to get from one part of the ship to another without passing it and it was always full of retail hungry passengers just longing to buy. Yet all it kept churning out was middle of the road fashions, some bling, a few toiletries, booze – very expensive and couldn't be collected until just prior to disembarkation – perfume, handbags, baskets and assorted trinkets.

Stella wondered how difficult it would be to have a lorry waiting at each port to take away the old goods and replace them with merchandise relevant to the country they were visiting; after all, food and waste had to be organised in this way. For Stella, and those like her who wanted to use the limited time available ashore for learning something about the place, shopping opportunities were rare and often rushed. They would have appreciated time to browse at leisure on sea days through souvenirs they had missed on shore.

Isobel's port lecture would focus on Darwin, Australia; and Benny Green would be giving a talk about Bette Davis. Father John was celebrating Mass at 5 o'clock and there was a reminder that a Remembrance Day service would be held at 11 o'clock the following morning. A new Cabaret Artist had joined the ship and finally an item at the bottom of the last page stated that at 8.30 in the morning the ship would be crossing the equator for the first time – North to South – but, apparently, news had arrived that King Neptune would be sleeping at that hour, though he assured them that he and his Royal Court would be

84

watching over the voyage and demanding everyone's attendance at the ceremony of the next equator crossing later in the journey. Stella wondered what that would entail.

Stella managed to catch Denny during a rare moment of calm in his busy life and ran her 'Spirit of Christmas' ideas past him, leaving a copy with him. Looking as though he was, at least, half listening, he muttered,

"Yeah, OK darlin'...great stuff. I'll put a note in Cruisenews tomorrow...we'll get everyone togever...see what they fink...." before rushing off somewhere.

The meeting was scheduled for 2.45 in the afternoon and when Stella got to The Club a few minutes early she found Denny already waiting.

"'Ello, darlin'...Now look, about this new script you've written...I love it...it'll work, but I don't want people upset, see. You know...I've seen 'em around the ship already learnin' their parts an' that...don't want to upset anybody."

Stella sat back and thought for a moment, wondering how she could tactfully tell Denny that he had, as her old granny used to say, 'picked this up all wrong!' Far from people learning their scripts, everyone who had spoken to her had made it clear that, unless something drastic happened, they would be following Desmond's example and walking away – no show. She suggested that they should wait and see what the reaction was when she explained her ideas to them.

"Yeah...OK...that's OK, darlin'...just as long as no-one's upset...know what I mean?"

Assuring him she could grasp his meaning without too much difficulty, Stella sat back, once again feeling very nervous as the potential cast filed in and sat down. Reminding herself that if they hated it she could just quietly disappear and let them get on with the pantomime, she handed out the scripts and talked them through the show. They loved it, and Denny looked relieved when he saw how enthusiastic everyone was.

"OK, people, rehearsals start next sea day; look out for the times in Cruisenews," and flashing his cheeky-chappie grin he was off.

'I'm going to enjoy this,' Stella thought, as she made her way back to the cabin; though she was feeling just a little bit apprehensive about Denny's replacement who would be joining the ship in Australia. What would he be like and would they be able to work together?

With huge, bear-paws raised for silence and dark eyes twinkling, Adam leaned forward across the dinner table. The others did the same, knowing that something good was coming.

"Have you seen them…? Well have you?"

Dramatic pause, during which Stella wondered, not for the first time, why Adam wasn't taking part in the show.

"Who? Have we seen who?" Asked Bernard.

"Whom," corrected Sheila, then turned back to Adam as they all waited for the revelation.

"Well…they joined the ship in Singapore…you can't miss them. Cor!…A right couple of…"

Denise glared at him and he mentally moderated his language,

"I mean…sexy or what!? Just keep a look out wherever there are men for two very, VERY, exotic ladies and I mean…" He made the outline of a voluptuous woman, exaggerating the curves, "really flaunting it. We shall call them Naga and Saki. One has long, black hair – that's Naga – and the other one's hair is short and yellow with black roots." He gave a bark of laughter, "not that you'll notice the hair."

Another glare from Denise, who was obviously wondering for how long Adam had sat looking at them to take in so much, and they changed the subject; but not before glancing surreptitiously around the dining room to try and catch a glimpse of these extraordinary creatures.

They didn't have to wait long. Relaxing together in The Club with drinks after dinner, Stella looked across to the dance floor where she saw an extremely curvaceous woman, probably in her late thirties, with long black hair and a dress that left very little to the imagination, sashay up to Antonio and wrap herself around him. The following dance was so suggestive, much to Antonio's amusement – and some obvious pleasure – that it had everyone clapping and cheering. Everyone except Edie.

"Oh, look out...look out. Trouble's brewing," Adam chortled, and they all watched as Edie, unable to bear it any longer, stomped down to the dance floor and tapped Naga smartly on the shoulder. Still clinging limpet-like to Antonio, she turned to face her adversary who was standing with one hand on her hip and the other raised, thumb indicating the direction in which Naga should go. Full mouth twitching to suppress a smile, Naga turned back to Antonio and, again wrapping both arms tightly around his neck, kissed him slowly and seductively on the lips before, with a careless shrug of her shoulders, gliding across the floor to where Saki was sitting – also dressed to show off every asset. This whole pantomime was accompanied by cheers, wolf-whistles and cat-calls. Paid only to keep the passengers happy and caring little whether his partner was an over-sexed siren or over-weight matron, Antonio waltzed an ecstatic Edie off around the floor.

"....my friend and I like very much the men, but she more adventurous with men than me. We have nine days at sea and men in white uniform have much sexual...."

Freddie kept his eyes tightly shut as he pretended to be asleep in the library while listening to Naga talking to another passenger,

"We buy drinks for them and then go to cabin...have much fun...give pleasure while they are away from wives..." she paused and laughed, a husky, throaty sound, "Some are...how you say?...A challenge. I like very much the new singer on board and buy him champagne...write poetry for him and put under cabin door, but he say he love his wife…no matter. There are more."

Freddie peeped out through a half closed eye and saw Naga curled up in one of the chairs like a cat while her listener, a plump, middle-aged woman, was straining forward to hear more, cheeks pink and lips slightly parted. Obviously happy to have such an appreciative audience, Naga uncurled and leaned forward; her voice dropping to a whisper as further revelations had her listener blushing a deeper shade of pink and occasionally moistening her lips.

"So what else did she say? Come on, tell all." Adam leaned across the dinner table as Freddie relayed the incident that evening.

"I don't know…couldn't hear any more as she was whispering."

"Aaaawh." Adam sat back.

"I think we can imagine, though, can't we?" Said Sheila, colouring a little just at the thought of what might have followed.

CHAPTER FIFTEEN

Sheila hung on tightly as the tender boat bobbed and splashed its way to the quay.

"Padang Bay, Bali," Bernard jostled against her, reading from the little guide book but was unable to continue as a large wave rocked him back the other way.

"Bernard, for goodness sake hang on and sit still. I know where we are."

Honestly, he can be so irritating at times. Still clinging to the bar in front of her, she thought about Bernard – husband number three. He was kindly, that's for sure, biddable and seldom answered back, so why did she find him so annoying? After what Hugo had put her through, she knew she should be profoundly grateful for someone like Bernard.

Young and full of romantic notions about life as the ideal wife to a handsome husband, Hugo had fitted the bill perfectly. It had been as if her dream man had materialised before her eyes and carried her off to live out all her fantasies which, at the tender age of eighteen and just out of finishing school in Switzerland, she couldn't separate from reality. He was rich as well as good-looking; experienced where she was naïve – and, yes, still a virgin – what could be more perfect? She could belong to him and him alone for ever, and he to her. Without a moment's doubt or hesitation she had said, 'yes…oh yes, Hugo…' when he had asked her to marry him, crying tears of joy which he had gently kissed away. They were, she thought, blissfully happy until that terrible day when, for no apparent reason, he had hit her very hard across the face. She had been refusing to argue with him, just keeping quiet as he had shouted, waiting for his temper to subside, and then he hit her. Deeply shocked, and with blood from the cut above her eye still running down her cheek, she had forgiven him, even thinking it must have been her fault for provoking him beyond endurance. He had been so contrite, so very sorry, tenderly kissing her while gently bathing her eye, promising it would never happen again. It was the stress of the new baby, he said. Oliver had arrived by then and he was finding it so difficult sharing her because he loved her so much.

She believed him; in fact it was almost with a sense of pride that she assumed the role of understanding wife, loving being loved so much that even sharing her with a new baby was a problem for her husband. But it did happen again, and after the third time, when he broke her jaw, she realised she couldn't go on. But even after that, when she sat in the back of the old Rover, clinging to Oliver, as her father drove her away, she wanted to return. Looking back out of the rear window at the home she had so lovingly furnished for her husband, she saw Hugo watching her go. Shoulders drooping, he looked so forlorn and empty it was all she could do not to ask her father to stop the car. She still loved him so…he loved her…she knew he loved her…he couldn't help…didn't mean to hurt her. She had to fight the overwhelming urge to rush back and forgive him again refusing to accept that the dream could end like this. Glancing at her father's back, stiff and straight with suppressed fury, knuckles, bone-white on the steering wheel, she knew he wouldn't stop. With a super human effort she turned and, burying her face in Oliver's blanket, cried as though her heart would break.

It had been a while before she could love again, but when she met Julian she was sure she had found her partner for life. Feeling brave, she had ventured out alone one evening to a ballet at the local theatre and was fine sitting by herself in the darkness, letting the exquisite music and delicate movements of the dancers lift her into another world. It was only in the interval that she began to feel awkward, hovering near the bar trying to pluck up the courage to push her way through the crowd to buy something – just a mineral water or ice-cream – anything to feel she was doing the same as everyone else.

"Come on, let's scrum in together. It's easier with two."

She had turned and the warmth of his smile encouraged her to follow him to the bar. He had wanted to buy her drink, but she insisted on paying for it herself – something which he said afterwards he admired her for. They stood to one side chatting and she was charmed by his gentleness and sensitivity, his appreciation of the finer points of the ballet.

Afterwards she had loitered outside the theatre pretending to look for something in her handbag, but all the time glancing anxiously around until she saw him. He was also looking around and a smile lit up his face at the sight of her. They spent many afternoons reading poetry on the downs near her parents' home and Sheila loved the way Julian treated Oliver, an energetic toddler by this time. He had endless patience with the child and never minded him being with them. Looking back she realised this was what endeared him to her the most. He was very respectful towards her and never tried to push things too far when they were alone together; in fact if it hadn't been for Sheila making the first move they would never have got into bed at all.

She thought this was all rather lovely after Hugo's passionate demands and didn't mind too much when, after they had been married for a few years, the sex stopped altogether. She had Rosalie and Andrew by then, so was too busy to worry about it, and anyway she and Julian got on so well she was sure things would come right eventually. He was a designer, a very talented one, and as she admired his work, feeling sure he would be famous one day, she was happy to support and encourage him. It was therefore a total shock when he came home one day and told her he was gay. Just like that, out of nowhere. It is raining. What's for dinner? I am gay. To be fair he had made her a cup of tea and sat her down, saying he had something important to tell her, and she would have expected something exciting if he hadn't looked so miserable.

"There's no easy way of saying this, Sheil, so I'd better just come straight out with it."

Then he told her that he'd fallen in love with a window dresser at the local department store, they'd been having an affair for eighteen months and wanted to move in together. He looked so wretched and she was so stunned that they just sat there in silence. She was still numb as she listened to him telling her that he would always care for her and the children; he'd look after her and perhaps…perhaps they could be friends? She had agreed as she realised that was all they should ever have been, and Julian kept his word. He continued to be a good friend and loving father; Sheila met James and liked him, and sometimes the three of them would go out together. It was bizarre, but it worked, and it was then that she learned relationships simply are what they are and cannot be changed, any more than people can.

Many years later, after the children had grown, she met Bernard – dear, good, kind Bernard. A friend persuaded her she needed to get out more so she had agreed to make up a team for a quiz in the local pub. It was one of those smart, upmarket places with beams and very good food, so she decided to give it a try. Bernard was part of the same team and she found his bumbling ways quite endearing. He seldom got an answer right, but nobody minded – and he did make her laugh. His bluff good humour was refreshing, so when he asked if he could see her home she agreed; Sheila felt safe with Bernard right from the start.

He was a widower and she could see from his slightly grubby, frayed collars that he needed looking after; they got on well enough and she began to feel that they could enjoy a very comfortable, companionable old age together. Mothering him filled the gap left by the children's departure, so why was she so impatient with him? How did his shuffling dependency, endearing at first, so quickly become incredibly irritating? Honestly there were times when she could give him a sharp slap; and it was this thought one day that pulled her up with a jolt. She realised, with some horror, that she was replicating her relationship with Hugo, but the other way round. Had it been her eagerness to please, her worshipful devotion that had got on his nerves to the extent that it had caused him to lash out? There was no excuse for it, but she had to acknowledge, reluctantly, after all these years, that she could see it. She also saw suddenly, and with great clarity, that the only way to deal with a man like Hugo was to stand up to him. If she had hit him back, or even just screamed, argued, fought him in some way, he may not have hit her again. She would probably only have had to do it once, but it was too late, she would never know. And anyway, with hind-sight and the benefit of experience, would she have wanted to stay in a relationship with such a volatile man? There was no excuse for hitting a woman, or for a woman to bully a man.

With this revelation came a resolution to try and be kinder to Bernard. After all, he did love her, she knew that, and probably far more than she deserved. They'd decided to embark on this world cruise in the hope that it would bring them closer together. The trouble was, try as she might – and she really did try – Sheila knew she was still snapping at Bernard, and he just didn't deserve it.

"Oh, where are the dancing girls? The people who came over earlier said there were dancing girls. I can't see any dancing girls."

Bernard was shuffling forward waiting for his turn to get out onto the quay, his search for dancing girls making him pause longer than was necessary after the way ahead was clear. Instead of hustling him along, Sheila bit her tongue and waited patiently,

"Never mind, darling, there'll be plenty of interesting things to see soon."

When they finally stepped out onto the quay they were greeted, not by dancing girls but by vendors, and the hassling was beyond belief. Sheila clung to Bernard as they ran the gauntlet between boat and coach while merchandise was pushed under their noses with cries of, "you buy…you buy…!"

Hiding against Bernard's shoulder, Sheila declared she wouldn't buy anything in the face of such rudeness and Bernard, emboldened by Sheila's sudden, apparent, frailty, pushed the intrusive hands away, commanding gruffly,

"Go along…be orff…get orff with you."

It was with some relief that Sheila reached the safety of the coach and flopped down in a seat next to the window. She looked up at Bernard and smiled,

"Thank-you, darling. Honestly, what a nightmare."

Then turning to the window, she looked out to where the vendors were still jostling the last of the passengers trying to get onto the coach,

"I thought Cairo was bad, but this is just dreadful."

Composing herself, she smoothed her hair and frock, while Bernard eased himself down into the seat beside her, his cheeks pink with the pleasure of feeling he had been of some use and his shoulders just a little further back than usual.

Sheila linked her arm through Bernard's as they wandered slowly round a beautiful garden with two swimming pools of clear water surrounded by statues and pots of exotic flowers. Sheila pointed towards the statues,

"Oh look…look at the funny little skirts they are wearing – green and white check, just like my school uniform."

Still feeling bold, Bernard decided to take a risk.

"By golly, I'd like to have seen you in that, old girl."

He nudged her and was pleased when, instead of scolding him, she gave a little laugh and tapped him playfully on the arm,

"Oh Bernard…really. I wonder why, though…why the little skirts."

"I have no idea, but just look at those gruesome devils."

He was indicating two large and very ugly gargoyles representing good and bad spirits, set one each side at the top of some steps.

"And just look beyond!" Sheila burst out laughing and pointed to where a nearby tree had a notice pinned to it bearing the intriguing warning: NO MASSAGE!

They wandered on past shallower pools with rows of statues built in them and gargoyles spitting water round the edges. Sheila even listened attentively while Bernard read a piece from the guide book which told them that this was the Water Palace of Tirta Gangga built in 1948 by the last Raja of Karengasem as his private bathing pool, given over now to the public and used by the locals for swimming. As if to prove the point, they did, in fact, pass a group of honey-skinned boys enjoying the water and showing off by jumping in when they saw people watching. Sheila and Bernard started clapping and noticed that the harder they clapped the more spectacular the jumps became.

"Let's just stick together, put our heads down and go."

Jack took command of the situation, swinging into military mode as he came up behind Bernard and Sheila, hanging back in the face of the approaching hoard of vendors planted firmly between them and the safe haven of the coach.

"Quite right old chap."

Emboldened by Jack's presence, Bernard put his hand under Sheila's arm; Jack took hold of Chrissie's elbow and, seeing this, Kieran put his arm round Nancy, but it was immediately shuffled off as she told him crossly,

"I can manage just fine, Kieran. You look out for yourself, and hang on to them glasses."

Kieran blushed and removed his glasses which had almost got knocked to the ground by the vendors as he was getting off the coach. Jack and Chrissie strode ahead with Bernard puffing along behind, marshalling Sheila who was trying very hard not to push him away. He was, after all, just being kind and protecting her, though she did feel that she could have managed perfectly well on her own. However, she'd set a precedent by clinging to him on the way out and had sensed that her 'helpless little woman' act had made him feel good. No going back now.

They reached the safety of the coach and sat back to enjoy a peaceful ride through beautiful countryside – wet fields of rice on every side and even a group of excited monkeys – before arriving at Puri Agung Karengasem, the Palace of the former Karengasem Rajas.

"Charming…quite charming."

Jack had stepped inside the Palace gate and was enchanted by the small group of dark-skinned children with coal-black eyes staring up at him from round, serious faces. They stood quite still, hands clasped in front of them, bowing respectfully, the beautiful young girls handing out sprays of frangipane blossom to the ladies. Jack turned towards Chrissie and waited for the usual expression of delight he had come to expect as her natural response to such a scene, but she just accepted the flowers and walked on into the Palace courtyard. He frowned. What was wrong? Were her injuries causing her pain? He hurried after her, past a small group of men playing instruments that looked like giant xylophones with huge bamboo keys, and caught up with her as she accepted a cup of coffee and a small basket containing Balinese snacks. She moved quickly away and, hastily taking his own drink and basket, he followed her. They stood in silence on the terrace staring out over the surrounding countryside. Jack cleared his throat,

"It's breath-taking, isn't it?"

"Mmmm,"

was all Chrissie said in response and, glancing towards her, Jack saw that she was looking at the floor, not the view. He plucked up courage,

"Chrissie, what's wrong?"

"Nothing."

Oh dear. Jack remembered this from his marriage to Gwennie; it had been a happy one but, like all marriages, had gone through challenging times. He knew only too well that this 'nothing' was very much something, but his chances of finding out what were slim unless negotiated very carefully. The territory he was entering now was as dangerous as any minefield he had ever crossed.

"I wish you'd tell me…I'm quite a good listener, you know."

Chrissie turned and looked at him. She knew she was behaving badly and felt dreadful when she saw the genuine concern in his kind, grey eyes.

"Jack…. I'm so sorry. Do you mind…I'd just like to be alone today? There's something I need to think through."

"Yes…yes, of course. I'll…em…just go off and have a look around…and maybe see you back on the coach."

"Yes."

He moved away, resisting the temptation to look back, as he very much wanted to respect her wishes, and stared instead at an elaborate water feature full of exotic fish before sitting down on a strange-looking 'sofa' made of a heavy concrete material set with smooth black and white pebbles and topped by cushions. Although he wasn't really hungry, he opened the paper bag inside the basket and sampled the snacks, thinking sadly, as he nibbled the sticky rice wrapped in coconut leaves and fried bananas, how much he would be enjoying these if Chrissie was by his side, exclaiming enthusiastically at every mouthful.

"This next Water Palace is a bit of a ruin, I think. It's called 'Taman Ujung' and was constructed in 1919 by the last Raja."

Back on the coach Jim chatted to his friend, hoping to improve his mood, but Jack's grunted response told him it wasn't working, so Jim gave up and stared out of the window. He had no idea what was wrong; all he knew was that Jack had sat down next to him instead of Chrissie, which was a great relief as it meant he escaped from

Margie. The scowl on Jack's face had also made short work of the vendors, so it wasn't all bad, but he did feel sorry for his friend. Although they hadn't known each other for long – the tale of their meeting at the port for the first time was now common knowledge – they had become quite close and were generally popular with their fellow passengers. Jim knew that Jack was falling for Chrissie and sensed that this was at the heart of the current problem. Oh dear. Jack had told him a bit about his long, happy marriage to Gwennie and he had been a little envious. His own miserable marriage to Doris had ended in an acrimonious divorce which had left him penniless and living in sheltered accommodation while, following the death of his wife, Jack had kept his own home – and quite a luxurious one judging by the photos he'd seen. If he was honest, one of the reasons he was so fed up with Margie's attentions was that she reminded him of Doris, and that was the last thing he wanted on a 'get away from it all,' round the world cruise.

Feeling wretched, Chrissie wandered alone along pathways with huge lakes on either side and the tumbled remains of this former Royal pleasure ground all around. She found a deserted bench in a shady spot and sat down, removing her straw hat and slowly fanning herself. The haunting sound of plain chant drifted across the water from a distant building, soothing her senses while at the same time making her feel emotional.

"Hello, love, just taking a bit of a break?"

Nancy plonked herself down on the bench while Kieran hovered uncertainly on the path. Nancy looked at Chrissie's face then turned to Kieran,

"You go on, chuck, I'll catch you up."

Kieran cleared his throat and hesitated, looking more unsure of himself than ever.

"Kieran…"

The stern note in Nancy's voice and her raised eyebrow were enough. He got the message and walked off down the path, giving a little wave then putting his head down and hands behind his back.

"Now what's up? You look as though you're at a funeral instead of a pleasure Palace."

To her surprise Chrissie found that she welcomed the presence of this chirpy northern lass, down to earth and often able to cut right to the chase. Maybe Nancy's plain speaking was just what she needed.

"The truth is, Nancy, I've got myself into a bit of a situation. It's Jack…."

"…He's dead keen and you're not so sure."

Chrissie smiled in spite of herself,

"Something like that. He's so lovely I don't want to hurt him, but I think I'm going to and I feel absolutely dreadful about it."

"What's the problem though, Chrissie? You're both single, you make a lovely couple and you obviously get on really well together…"

She trailed off, frowning, and Chrissie could see that in her eyes they were two elderly people who could stave off the loneliness of old age by pairing up. Nancy knew nothing yet of the difficulties of commitment; she had no experience of looking after a very ill person as she had nursed Maurice, and to her horror she found herself saying,

"I just don't want to look after another old man."

There. It was out. Nancy was still frowning. Chrissie had told her a bit about being Maurice's carer, but nobody could know what it was like unless they had been through it.

"Well, you'd look after each other wouldn't you; and the thing is, Chrissie, you'd have some fun along the way."

That was certainly true. They were having fun and really enjoyed each other's company. Was she making problems where none existed? After all long term commitment…marriage…they hadn't been mentioned. It was just that she was pretty sure Jack was serious about her and she didn't want to build up false hope then let him down. Nancy lifted her sunglasses and looked around,

"It's lovely here, in't it? Hey, weren't it a hoot our guide getting all embarrassed tying to explain what the Raja and his concubines got up to? As if we didn't know!"

Chrissie laughed,

"Yes, it was rather." She paused, "How are things with you – you know, Kieran, Wayne and Sean?"

"Oh fine. I've decided to just let things take their course. Me and Wayne have a right giggle and Kieran comes in handy for carrying things. As for Sean, well, I'll cross that bridge when I get home. Meanwhile I'm just enjoying meself."

'Oh to be young again…' Chrissie gazed out over the lake then, out of the corner of her eye, saw Kieran heading in their direction. Nancy saw him too and, as he drew level with them, said angrily,

"Bog off Kieran! I've told you once already."

He cleared his throat,

"The thing is…the guide is waiting. We're leaving now."

"Come on then, we'd better get going. Walk along with us Chrissie."

And thrusting her bag and cardigan onto Kieran, she linked arms with Chrissie and they set off down the path. Kieran followed like a spaniel that's just been kicked but glad to be back in favour and of use to his beloved master.

"CLEAR OFF! I said clear off and I meant it!"

Still holding on to Chrissie, Nancy barged her way through the ubiquitous vendors who had been lounging against their cars until the arrival of the 'Matisse' passengers had the effect of a switch being thrown. They leapt into action, swarming and pestering with a desperation borne of the fact that it was almost the last chance to wring some money out of these tourists. Kieran followed on behind muttering,

"Excuse me…sorry…just let us through please."

100

"You buy…you buy."

A thin, brown-skinned woman wearing a brightly-coloured sarong and a scarf pulled so tightly round her head it gave her face the appearance of a skull, placed herself firmly between him and the entrance to the coach. Sensing his weakness, she glared at him, black lips pulled back against white teeth, and thrust a bony hand gripping a pack of post cards into his face. Kieran started to fumble for money,

"Well, perhaps just one pack…how much?"

"Five dollar…you give me five dollar." Then she saw the money in his wallet,

"No…you give me ten…ten dollar…"

"Oh…er…"

Kieran was floundering when suddenly Nancy appeared at the top of the steps. She jabbed the vendor in the back,

"No, no dollar. Now CLEAR OFF…AWAY."

She shooed the woman whose scowl and bared teeth were no match for Nancy's fury. She knew she was beaten and stormed off as Nancy pulled Kieran up the steps onto the coach.

From the safety of her seat Chrissie watched this little pantomime then instinctively flinched as several vendors jumped up at the windows, waving hands full of fabrics and carvings. She found herself entertaining the blush-making thought that the Balinese all seemed to look alike, when she suddenly felt sure that she really had seen at least one of them before as they got off the tender boat. How strange when they were miles away from the quay-side. She mentioned it to the guide as he passed her doing the head-count and, smiling, he told her they were indeed the same people who had been following them all afternoon. Well…full marks for persistence, but nought out of ten for sales technique, though she noticed that several passengers, without Nancy to rescue them, did succumb to the pressure and buy just to get back onto the coach.

As they made their way through the lush country side, Chrissie looked out of the rear window and saw the vendors clamber into their cars and set off in pursuit, leaning out of their windows and smoking as they followed the coach back to the quay for one last assault.

CHAPTER SIXTEEN

Two days to Darwin, Australia, and Stella's time at sea changed as rehearsals began. They were going well, but her table companions were mystified.

"Do you really want to do this, Stella? What about relaxation?"

As if to emphasise the point Adam stretched like a large and very contented cat. He had spent his day 'soaking up the rays' on his now well established spot – christened the poop deck – above the swimming pool at the stern of the ship. As someone who had to return to the world of work, he couldn't understand the concept of retirement. Stella could now, after more than thirty years in education, lounge about all day at home if she wanted to – she didn't, but she could – and the pace of life for her was totally different. The activities she chose to engage in were manageable with far less stress so the need to re-charge the batteries no longer existed and, as she was not fond of sun-bathing, 'The Spirit of Christmas' was providing a welcome focal point for days when all normal chores and decisions were taken care of. She was in her element.

"Don't forget the bun-fight this afternoon; you'll need to come down from the art room a little earlier than usual,"

Stella was just leaving the cabin when Freddie reminded her about this special event:

'Patisserie Buffet – come along and sample some of the wonderful pastries and cakes our chefs have made for you.'

So said the advertisement in Cruisenews that morning, also reminding people to take their cameras so they could photograph this banquet before it was eaten. But no, not on 'The Matisse.'

Geoffrey finished the class early and Stella hurried along to The Nautical Restaurant with everyone else, well in time to view the edible works of art before eating began.

She walked in and froze to the spot, unable to believe what she was seeing. The display had been decimated and old ladies with laden plates were pushing and shoving round the table to get more. The Maitre d', his assistant and the waiters looked confused and the noise was horrendous. The Maitre d' had one last try,

"Ladies please…you stand away from the table…please to make a queue for everyone to get some food,"

"Shove off, mate. I want some of that chocolate gateau before them other greedy buggers get it." and so saying, Gracie pushed her way to the front.

"Stanley fetch me some profiteroles and cream…and a slice of that white chocolate bomb thingy."

Ensconced in her wheel chair at a safe distance from the scrum, Edie was directing Stanley with her stick. Looking at the table, it wasn't difficult for Stella to imagine from what was left how exquisitely beautiful the array of food had been before it was prematurely attacked, and she was sorry not to have seen it in all its glory. She found Freddie sitting with Adam, Denise, Sheila and Bernard, all with expressions ranging from disgust to fury.

"Honestly, Stella, you've never seen anything like it…" Adam was red in the face, "…appalling behaviour from people who should know better…"

"And I didn't get my photographs!" Sheila fumed, while even Bernard looked a little annoyed, aware that something unacceptable had happened and hoping that he would very soon work out exactly what it was – or Sheila would tell him.

Stella sat down next to Denise who quietly described what had taken place before she arrived,

"It was the worst example of sheer greed that I've ever seen. We were all admiring the beautiful array of cakes and savouries and, just as we were about to take our photographs there was this stampede – mainly elderly ladies – who just ploughed in and started loading their plates. The Maitre d' came forward and asked them to wait until 4.15, but I heard one old lady shout, 'we're not taking any notice of that, mate,' as she charged forward. Honestly it was unbelievable."

Stella looked up and watched Stanley push a very self-satisfied Edie past them balancing a huge plate of goodies on her lap.

"I hope it chokes you, love," Adam growled, but Edie didn't seem to hear him.

'Spectacular Jumping Crocodiles! Take a cruise on the Adelaide River for a pure Outback experience and see the famous 'jumping' crocodiles as they shoot out of the water in pursuit of their prey.'

When Stella re-read the blurb in the excursions brochure aloud to Freddie she had visions of great scaly crocodiles, completely clear of the water, snapping at…what?

"What do you think they are chasing as they fly through the air?"

Freddie laughed,

"I have no idea, but I think 'flying through the air' may be a bit of a stretch of your fertile imagination. They'll be jumping to catch something."

"Yes, but what?"

"I think we'll just have to wait and see. It does sound exciting though."

Stella agreed and looked out of the coach window as they set off through Darwin and then southwards on the Arnhem Highway towards the wetlands area at the mouth of this famous river. The country-side was green, scrubby and unremarkable; the river wide, murky and lined with trees on each bank. As they boarded the boat the rain, that had been threatening to fall all day, came down with a vengeance making Stella and Freddie glad they had opted for an inside seat.

"It's much better for seeing the crocs anyway,"

Smiled Melissa, a pretty female crew member, before taking her place at the side of the boat next to a bucket containing several large lumps of meat.

A fit-looking young man with dark curls and dimples, wearing shorts and a 'T' shirt sat at the helm and the boat glided out onto the rain-spattered water. His commentary, delivered in a low, lilting Australian accent, began as they drew away from the bank and lasted throughout the whole trip with scarcely a pause.

"...and so, ladies and gentlemen, we are looking for ...hoping for...sight of one or two crocs this afternoon...the river is full of them...they are highly dangerous and I don't think we need worry that the rain will keep them away...just keep looking and shout if you see one. There are many of them just lurking around...they will appear silently as if from no-where – and still people swim here...still people say there is no need to be afraid of the crocs."

The last sentence was repeated many times during the afternoon. He was an entertainer with an obvious love of drama and, as the boat reached the centre of the river, he was clearly delighted to be able to say that he could see not one, but two crocodiles. Stella and Freddie looked and, yes, sure enough, there were two shapes, barely discernable above the surface of the water, gliding towards them. They could easily have been mistaken for logs floating down the river; in fact several times during the afternoon Stella did have trouble distinguishing crocs from lumps of wood. They came nearer and she peered through the glass at the creatures – sinister, menacing and ugly. One of them flicked its tail and disappeared round to the other side of the boat while the other approached and regarded all on board with eyes that rolled and stared.

"Oh...I say...!"

This exclamation was followed by a tiny shriek and, looking round Stella saw that their nearest companions in the seats behind were Colin and Venetia and, behind them, two other couples from the expensive cabins. Venetia had

106

her hand over her mouth and was wrinkling her nose as the croc continued to stare, opening its mouth very slightly to show the tips of tiny, needle-sharp teeth. She clung to Colin's arm exclaiming,

"Thank God for this thick glass, that's all I can say. What a grizzly looking creature. Marcia just look at its teeth – and those scales – positively pre-historic."

Her friend was already looking and they all continued to do so as a lump of meat tied to a piece of string was dangled over the side of the boat and waved around above the crocodile's head. At first it appeared to be taking no notice, its body motionless in the water, but Stella saw the eyes swivel up and fix onto the prey. Suddenly it jumped, its tail thrusting it upwards, armoured body vertical, small front legs dangling and huge jaws fully open now to reveal two rows of deadly pointed teeth. They snapped shut but the bait was pulled quickly away and the crocodile fell heavily back into the water with a loud splash. This was repeated three times and on the third jump Melissa allowed the animal to 'catch' the meat before pulling the empty string back into the boat.

They actually saw fifteen more crocodiles that afternoon, but the 'show' was only repeated nine times as six of them went straight past the boat, ignoring the passengers and the opportunity for a free lunch. Delighted to be producing so many crocodiles for his passengers' pleasure, the curly-haired commentator told them, with great relish, that crocodiles are cannibalistic and many bear hideous wounds as the result of fights they have with each other. He was particularly pleased when he saw that the fourth croc to approach the boat was Lucy, one of Melissa's favourites ('…she names all the crocs…'), as he was able to point out that one of her front legs was missing, apparently bitten off by one of the other crocodiles. His joy was complete when croc eight turned out to be an old favourite of his, minus three of its four legs! Stella thought it looked particularly sinister with skin the colour and texture of old stone.

"Well that was a good show, wasn't it?"

"Yes…absolutely…most entertaining."

"I'll say so. Well worth the money. The Aussie's have done us proud so far."

Freddie was chatting to Colin, Peter and Steven as Stella climbed back onto the coach followed by Venetia, Marcia and Julia, clutching heads and stomachs while still exclaiming at the grizzly inhabitants of the Adelaide River.

The next stop was a well set up Wetlands Centre that reminded Stella of the one near her home in the fens, but with different birds and animals; and then on to the last stop of the day – The Humpty Doo Hotel. A single storey, flat-roofed building, it squatted at the side of the busy Stuart Highway thirty miles south of Darwin and was described as 'a traditional Aussie bush pub' where cold beers and refreshing soft drinks would be available. The outside was painted pink and green with beer advertisements scrawled in giant letters across the tops of the walls. A few sparse palm trees grew on either side and the passing traffic created clouds of dust that billowed into a noisy covered area with picnic benches, entered through archways and cooled by several ceiling fans running at high speed. Stella looked round and was not impressed. It was one of those really dirty scruffy places, full of smoke and people with lank hair and no shoes, which the guides said they would all love as it was part of the 'real Australia.'

"Oh what fun!"

Venetia, who Stella imagined wouldn't normally frequent even a clean pub, suddenly jumped forward and sat down on a bench with a group of the dirtiest, greasiest men she could find – obviously regulars as they looked very much at home.

"Oh yes…this is the real deal isn't it?" Marcia cooed as she followed, then the rest of their group squeezed in anywhere they could get a seat. Pink-faced, they laughed – too loudly – and chatted to men in string vests and baseball caps with arms covered in tattoos. The men laughed too, but as Stella watched she realised they were laughing, not with but at the bus load of English tourists who had suddenly appeared. She also noticed that, although they looked as though they wanted nothing more than to get on with their usual pint out, they weren't averse to bumming drinks off the visitors who seemed only too pleased to pay up. One of them leaned back, waving his empty glass in Colin's direction,

"How about some more drinks for your new Aussie pals, mate?"

"Yes, of course. What would you all like?"

They shouted the names of various beers and he made his way to the bar while the one who had spoken first leaned forward again and ran his dirty finger down Venetia's back. She gave a mock shudder and giggled hysterically.

"Do you want a drink, darling?"

Freddie had appeared at Stella's elbow. She turned,

"No thanks. I'll just stay here."

She hovered outside the courtyard and couldn't wait to leave.

CHAPTER SEVENTEEN

Three more sea days. Rehearsals were going well and 'Cruisenews' was positively buzzing with all the activities available to pass the time:

'...Take part in the three day Skittles and Shuffleboard Tournament...Hurry along to the shop to purchase an evening bag (if you didn't get one last time) or some bling ready for tomorrow's formal evening...Make sure your costumes are ready for tonight's Rock and Roll party, after which you can go on deck to star gaze with our newest lecturer...After tea there's Cash Prize Bingo...And don't forget to book your hairdo ready for the formal evening...Guests are respectfully asked not to make too much noise when returning to their cabins, or to have televisions turned up too loudly; not to reserve (hog!) sun-beds on the open decks; to remember to use sun-cream and drink plenty of water (nanny will be checking later!). You can go and listen to talks about David Niven and Carmen Miranda...watch more films...see a show – Cole Porter tonight with dancing – or take part in the popular game of 'Mr and Mrs.''

And then there was Cairns where Denny was leaving the ship to be replaced by...?

'The Matisse' arrived in Cairns and anchored at Trinity Wharf for a two day stopover – the first one of the trip so far – and Stella found herself looking out onto civilisation. The town centre was only ten minutes walk from the docks and, in the course of a morning's exploration, she was delighted to find a couple of art shops where she bought gouache, water colours and brushes.

"This is great! Now I can paint in the cabin as well as in the art class for the rest of the trip."

"That's good." Freddie was pleased knowing that she would be happily occupied while he was reading in his favourite spot in the library.

The afternoon excursion took them through countryside that was lush and green, but led Stella to ponder again on the mismatch between the description in the little guide book – in many ways an excellent publication – and the reality of what they were experiencing. She was becoming certain that unrealistic expectations were at the root of the discontent and sheer misery felt by some of the other passengers, many of whom spent a lot of time at the desk complaining to Judy, the Cruise Director. Had they been seduced by travel brochures into parting with precious life-savings in the hope of 'getting away from it all' to paradises that simply don't exist this side of heaven? How much of their lives had they squandered while nurturing the dream that was slowly turning to dust? No-where on earth could live up to the hype as the descriptions of our world were out of this world:

'…Away from the coast there lies a high country of silent tropical rainforest, of rich plains where fat dairy and beef cattle graze, of waterfalls and swiftly flowing rivers watering avocado groves and fields of sugarcane, tobacco, groundnuts and maize. The cool, mist-shrouded tablelands nearby provide relief from the heat when summer temperatures reach 30 degrees centigrade…'

Maybe television was partly to blame with its enhanced picture quality and the ability to home in on and only pick out the best bits, accompanied by appropriate sound effects. The beauty of these tropical 'paradises' could be experienced from the comfort of an armchair without the inconvenience of excessive heat, unpleasant smells, aching legs and insect bites.

It certainly was lush and green, there were crops, and cattle grazing along the way, and it was exciting to arrive at the Rainforestation Cultural Park to experience a taste of Aboriginal life. The tropical rainforest, they discovered, is very ancient with some primitive plants such as tree ferns dating back more than a hundred and fifty million years. It is typified by a closed canopy of trees which cuts out the

111

sunlight, and two acres supports approximately 400 tons of plant life. Up to 14 tons of leaves fall in one year and are broken down by bacteria, insects and fungi. It also has a great diversity of life being home to more than 200 types of birds and more than 60% of Australia's species of butterflies. Giant Amethystine Pythons, which grow to a length of more than twenty five feet, can also be found there, along with giant tree frogs – up to six inches long – and large Hercules moths with wing spans of 10 inches.

"Come on…food…eat up…don't be shy…" Stella was feeding wallabies and kangaroos with some success as they were obviously used to the constant procession of tourists.

"Hey now, there's the really shy fella. Look at that dingo crouching behind a rock. Come on, old chap…come out and have a chat."

Although Freddie tried his best the dog-like creature stayed partly hidden from view.

"Oh look…look."

Stella pointed to some wombats, koalas and strange, gangly cassowaries before they were interrupted by the guide calling the 'Matisse' group and leading them to a clearing in the forest where rows of tiered seats faced a small stage. All went quiet as five stocky, brown-skinned men, scantily dressed and brightly painted, began stamping around the stage with strong movements, their bodies forming dramatic shapes. The little folded leaflet that everyone had been given said they were the Pamagirri Dancers, a troupe from different tribal areas of far North Queensland that formed in 1993 to perform traditional dances reflecting the aboriginal culture and telling little stories about their lives.

They began with the Welcome Dance during which everyone was summoned by the 'song man' playing a didgeridoo. This was followed by a Mosquito Dance showing how, when they hunt in the mangroves, they hit their bodies with leaves to keep the mosquitoes away. There was a Warning Dance, traditionally performed by the resident tribe when a new one moves to the area, warning them to stay away and avoid tribal war. A Snake Dance (Pamagirri means snake) brought them snaking out into the audience – quite scary – and was followed by a dance used to celebrate the finding of the Makor tree which has a sweet-tasting centre and is chopped down to share among the tribe. The Cassowary and Kangaroo Dances had the men imitating the animals' movements in a very amusing way; and the show finished with the Shake-a-Leg: Warran-Jarra.

Stunned by the powerful dances performed in such an amazing setting, the group filed slowly out of the clearing.

"A few new moves there for you to try, Margie." Freddie couldn't resist the quip as the dour Cornishwoman shuffled past. She didn't smile,

"No, I don't think so. I'll stick to me line dancing; I love me line dancing."

"Yes, quite right, and we enjoy watching you."

Stella smiled and dug Freddie in the back, daring him to say another word.

Then it was off to the steaming forest where everyone clambered into an old amphibious army 'duck,' actually spelt DUKW – D meaning its first year of operation was 1942; U signifying that it can operate in water; K for front wheel drive and W because it has two rear axles. It was large enough to take most of the group, has ten forward gears and two reverse and can travel at a speed of 85kph on land and 16kph in water. It has a propeller, rudder, bilge pumps and winch on board, and the driver can inflate or deflate the tyres while moving using an engine driven compressor.

The group knew all this as before they set off Freddie fired questions at the driver who was only too pleased to share his enthusiasm for this rather battered old machine with anyone who was interested. Freddie was in his element and all the other blokes were nodding, just as fascinated as he was by this relic.

"Now shut up so that we can get going," Stella hissed in her husband's ear.

"Well, if I hadn't asked, someone else would have done. Anyway, it's jolly interesting." Freddie sat back and got out his video camera as the ancient machine croaked into life and jerked off along the track.

The forest was hot, damp and full of strange, exotic trees and shrubs, many described by the guide as dangerous, and one so deadly they were warned to take careful note of it in order never to touch or even go near it. They bumped along over rough ground until they were suddenly faced with a lake and it looked as though the only option was to go in the water until the driver pointed to a steep track over to one side. Smiling, he turned to the group with eyebrows raised,

"Roadway or water?"

"Water!"

Everyone shouted in unison and he pretended to be surprised, rolling his eyes as he exclaimed in mock astonishment,

"You're sitting in a sixty five year old vehicle full of bullet holes and you want to go in the water?!"

It was obviously a practised routine and they did, of course, float safely through a very dirty, muddy lake and out the other side.

"I thought these things were meant to come back when you throw them." Hands on hips, Edie was staring crossly at a boomerang she had just thrown which had lodged itself in the grass and was sticking up at an odd angle a few feet from where she was standing. She was not happy. The forest was hot, smelly and full of weird insects; a kangaroo had tried to eat her fingers and as for them dancers – well, disgusting! dressed just in them little cloths round their waists. I mean, when they was moving you could see nearly everything they'd got! She'd had a go at playing one of them didgeridoo things and couldn't get a sound out of it; went to try spear-throwing and couldn't lift the blessed thing and now this boomerang wouldn't come back.

From a discreet distance Freddie and Stella were laughing as they watched her antics, then Stella turned in time to see Jack make a perfect throw. The boomerang sailed into a clear blue sky, circled round and landed back at his feet. The watching group applauded and Stella looked round for Chrissie. She was standing some distance away with Margie and, although she didn't applaud Jack's achievement, she was watching him. Stella wondered why she wasn't with him…come to think of it, she hadn't seen them together for a while. Then her attention was drawn back to Edie who had turned her back on the boomerangs and was stomping towards her across the field. Stanley marched by her side and, as they drew nearer, Stella heard him trying to cheer her up by saying brightly,

"Come on, love. Tell you what, we'll go and let you have a taste of that Jak fruit they're handing out over there."

Edie looked pleased and headed for the table where slices of this strange fruit were available for anyone who wanted to try. Stella groaned,

"Oh no!" She had already sampled this 'exotic delight' and was pretty sure she knew what Edie's reaction would be.

"THAT REALLY IS… D-I-S-G-U-S-T-I-N-G!"

Edie's vehement cry echoed round the field as she spat the offending fruit out onto the ground.

CHAPTER EIGHTEEN

The second day in Cairns and this was it – the apex, the absolute zenith of the entire trip – their eagerly anticipated visit to the world-famous Great Barrier Reef. Here the guide book surely couldn't be wrong. Stella read again the flowery description of the

'...awe-inspiring phenomenon and one of the natural wonders of the world...a 1200 mile palette of turquoise, emerald and aquamarine, dotted with coral islands and fringed with a white plumage of breakers sheltering an ancient realm of petrified gardens inhabited by an unbelievable range of creatures...'

She looked again at the picture in the excursions booklet which showed one of the islands and, eager to experience this unique adventure, set off with a large group of about a hundred and thirty fellow passengers just before nine o'clock. As she and Freddie climbed on board the waiting catamaran, they were encouraged to sit outside, which they were more than happy to do, though Stella noticed a good-sized seating area available inside.

"We'll leave those for the halt and lame," Freddie whispered as he watched Edie commandeer a comfortable looking padded seat, closely followed by Stanley, 'Central Eating' and 'Two Sticks.'

Then they were off, transported across the ocean at high speed, the combined noise of wind, spray and engines making conversation almost impossible as well as drowning out the running commentary they were vaguely aware of coming through the PA system. It was obviously accessible to people inside the craft, but Stella assumed it wasn't of great importance as they couldn't hear a word of it from their seats at the stern where they just sat back and enjoyed the sensation of speed, the sunshine and the thrill of anticipation – they were on their way to The Great Barrier Reef!

After an hour and a half the catamaran slowed down and Stella looked round for the island where they would be spending the day; but there was nothing, no land anywhere, just sea and a sort of floating platform towards which they seemed to be heading. They stopped alongside this moderately sized pontoon and people started to climb onto it. Somewhat mystified, she and Freddie followed and got swallowed up in the general hustle and bustle: Bright young things, male and female, handing out tickets for something; people hurrying along the wooden platform into a sort of shed at the end and emerging a few minutes later clutching hideous lycra body suits, the colour of pink bubble-gum, into which they heaved and squashed their various lumps and bumps of flesh. There was a lot of jostling and laughing as they flapped about the deck in flippers, holding masks and snorkels, and then headed purposefully towards the side of the pontoon.

Stella and Freddie were not part of this bustling activity and, still feeling confused, they joined the green-faced 'stick' brigade in the quiet seating area. The catamaran had made several of them sick, or just queasy, and they were doing their best to recover now that there was relative stillness, though their faces registered a fervent wish that they hadn't come on this particular trip. Stella and Freddie had a cup of coffee then, still wondering what they were supposed to be doing, wandered out onto the platform and peered over the side. Many of the group, clad in the 'pink bubble-gum' outfits, were floating face down in the water, snorkels sticking up in the air, clutching a rubber ring while others waited on the side, chatting and splashing.

Stella was torn. Part of her longed to join them, especially when she saw a giant blue and yellow fish playing with them like a puppy, but she was nervous, having had a scary experience with a mask and snorkel in Crete on a previous holiday. She wanted to conquer her fear, but needed encouragement and there wasn't any; everyone else looked so confident, so in the midst of all this noise and busyness how could she expect anyone to have the time to coax her gently into the water. And anyway, she still hadn't the faintest idea what to do. Sensing her misery, Freddie squeezed her hand,

"Shall we have a go, love?" He wasn't particularly keen to don pink lycra and flap about in the water, but was quite prepared to do so if it was what Stella wanted.

"I don't know…not sure."

Freddie turned and saw a semi-submersible glass-bottomed boat about to leave the side,

"Tell, you what, let's go in that while we think about it."

They peered back at the strange fish staring goggle-eyed at them through the glass and listened as the young guide told them about the amazing coral formations they were seeing in the murky depths of this underwater phenomenon.

"…that one is called Staghorn Coral. It's very fast-growing – about 26 to 28 centimetres a year – and is found mainly in the more sheltered areas as the horn-like growth could easily be damaged in exposed water…Now this big fella here…" she indicated a huge rock they were passing, "…this is Boulder Coral – a much slower growing species – only about 10 to 12 centimetres a year. These are both hard corals, but you will notice some strange-looking soft formations wafting about in the water…" they did, "…these are species of soft coral known as Spaghetti or Cabbage Corals and are quite squishy."

The guide also told them that The Great Barrier Reef has been listed as a World Heritage Sight since 1981, and the Reefs, Islands and Coral Caves have also been separated into different zones, each one characterised by a different colour. They were in the green zone which meant no fishing or coral collecting was allowed and water sports were limited, all of which helped to protect the reef for a little longer.

Stella found all of this very interesting, but climbing back onto the pontoon she still felt she was missing something so, in an attempt to try and redeem some of the upbeat mood from the earlier part of the day, she plucked up courage and grabbed Freddie's sleeve,

"Come on, let's have a go at the snorkelling."

They approached one of the young women who was now pre-occupied with removing tin foil from trays of 'tropical smorgasbord lunch,' and asked what they had to do to get in the water. She had started to dig the food out of the tray with a fork but paused for long enough to inform them casually,

"The snorkelling tours have now finished for the day. After lunch the men will be taking the intermediate group further out." But then, on seeing Stella's disappointed face, she added brightly, "...but hey, you might be lucky...go over there and talk to Craig...he may have one more group going just before lunch."

She returned to her digging and they went to find Craig who said yes, he would take them if they hurried, they just had to go and purchase their suits for twelve dollars each and they could pay their thirty dollars each for the snorkelling tuition at the end of the day. WHAT!?!...Stella was reeling. The trip had already cost a hundred and thirty pounds – sterling – each and there had been no mention of extra money for snorkelling. What a rip off! Freddie agreed so they declined the offer and collected their lunch, which was not impressive, then spent the afternoon sitting around on the platform. They did go in the semi-submersible again and saw a shark. 'How does that work?' Stella wondered, knowing that many of their companions were snorkelling just a little way off.

At last it was time to return and the catamaran ride back in the evening sunshine was pleasant, but people were subdued and, although many had enjoyed themselves, Stella sensed a lot of genuine discontent. With a face like a slapped bottom, Edie made her way slowly and painfully down the gangplank, declaring when she reached the safety of dry land,

"If I never see another catamoorangue in me 'ole life it'll be tooo sooon."

It niggled. And when Stella woke up the following morning she was still cross so, for the first and only time on the trip, she found herself in sympathy with the complainers. She checked the booklet carefully and nowhere did it say they would be spending the day on a pontoon; nowhere did it say they had to pay extra for snorkelling tuition. It did refer to 'snorkelling tours' being, like helicopter flights, one of the optional extras but Stella and Freddie, along with most of the others, didn't realise that a 'tour' meant floating about a little way from the pontoon.

'Don your complimentary snorkelling gear' did seem at odds with the charge of twelve dollars each for the pink suit that people were strongly advised to wear to protect themselves from the jelly fish – no-one saw any. Apparently, they learned afterwards, they could have been given the basic mask and snorkel and just splashed around on their own if they wished. Even genial Geoffrey, the art tutor, who had had a marvellous time, said,

"More money here, more money there – it were a bit of a rip off, weren't it?"

Stella made her way along to the office to see Pete, the excursions manager. She just had to get it off her chest, partly so she could put it behind her, but mainly so that he would have the opportunity to change the misleading blurb in the brochure saving others from a similar experience to hers. He was defensive:

"…It doesn't say we'd be on a pontoon, Pete…"

"…It doesn't **say** you'd be on an island…"

"…No…but the picture…"

"…It still doesn't say anything about an island…" He jabbed the booklet with his finger.

"…We didn't know what was going on…"

"…Everything was explained quite clearly over the PA system during the trip out there…"

"…Yes, but we couldn't hear it. We were sitting outside…"

"…you should have sat inside…"

"…Pete, we were **encouraged** to sit outside and no-one told us we would miss vital information if we did so…"

Stella had arrived at the desk feeling quite calm, by this time she didn't. She tried again,

"Look, Pete, I didn't come here for an argument and I don't want any money back," – he looked relieved – "I just wanted to tell you how I felt. The advertising material for the trip is very misleading, and there are many of us who would not have gone if we'd known exactly what to expect. I just thought you could change the advert for the next voyage, or arrange for a trip to one of the islands which is what most of us had been expecting."

Pete didn't look convinced and Stella was disappointed that he hadn't taken her comments as the positive evaluation they were meant to be.

Three more sea days and the shop brought out its Baltic amber again – very expensive – as well as a selection of Timex watches. There was another three day tournament – kalooki and table tennis this time; people were invited to get their faces painted for the Australian Deck Party and go out again after dark to 'Star Gaze with Jonathan.' Stella and Freddie had tried this and thoroughly enjoyed staring into the velvet blackness, steadying themselves against the motion of the ship, while he probed the night sky with his special laser light, informing, educating and generally infecting them with his enthusiasm.

People could take up a sudoku challenge, try golf-chipping into the pool or even learn how to navigate "The Matisse" as one of the passengers was beginning workshops to provide their 'first informative insight into the world of navigation.' They could get their feet massaged – ABSOLUTELY FREE – if they booked a foot spa and pedicure; buy a 'T' shirt advertising the fact that they had crossed the equator, take part in games to identify sounds or even see how many words they could make from CRUISENEWS.

Following the Australian deck Party on the first of these three 'at sea' evenings, made complete by a promotion in the form of a 'Beach Bum Cooler' – rum, banana, pineapple juice etc. they could, on the second evening, enjoy the performance of a new cabaret artist; and on the third they were urged not to miss the fun when 'Mr. Matisse' would be chosen from a crowd of hopefuls.

Stella and Freddie were genuinely impressed by the versatility of the Sailaways staff who worked tirelessly to ensure that there wasn't a moment from dawn till dusk without a variety of activities on offer. They quizzed, walked, exercised, played games and generally frolicked with all and sundry. If people were bored it was not for the want of effort to stimulate on the part of the staff. As all this became a way of life, they were further reminded how odd it was to be part of this strange community where many of the passengers seemed to have reverted to childhood; their decisions were made for them and, like children in a nursery, they demanded constant entertainment or they would complain, grumble, generally make a nuisance of themselves or kick their toys to pieces.

Stella was very glad to be absorbed in 'The Spirit of Christmas' and felt it was a privilege to have the opportunity to create a show in which she was working with both amateurs and professionals. And then there was Stuart. Having said goodbye to the chirpy Denny in Cairns, wishing him all the very best with his pantomime in Norwich, she waited with baited breath to meet his replacement. She didn't have to wait for long.

On the first sea day the cast assembled at ten o'clock and there he was – dark hair, clear eyes and a lovely smile. He introduced himself and listened attentively as she explained what they were doing and how far they had got. Apparently Denny had said some good things about the show and Stuart was keen to get started as co-director. They rehearsed, then Stella stayed behind to talk to him and plan further rehearsals, glad of his intelligent contributions and his ideas, sensitively shared without making her feel that he really should be somewhere else as he was the professional and she, these days, merely an enthusiastic amateur. But most of all – he listened! She breathed a sigh of relief sensing immediately that they were going to get on – and they did. They worked well together, and the harmony between them benefited the whole cast – almost sixty altogether by the time they had added a choir. It was great fun and proved to be one of the most trouble-free projects Stella had ever been involved in.

CHAPTER NINETEEN

'Picture a handful of sunny islands surrounded by coral reefs and blue lagoons, shell-strewn beaches and a warm Melanesian welcome, and you'll start to feel the atmosphere of this fragment of France in the South Pacific. Beneath the flame trees shading public squares, petanque enthusiasts play with fierce fervour and, as on every village square in Southern France, they're applauded by onlookers sipping pastis outside the nearest cafes.'

So said the Disneyesque description in the guide book of Numea, New Caledonia, but the reality, again, was somewhat different. To be fair, perhaps a longer stay would have allowed 'The Matisse' passengers to experience at least some of these pleasures. As it was, the 'birds' eye view' excursion had been cancelled, so not for them the thirty minute flight during which they could 'marvel at the wondrous bays, beaches and off-shore islands of Duck, Escapade and Amedee while admiring the vibrant shades of blue over the lagoon's waters – and all the while looking for turtles.'

Freddie closed the guide book and turned to Stella who looked a bit disappointed,

"Never mind, love, let's go down and see if there's something else we can book."

And they managed to get two seats on a glass-bottomed boat trip in the afternoon, so had some time free to explore. Leaning on the rail at seven o'clock that morning as the ship sailed along the coast towards the quay, Stella and Freddie had been enchanted by the mixture of little bays with blue seas and bobbing boats, fringed by blocks of flats and houses with quite large mist-covered hills in the distance. They learned that it was one of the French Overseas Territories from 1956 to 1998 but was now well on the way to independence. Their arrival was further enhanced by a Polynesian dancing group performing on the quayside, a swirling mixture of vibrant colours and energetic movements.

After breakfast they set off, along with many of the other passengers, to explore the town of Numea and found it to be a strange mixture of shops. Gifts, jewellery, clothes and bags were all jumbled up together alongside boutiques selling upmarket French fashions. They had been assured that US dollars and euros would be accepted, but they weren't, which wasn't too disappointing as there was very little they wanted to buy. Stella did try to purchase a few toiletries but the chemist, who reluctantly said he would take dollars, then put such a high price on the items that she returned them to the shelf. They fancied a cup of coffee but the vendor, in a sort of snack shack that formed part of a covered market of different shops and stalls, insisted that coffee could only be bought with pacific francs and then only if accompanied by food.

They strolled back to the ship for an early lunch then boarded a minibus for their trip out to an island and the ride in a glass-bottomed boat. After about three minutes Adam, who was sitting behind Freddie, tapped him on the shoulder.

"We're on our way back."

"No, surely not."

"Yep. We've just gone round in a circle."

And he was right. Freddie turned and looked out of the window just as 'The Matisse' came into view and, a few seconds later, the minibus pulled up at the quayside in exactly the same spot from which they had departed five minutes earlier.

Looking a little nervous, Pete, the excursions manager, greeted them as they got off the coach. He cleared his throat,

"I'm very sorry, but owing to an increase in the strength of the wind you wouldn't be able to see anything in the water so I'm cancelling the trip. I'll refund your money in the morning."

This announcement was, predictably, met with groans and, shoulders drooping, people dispersed in small groups, muttering and shaking their heads.

"Oh well, can't be helped. Denise and I are heading over there to stock up on pre-dinner supplies."

Adam pointed across the road to a large building that Stella and Freddie hadn't realised was a supermarket and they watched him amble off, the ever patient Denise at his side.

"Shall we give it a try? Freddie suggested, "They must surely take US dollars." And they did. Stella was able to buy the toiletries she had failed to get in the town with the added bonus that the refund from the trip would cover the cost of these.

"Hello shipmates."

It was Ray, a cheery grin spread right across his face, also, like Adam, stocking up on pre-dinner supplies.

"Bit of a shame about the excursions, weren't it? Still we're making the best of it." He pointed to his basket, groaning under the weight of red wine bottles, and chuckled.

"Vera's over there, looking for stuff for the grandchildren – as usual. No change there."

It was said with affection, and Stella looked over to where Vera was browsing amongst the toys and baby clothes. She turned and waved.

"Oooh…watch out. Cranky alert."

Ray gave a nod of his head to where, further down the aisle, Jeannie and Donald were studying the bottles of whisky, taking them off the shelf in turn, looking at the price, then either returning them or putting them into their basket, already laden with wine and gin.

Ray turned away from them and, lowering his voice, muttered,

"They hardly ever come down to dinner now and if you see them around the ship they are nearly always the worse for drink – especially her. Rumour is they're killing themselves with booze. Sad ain't it? Still I suppose there's worse ways to go. See you later,"

And he staggered off towards the checkout, his bandy legs buckling under the weight of his basket.

Back outside the supermarket Stella and Freddie browsed among the 'T' shirts, gifts and knick-knacks for sale at some stalls in a small square nearby then returned to the ship where they enjoyed watching more local dancing as they prepared to leave. They had already noticed throughout the trip that if 'The Matisse' was due to sail at a particular time it did so, almost to the second, and that day was no exception. Their published departure time was 5.00 p.m. and, sure enough, they slid away from the quay on the dot. Along with several others they watched the crew manoeuvring the huge vessel, and admired the way it glided effortlessly through quite a small opening in the bay and out onto the open sea.

CHAPTER TWENTY

"Blimey, look at them, Denise…look…those trees over there"

Denise leaned forward and peered out of the coach window to where Adam was pointing at some unusually shaped trees spreading over the fields like giant green mushrooms. She continued to look as they travelled through several villages composed of small groups of straw huts and very basic shed like houses that reminded her of the pre-fabs put up in England just after the war.

'The Matisse' had docked the previous evening at Suva, the capital of Viti Levu, the largest of the two main islands of Fiji, and Adam and Denise, along with most of the other passengers, were heading towards the Pacific Harbour Arts Village.

"Captain Bligh…Mutiny on the Bounty…shiver me timbers, Jim lad…Aaahaaa…"

Denise smiled and covered her ear as Adam growled his mock pirate imitation so close to it that she felt his breath tickling her neck.

"Isobel made a lot of that connection during her talk about Fiji, and of the islanders' tendency towards cannibalism…" she told him, and Adam recoiled in mock horror until she added hastily "…that she assured us is no longer practised here," at which he made an exaggerated show of relief. Denise continued,

"She also said that the Dutch explorer, Abel Tasman, was probably the first European to sight the Fijian islands in…." she paused and bent down to extract a notebook from her straw bag, "…in…1643. Then in 1774 Captain Cook's 'Resolution' anchored off Turtle Island and, following the 'Bounty' mutiny in…in…ah, yes, here it is…in 1789, Captain Bligh evaded hostile islanders and still managed to give the first accurate charting of the islands. In the nineteenth century missionaries arrived and converted many of the islanders to Christianity, though some of them did get eaten for their trouble."

"Oh very nice," Adam chortled. Denise giggled,

"Yes, but it's OK. Apparently the islanders only ate people to absorb their good qualities!"

"Do you know what, Den, if I was up to me neck in a cooking pot full of boiling water with the steam, fragranced by a few well-chosen herbs, of course, pervading me nostrils, I don't think I'd find much consolation in that fact."

She laughed then continued to read,

"In 1874 the islands were officially ceded to Queen Victoria and today the population, a real ethnic melting pot of Melanesians, Polynesians, Indians and even some Chinese – around 893,000 altogether, all live largely on the two main islands, Viti Levu – where we are – and Vanua Levu."

Adam was only half listening as he continued to stare out of the window at the passing countryside. He admired Denise's intelligence and the way she liked to learn all the facts about the places they were visiting, but he was on holiday and attended very few of Isobel's lectures, preferring to soak up the sun's rays on his specially chosen spot – the poop deck – and let the world drift by. He was endlessly fascinated by the behaviour of the other passengers, having quickly realised you couldn't make it up, you really couldn't, it was unbelievable; so he indulged in a fair amount of people watching while pretending to dose under his pork pie hat, legs stretched out in front of him and waves gently splashing against the side of the ship. He loved absorbing the atmosphere of the exotic places they were visiting, but as to the facts, well he'd leave all that to Denise.

Denise. He glanced quickly at the pretty blond woman next to him and, not for the first time, marvelled at his luck. He was not a religious man and continually wondered what providence, what stroke of good fortune had brought her into his life. Plunged so deeply into a pit of depression following his bitter divorce from that stupid, fat cow he'd married, he'd actually considered suicide, especially after she had managed to turn his two children against him, and it was Denise who had saved him, Denise who had convinced him that life was still worth living.

'What on earth that gorgeous, 'fragrant' woman sees in you we will never know,' was only part of the ribbing he'd got from his friends at the pub on Friday evenings after he had proudly introduced her, announcing that they were moving in together. And he agreed with them. He knew he was grossly over weight, but his love of food prevented him from doing anything about it. When he gave it some serious thought, which was rare, he acknowledged that the failure of his marriage was partly the cause of him turning to food for comfort, as comfort had been seriously lacking in that relationship. Denise now provided all the love, stability and comfort he could want, but his addiction to food remained. Luckily, she didn't seem to mind, but accepted him just as he was. Yes, he was indeed, very, very lucky.

"Cor…makes you feel like royalty, don't it!"

Adam observed as he struggled down the coach steps at the Arts Village where their arrival was heralded by the reverberating sound of a hollow drum beaten by a Fijian warrior. They were then serenaded by a group of young people with grass skirts and painted bodies, singing and playing guitars, before being given cold drinks and led to tiered rows of seats. As they sat down, Adam and Denise looked across a moat of very dirty water to a patch of ground surrounded by trees with a pile of smouldering wood and stones at the front, a little to one side. A stone building, only one storey high but topped with an extremely tall thatched roof, was set some way back at the top of a small incline. Adam pointed across the water,

"That's where it's all going to happen then. I'll bet they come out of that weird building to do their bit of pageantry and fire-walking."

And he was right. But before any of that, a very attractive young man came out onto the platform directly in front of where they were sitting to tell them all about the value and versatility of the coconut, used extensively by the Fijians. He was accompanied by a lovely young woman who stood next to him as he explained the significance of the flower she was wearing in her hair. If placed behind the left ear she is still single, behind the right, she is married – "right is cooking, left, still looking," he quipped, then added, "If it's in the middle, she hasn't made up her mind!" Denise laughed and whispered to Adam,

"I know he's dressed in a green grass skirt with foliage all over him and a circle of leaves on his head, but he still looks very macho."

"She's not bad either," whispered Adam, admiring the young woman's voluptuous figure, "Strange head dress though – looks like a collection of long hat pins stuck in her hair with bits of ribbon at the ends."

The pretty young woman left the stage and the man, using the basket of props he had with him, proceeded to tell everyone about the way in which Fijians make use of every part of the coconut. The leaves can be woven into baskets or fans – ('Fijian air conditioning!') Branches are used in the cooking process; the fibres inside the coconut husk, called magi-magi, are made into string used for fishing nets or binding together the joints of houses and boats; they can even be woven into ropes for tying up prisoners, mooring canoes or making belts.

He showed examples of green coconut shells made into soup bowls – with stands – and mature coconut shells used to make cava bowls. Adam nudged Denise, "There you are, love, that'd do for you on a Friday night; bit of a change from your champagne glass; you'd certainly get more. I'd end up carrying you home!"

He guffawed, not realising that his 'stage' whisper had echoed round the seating area and reached the ears of the young man in front of them. Denise's face was scarlet as everyone laughed and the man looked at Adam.

"No, my friend, you would not give your lovely wife this cava; it's not like that gentle drink you have in your country." He looked round at the assembled company before continuing,

"Here I give you all a serious warning not to touch this cava. It is a traditional drink made from the root of the cava plant which is pounded into powder and mixed with water. The mixture looks muddy and is very intoxicating but to the Fijians tastes good. After a few bowls of this the lips and tongue become numb." He paused again before adding ominously, "the more cava a Fijian man drinks, the less family he will have."

"Thanks for the warning, mate," then, still playing to the gallery, Adam looked round, "Not much of a worry for us, eh chaps?"

Everyone laughed again as the average age of 'The Matisse' passengers was about fifty!

The young man concluded by explaining that the trunks of the coconut trees are used to make furniture and, years ago, even for building bridges; while the roots are believed to cure breast cancer in women. "In Fiji it is a compliment to be called 'as useful as a coconut.'"

Everyone applauded loudly and Denise sat back looking thoughtful,

"I found all that really interesting, but you know one of the things that impresses me most is the fact that he delivered it in faultless English, even pausing in the right places."

"Yes," agreed Adam, "Very humbling."

The young man left the stage and his place was taken by Scott whose job it was to prepare the audience for the main event of the day – Fijian fire-walking. Everyone listened attentively as he began by telling them the fascinating legend behind the ritual:

'Many years ago on a neighbouring island lived a tribe called the Sawau who had among their number a famous story-teller. He would entertain them with his tales and, in return, it was customary for the members of the tribe to take him gifts as a show of their appreciation. On one occasion, when asked what he wanted, he requested that each member of the audience should bring him the first thing they caught when out hunting the following morning.

One of the warriors, a man called Tui, went fishing for eels in a mountain stream and the first eel he caught assumed the shape of a little man when he pulled it out of the mud. It spoke to Tui who immediately recognised the voice of the spirit god. Pleased with his catch, the hunter set off to present it to the story-teller, but the spirit god pleaded for his life and offered all manner of gifts in exchange for this. Tui refused to let him go until finally the spirit god offered to give him power over fire at which point Tui's interest was aroused to the extent that he built a fire under a pile of stones and watched as the spirit god leapt onto them, calling on Tui to join him. When the hunter plucked up enough courage to do so, he was surprised to find that he felt no effect from the heat. To this day the ritual is performed only by members of the Sawau tribe who can claim to be Tui's direct descendants.'

Conch shells were blown to indicate that the ritual was about to begin and, first to emerge from the thatched hut was the High Priest who walked slowly down towards the water and pile of stones from which smoke still spiralled upwards. Scott explained that this priest was in charge of the ritual and, as they watched, he made quite a drama of calling the rest of the walkers to come down and remove the smouldering logs from over the stones, which they did, adding to the drama with a great deal of shouting. They pulled the wood off using poles with loops – (most probably made from coconut fibre) – tied to the ends. Much was made of the fact that the stones, which are taken from the river, have to be white hot, so the fire had been alight since eight o'clock that morning.

There followed about half an hour of raking around in the ashes and pulling the stones about before a long pole, strung with four garlands, was carried in and held over the stones. Scott explained that this is an important part of the ceremony as the fire-walkers believe that spirits dwell in the garlands. A vine was then used to turn the stones over again and, at the same time, the men shouted a prayer to the fire god asking him to send down his blessings on the ritual before the stones were again re-positioned. Scott also added that since Christianity had been introduced into Fiji by missionaries, the fire-walkers also pray to God before each ceremony. For two weeks before the ritual the participants must segregate themselves from all females, having no contact with them at all, and must not eat any coconuts,

"Nor drink any of that cava either, I should think,"

Adam whispered. Denise nudged him to be quiet.

Another rule was that the rest of the villagers must not cook in an underground oven at the same time as the fire-walking ceremony is being performed as they believe that the food will never be cooked.

Leaves and branches were carried down and put near the stones ready to be placed over them after the ritual, though some were used before it took place to brush the stones in order to sweep away any evil spirits that might disrupt the ceremony. Adam leaned towards Denise and whispered,

"You know what, with all this faffing about the stones will have had plenty of time to cool down before those blokes actually step onto them."

Denise was glad they were far enough back for Scott not to be able to hear Adam's cynical comment, but his 'whisper' was loud enough to evoke a few titters and nods of agreement from some of the people nearby. Freddie, who was sitting behind, poked him in the back,

"Do you fancy having a go then, mate, show us all how it's done?"

Adam looked to where smoke was still rising from the pile of stones and heaved his bulk round towards Freddie,

"Nah…I'll leave it to the men in the grassy skirts. Too many evil spirits hanging about me; I'd need to be pooorified first and that'd take too long!"

Denise raised her eyes to heaven, then they both turned back in time to see the High Priest make quite a show of checking that all was in order according to tradition before he squatted down, clapped his hands and shouted to signify that everything was ready. Slowly and carefully he stepped up onto the large stone in the centre of the pile then he signalled to the rest of the walkers to join him, which they did, making a great show of it by walking on each stone in turn and posing at the top, indicating that they expected the audience to applaud.

"They're milking that for all it's worth,"

Grunted Adam, slapping his bear paws together.

The High Priest who had been the first to walk on the stones was also the last and, as he stepped down, leaves were placed over them. Denise pointed to where smoke was still rising from the pile as the tribesmen walked away,

"There you are, cynic, they must be hot."

"OK…OK…I take your point," Adam conceded, but couldn't resist adding,

"I just wish they'd chucked a bucket of water over them so I could see if they hissed and sizzled."

Next came Fijian dancing during which the men performed a spear dance with strong movements and much stamping, while the women sat clapping and singing to music supplied by a man banging a hollow tube with a stick. The men then sat down and the women danced,

"When they dance they smile to attract men,"

Scott told them,

"The men, of course, don't bother to smile. Typical!"

Denise whispered and glanced at Adam who grinned,

"Quite right too. We don't have to; we just draw you in with our macho charisma and winning charm"

Denise said nothing.

Then came the finale – a pageant in the form of a tribal war challenge which began with a man stomping angrily up and down next to the water on the same side as the audience was sitting. He was shouting and waving a stick at the people on the other side then, amid gasps of delight from the onlookers, he threw himself into the murky water. As he climbed out on the other side he was asked why he had come.

"Sent by chief to get a lady,"

He shouted in reply, and was told there was no lady there for him and if the chief wanted ladies he must come himself with more men and fight for them. He was then chased back into the water.

"One chief can have as many as forty or fifty wives, so there are frequently battles of this kind. The women now come to purify themselves in the water,"

Scott explained as about a dozen women walked down from the hut, sat on the bank and started to wash in the muddy water. They were all voluptuous but some were young and quite beautiful while the others were middle-aged and running to fat. Adam was amazed,

"Purify!? Blimey how can anyone purify themselves in that soupy stuff? Contaminate more like. If they were my 'wives' I'd have to run them under the shower before they performed their 'wifely' duties for me."

Denise dug him in the ribs,

"Ssssh. Be quiet and listen."

Scott continued,

"The chief who wins these battles takes all the women. He keeps the beautiful ones as wives and the rest are killed and eaten, while their children are tied to the trees and used for target practice."

Adam gave a loud bark of laughter.

The chief from the other village arrived and there was a fight during which he was 'killed,' then the victor walked down to the bank. He glared over the water at the audience and, looking slowly from right to left with a fierce expression on his face, asked if there was anyone else who wanted to challenge his supremacy. Knowing it was just the daft sort of thing her partner would rise to, Denise fixed Adam with a look every bit as menacing as that of the warrior and he got the message. There were no takers.

A hollow log was beaten slowly to summon tribesmen who came and carried away the 'body' which would apparently be presented to the god of war.

"That's it then,"

Adam got up to leave but Denise grabbed his arm,

"No look, the first chap has come back."

Adam sat back down again as they watched the original protagonist leap into the water, scramble up on the other side and challenge the chief to a battle. There followed another well choreographed fight which ended with him being 'killed' by the resident chief. A drum was beaten to signify this victory while the women showed their gratitude to the chief for protecting them and Scott announced that the 'dead' warriors would be cooked and eaten at a feast! The men and women who had entertained their audience for well over an hour then gathered on the opposite bank and sang a hauntingly beautiful Fijian song of farewell that drifted out across the water.

"Very good...excellent," Adam mumbled as he shuffled after Denise towards a little group of shops and stalls selling souvenirs.

"Here Den, what do you think of this – just right for the Fijian party on board this evening – what?"

He was holding up a brightly coloured shirt and looking hopefully towards his partner for her approval.

Pretending she just wanted a closer look, Denise took it from him and had a sneaky peek at the size. XXXL – yes it just might fit him.

"Very nice. I should slip it on, though, just to be sure it's comfortable."

He did and it was; then they realised it was time to return to the coach so, even though they hadn't seen everything they wanted to, they made their way reluctantly back and climbed on board just behind Freddie and Stella. It was almost time to leave but they were still waiting for one or two stragglers when a woman in the seat across the aisle, seeing a Post Office just opposite, asked the passengers nearest to her if they minded if she dashed out to post her cards. Adam and Denise along with Freddie, Stella and a few others said yes, that would be fine, reasoning that it would only take a few moments. The stragglers arrived back and twenty minutes later the woman still hadn't returned, so the guide went to find her. A few moments later she was led back and sat down without a word of apology.

As the coach rumbled into life, Adam leaned forward and tapped the guide on the shoulder,

"What was taking her so long? She only went to post her cards."

The guide looked exasperated,

"No, not just posting her cards…she was sitting there writing them!"

Adam turned and said, loudly enough for the woman to hear,

"Of all the inconsiderate, stupid, selfish people! That behaviour really does take the biscuit"

He sat back and for once Denise didn't hush him up.

CHAPTER TWENTY ONE

"Honestly we couldn't believe it, could we Freddie? Silly cow! Sitting writing her post cards while we were all waiting to go...twenty minutes after the time we had been told to be back at the coach!"

Still incensed, Adam was relating the incident – 'postcardgate' – to Sheila and Bernard over dinner. They were tutting and nodding in sympathy; but Denise, feeling that quite enough had been said on the subject, sought to deflect him by reminding everyone of the date,

"It's the 27th of November."

Adam looked sideways at her,

"Yes, dear...and tomorrow it will be the 28th November,"

He spoke slowly as though addressing a rather backward small child.

"No it won't. It'll be the 27th of November again."

Denise calmly placed a piece of fish in her mouth and chewed,

Freddie clicked his fingers,

"Yes, she's right. It said in 'Cruisenews' we are crossing the international dateline so we have a day to live all over again"

Adam chortled,

"I'll bet they show 'Groundhog Day' in the cinema."

Bernard sat back, a huge beatific smile of satisfaction spreading slowly across his face. When advised to do so, everyone had been gradually moving clocks and watches forward as they made their way around the world; to some this was disturbing, to others, confusing. Poor Bernard became more distressed every time the announcement appeared in 'Cruisenews,' bewailing loss of sleep and quite miffed when he discovered that Sheila wouldn't accept this as an excuse for a poor performance at bridge. On one occasion, Adam was even cruel enough to kid him into believing that the clocks were actually going forward two hours. His expression of utter despair had made everyone laugh, but Stella couldn't keep it up and put him out of his misery by telling him the truth. Now he was gaining a whole day – twenty four hours – oh the joy of it! A joy marred only by the niggling suspicion that to Sheila it would mean extra time for bridge.

"I think the next port of call sounds rather fun,"

Sheila looked round the table and saw they were all waiting for her to continue. Like Denise and Stella, she enjoyed finding out a bit about the places they were visiting and she could see from their blank expressions that she was, on this occasion, ahead of the other two.

"It's a hat-shaped island called Alofi, Niue, but known locally as 'The Rock.' It is reputedly the largest upraised coral atoll in the world and the name means, 'behold the coconut' believed to derive from the first visit of the Polynesians in their canoes who would have seen the trees and exclaimed, 'look, coconuts.' Captain Cook visited in 1774 (she had memorised the date for just such an opportunity as this) and found the island less than welcoming, so much so in fact that he christened it 'Savage Island.'"

Not to be outdone, Denise bent down and retrieved the guide book from her straw bag.

"Yes, and after that we stop off at Rarotonga which sounds positively idyllic. Look...look...here it says it is a 'Pacific Paradise where no building is allowed to rise higher than a palm tree. It's full of silvery bays...white sand...blue-green volcanic peaks.' Just what we're all looking for. And apparently the villages are neat and clean and full of friendly people. There are flame trees...bougainvilleas and succulent vegetables..."

Adam gave his partner a withering look,

"Yes, thank-you dear. Perhaps you could record the guide book for us and we can play it as we go along – save you the trouble of reciting it."

Her cheeks crimson, Denise closed the little book and returned it to her bag. Stella was furious wondering, not for the first time, why Adam had to put her down like that in public when he clearly loved her and relied on her for support. She frowned across the table at him,

"Well, I think it's jolly interesting. Thank-you Denise. I shall look forward to seeing the island."

But she didn't. No-one saw either Alofi or Rarotonga as bad weather prevented the ship from being able to get anywhere near either of them. So instead of the planned excursions passengers were invited to wave goodbye to the islands – just a distant blur – as they pounded out a mile around the deck.

With the loss of the two island stops they were at sea for five days and 'Cruisenews' was simply buzzing with a revised schedule of activities. There was sarong-tying, Spanish lessons, French conversation and a darts tournament. Passengers were invited to play skittles, bingo or giant scrabble; they could watch 'Peyton Place' in the cinema, make a pirate costume for a 'Pirate Night – coming soon,' brush up on their foxtrot with Irma and Antonio or unwind and relax at yoga with Stuart.

'Take steps to better hair days' – courtesy of the on-board hairdresser – and 'hurry, hurry, hurry as all massage treatments are discounted for one day.' Leather jewellery boxes joined the wallets and purses which appeared again in the shop; while pictionary, taboo and scrabble were added to the selection of available games. Another new cabaret artist joined the ship – female this time – and bling came out again in the shop for a formal evening on Saturday 1st December.

Ms Matisse was chosen and crowned – quite a fun event during which the contestants were given a set of silly tasks to perform and eliminated along the way until a winner was left on stage. The billing had said, 'Who will be the fairest of them all?' which was misleading as it actually transpired that the winner was the most uninhibited of them all!

Stella was glad of the extra sea days for 'The Spirit of Christmas,' particularly as, having rehearsed all the separate elements of the show, including a pantomime excerpt (much scaled down from the original), they were ready to form the choir. Things were going well and they were knitting into a hard-working, congenial and mutually supportive group.

The people who least appreciated the unavoidable change of schedule were those who had joined the ship in Fiji.

"There they are. Look there's a group of them over there."

Adam pointed with his fork,

"Have you heard them? They are really seriously getting on my ti.." (glare from Denise) "...nerves. They just don't stop moaning. Poor Judy and the rest of the staff seem to be coping with a bunch of the sad-faced idiots propping up the reception desk most of the day."

Stella, refusing to let Adam's strong opinions dominate every meal time, intervened,

"I know what you mean, but it's possible to sympathise with their discontent up to a point. After all the limited duration of their voyage means the exact itinerary is important."

Sheila looked at her,

"That may be, but the whingeing is becoming chronic. I'm afraid my patience ran out when I saw one of them bang the desk in front of Judy as he shouted 'there's just too much sea!' I mean... how ridiculous"

Adam ignored Stella and turned to Sheila,

"Quite right, Sheila, they don't deserve to be tolerated. I shall call them the 'Fiwis' – Fiji whiners," he added in case anyone couldn't quite work it out for themselves – "and I for one shall ignore them."

"Me too," said Sheila quite forcefully.

Stella, Freddie, Bernard and Denise continued eating.

Father John's regular services of Mass and Holy Communion were a source of comfort to many. During the week they were held downstairs in the nightclub, while on Sundays, with the addition of an Ecumenical Church Service to which more people went, The Club was used. Father John was a lovely man, rotund and smiling with a gentle manner, soft voice and a kind face ringed with feathery white hair. His walk was a sort of toddle as he glided across the room in his white robes, body tilted back, taking small steps while his arms made a sort of paddling movement that rocked him from side to side. He was sweet and unfailingly courteous to all, calming everyone during the fiercest of storms with his gentle, lilting voice.

According to one of Stella's new friends in the cast, his innocent, unworldly air meant that he was frequently ripped off by unscrupulous shop keepers; but an anecdote he told her later in the voyage revealed a surprisingly steely side to him. He was describing how he was offered drugs at one port of call.

"What did you do?" Stella asked, intrigued and sure that he must have offered a gentle sermon on the evils of such things.

"I lied," he said, and her jaw dropped.

"What did you say?"

"I told them I already had enough."

She threw back her head and laughed, sure that God would approve of such quick thinking.

CHAPTER TWENTY TWO

"We expect 'The Matisse' tomorrow...you arrive tomorrow and all the shops open."

The disgruntled café owner jabbed at the dust on the pavement outside her shop with a stiff broom, then paused and added,

"If we know you come today, shops would open for you."

She continued with her sweeping while Freddie and Stella slowly turned away. Oh dear! What a failure on the part of the jungle drums! The loss of the two island stops meant that 'The Matisse' had docked at 8.00 a.m. in Papeete, Tahiti, one day earlier than planned. Pete had managed to re-schedule most of the excursions, but the one they had booked – sailing along the coast...snorkelling...enjoying the turquoise waters etc. – had been cancelled. Well, never mind they would 'do their own thing' – and why not? Lots of other passengers had at previous destinations – and very successfully too.

They reasoned that they would find plenty to do, after all they were in Tahiti, an exciting island, the name synonymous with Gauguin's dark-skinned girls draped in colourful sarongs and frangipane blossoms in their shining, jet black hair; or Marlon Brando and 'Mutiny on the Bounty.' And surely the advertisements for bars of sticky coconut wrapped in chocolate must be made here on beaches of white sand kissed by gently lapping, blue sparkling water.

It is the largest of the group of Society Islands lying halfway between Australia and South America, with an area of 402 square miles. This group of a hundred and thirty or so islands, known as The Sisters of the Wind, lies in the enormous span of French Polynesia and includes the Marquesas, the Tuamotus, the Australs and the Gambier islands. The total population of the group is approximately two hundred thousand, mainly Polynesians with some Chinese, Vietnamese and French Europeans.

In 1767, while searching for Australia, Samuel Wallis, in a British ship called 'the Dolphin,' came upon Tahiti by chance, raised a Union Jack and claimed it for England, calling it 'King George 111.' It was subsequently claimed for France, but Captain James Cook visited the island and was apparently uneasy about the unrestrained sexuality of Tahitian life, something The London Missionary Society tried to correct in 1797.

Stella had giggled when she read out this last piece of information from the guide book to Freddie and wondered how successful those earnest missionaries had been in their quest.

"What do you think they taught them? Safe sex and the 'missionary position'?"

Freddie quipped, and they'd both laughed as they set off, confident that they would indeed have a lovely day. The sun was hot on their backs and they refused to be discouraged by the dour café owner. OK, so it was Sunday and the shops were closed. So what. Buses and taxis would be falling over themselves to take them to see the island – anywhere they wanted to go, and at reasonable rates – they were sure to have a wonderful day – right? Wrong!

They wandered around looking in the windows of shops that were an interesting jumble of small stores and modern complexes. As they gazed into the dark, silent interiors at black pearls nestling in creamy-coloured oysters, they could only imagine the lively bustle of Papeete on every other day of the week, with people tumbling in and out of the doors. They headed for the market, described by both Isobel and the guide book as '...vivid with colour and commerce, selling everything from straw bags to sticky deserts wrapped in leaves; from live pigs to more species of bananas than you have ever seen...' And they had been assured by the ship's administrator that it would be open. They found it, but it wasn't! The streets were deserted, filled with that strange, litter-strewn emptiness of a town on its day off.

And it was hot, very, very hot. Stella looked up at the smoky, green volcanic slopes in the distance and longed to be there. They tried the tourist office,

"No…sorry…everyzing ees closed…you see, we expect you tomorrow…"

"Yes, we know, but we're here today and want to see Tahiti."

"I sorry…nozing I can do,"

The pretty girl behind the counter spread her hands and looked at them with genuine sympathy in her deep brown eyes. Stella grabbed Freddie and turned away, trying not to let her exasperation show, after all it wasn't her fault. They tried to hire a car but, although the place was open when they went in, it was closing at midday – one hour away.

"Come on…look there's a taxi rank,"

Stella pulled Freddie along, still determined to try and salvage the day, but the taxis were all either ridiculously expensive or driven by shady-looking characters who blew smoke at them while trying to work out exactly how much they could add to the price for these English tourists. It seemed nobody wanted to work on Sunday.

Feeling thoroughly dejected by now, Stella looked towards 'The Matisse' from where air-conditioning and a buffet lunch beckoned. As if reading her thoughts Freddie nodded and they both headed towards the ship, longing for the cool interior, something to eat and somewhere to collect their jangled thoughts. As they reached the quayside Freddie stopped and nudged Stella, pointing to where a noisy group of people were gathered round one of the tables that spilled out onto the pavement from a bar. She looked more closely and recognised Jeannie and Donald, along with a few other passengers, amid a crowd of locals. Judging by the level of noise, the party, united by the international language of alcohol, had been making merry for quite some time. As she watched, Jeannie, looking thinner and scrawnier than she had at the start of the voyage, let out a bark of laughter then took a long drink from the glass in front of her. She inhaled on her cigarette and blew out a cloud of smoke before saying something to Donald and laughing again – a strange, rasping sound.

"Oh well, they're happy anyway,"

Stella said, and followed Freddie along the quayside onto the ship.

But back in the cabin Stella had an idea. She just couldn't bear the thought that they would leave this intriguing place having seen nothing but the port town, and she knew there were two trips scheduled for that afternoon, one exploring the island's treasures and the other a jeep safari up into the hills. Suddenly lunch didn't seem very important, so as Freddie (wondering what she was up to) made his way to the dining room, Stella went along to see Pete and asked if, by chance, anyone had cancelled on either of the afternoon trips. She knew this sometimes happened as the result of over-indulgence in the bar, or at one of the meals or just plain fatigue – the average age of the passengers being what it was. He looked down the lists and shook his head,

"Nooo....sorry. all still fully booked."

Undeterred, Stella made her way up to The Club where Amanda, the cruise administrator, was sitting, ready to welcome the first of the excursion passengers. She explained her request, finishing with,

"...I know there are no places at the moment, but maybe I could just lurk by the information desk...then if anything comes up..."

She smiled, "OK, Stella, you go and lurk and I'll let you know if anyone cancels at the last minute."

It was unlikely but worth a try, and she went along to the cabin to tell Freddie what she had done, first of all explaining it all again to Judy, the cruise director, who she met on the way. Judy also said she would help if she could.

Smiling and shaking his head, Freddie watched as Stella packed a bag containing a few essentials for a trip plus their swimming things.

"What exactly are you doing?" He asked. Stella paused and looked up,

"I'm packing ready for the call. If we get on the jeep safari it says there is the opportunity to 'take a refreshing dip in the clear, sparkling water of a river on the way,' and we wouldn't want to miss that, now would we."

Amused as always by his wife's unfailing optimism, Freddie settled down in the cabin to read, quite convinced that this was what he would be doing for the rest of the afternoon. Stella lurked by the front desk and felt like Cinderella as she watched everyone gathering for the two trips, chatting and laughing in small groups. She didn't wish anybody ill, but surely someone was suffering from the heat and had changed their minds...surely... 'Still, we are not children,' she told herself firmly, 'and if we can't go – which looks increasingly likely – we shall clock it down to experience and not make the same mistake again...but...if only...'

Suddenly Judy was leaping towards her waving a small scrap of paper,

"Here you are, Stella, one ticket for the 'Island Treasures' trip."

She looked so pleased, but Stella couldn't hide her disappointment,

"Only one?"

"Sorry, it's the best I can do."

Stella thanked her for taking the trouble and made her way to the cabin. Even before she told him she knew exactly what Freddie would say. Solicitous as always of her welfare and happiness, he said straightaway that she should go, assuring her he would enjoy reading in the coolness of the quiet lounge until she returned. She knew this was true and was grateful for his unfailing kindness, but she really didn't want to go without him. There was a knock at the door and Amanda stood on the threshold bearing two tickets for the jeep safari (you shall go to the ball!!).

Not stopping to ask how they had become available, Stella grabbed the bag and was off down the corridor, closely followed by Freddie, and together they dashed out into the sunshine, shouting to Judy as they passed the desk that they would settle the money in the morning.

Perhaps because it was the afternoon they nearly didn't have, but everything about that trip was an absolute joy: bumping along the coast road in an open-topped jeep, waving to anyone they thought would wave back; watching surfers and swimmers bobbing on waves that crashed onto black sand made them feel about sixteen again.

After a little while they went off road and were allowed to stand up as the jeep rattled along rutted tracks, heading up into tree-covered mountains. And what a staggeringly beautiful place Tahiti turned out to be! The highest slopes, lush and green, were ringed by wreaths of mist, and the very tops of the mountains disappeared altogether in a white shroud. The air became cooler as they climbed higher and they drank in the beauty of their surroundings – waterfalls that cascaded down through the many shades of green and rivers in valleys, splashing over stones.

Families were picnicking and swimming; smiling brown children shouted and waved as they passed, and several teenage boys amazed them by jumping from a high bridge into the water beneath with, Stella suspected, a little more attitude than if they hadn't been watching. The jeep stopped so they could swim in a wide part of one of the rivers – it wasn't 'sparkling' or even particularly 'clear,' but a truly lovely, memorable experience nonetheless. Stella swam away from the group to a quiet spot on her own and trod water while she gazed up at the surrounding hills.

'I am in Tahiti swimming in a river on a Sunday afternoon. This is mine forever...abiding...enduring.... I will only have to close my eyes...focus...and I will be here again in this moment. It will be one of my special memories. It is mine forever. Never again will I be the one on the outside looking in…wondering what these places are really like. I have been…I have tasted.'

And so it was to be with many of the destinations and experiences of the journey, made more poignant because she was with Freddie. It was, on reflection, to become extra special as nothing like it could ever be theirs again, though she didn't yet know this.

At that moment he called to her across the water and she swam over to where he was joking with a crowd as they plunged in and out of the river, splashing each other and laughing. A little way off she saw Jack and Chrissie swimming close together in a little circle, deep in conversation.

Back in the jeep and up even higher they went before stopping again, this time for a drink at a restaurant that nestled in amongst the lush, green mountains. They sat outside on a veranda staring down at the tops of trees which looked like a collection of green cushions into which they could comfortably fall. The restaurant itself was remote and isolated, accessible only by the steep upward climb on the single track road along which they had travelled. It was shabby and in need of some tender loving care. 'What a shame,' Stella thought, redesigning it in her imagination and creating a fantastic Arts Centre where people could come for painting holidays. She discovered that it was for sale and it was obvious that the current owner was just letting it tick over until a buyer could be found. The only other people on the terrace that afternoon were members of a French family, lingering over their Sunday lunch, wreathed in cigarette smoke, chatting, laughing and ordering large quantities of coffee, liqueurs and ice-creams for the children.

Rain started to fall and from their vantage point they watched it sweep across in front of them in huge sheets. People were chatting in small groups with the occasional bark of laughter coming mainly, Stella noticed, from the one that Freddie was in. Still in reflective mood, she was enjoying sitting quietly by herself, looking out at the rain that moved in waves over the tree tops. Also by themselves at the end of one of the tables Chrissie and Jack were still deep in conversation, looking into each other's eyes and, as she watched, Stella saw Jack reach tentatively across and take Chrissie's hand. She didn't withdraw it.

"It's such a privilege to be able to enjoy an experience like this, isn't it Stella?"

Sharon sat down next to her and they watched the rain together. She continued quietly,

"I mean…Round the World, Stella. Isn't it fabulous?" she paused, "And we're the first, aren't we…? The first generation who can do this. My mum couldn't have done it. I just think I'm so lucky."

She sat back reflecting on the wonder of it all and Stella smiled, so glad to have met people like her among the moaners. Sharon, down to earth but with such creative ideas; so full of life and ready to have ago at anything. She was playing the part of Aladdin in the show, even though she had never set foot on a stage before and was, of course, giving it her best shot. Stella was helping her, but she was a natural and very easy to direct. Having brought up her five children, she was now enjoying time with her husband, the trip round the world being a special treat they had awarded themselves and they were both determined to make the most of every moment.

Time to go – back along the bumpy tracks and then the coast road again from where they could see the locals still enjoying the rolling surf.

That evening The Club was full as everyone crowded in to watch a dance troupe called 'O Tahiti.' Stella, arriving there ahead of Freddie and their table companions, duly reserved the five seats next to her. She glanced to her left and saw Chrissie sitting alone at the next table, the bags and cardigans draped along the banquette indicating that, like her, she was expecting company. Stella leaned across,

"Did you enjoy the jeep experience?"

"Oh yes."

Chrissie smiled and Stella thought again how much she admired this beautiful, elegant lady. They had managed to have several chats over coffee and she knew all about Maurice and the years Chrissie had spent tirelessly…selflessly nursing her errant husband.

"You want to know about Jack, don't you?" Chrissie blushed very slightly, but Stella, unashamed, just raised her eyebrows and waited.

"Well, I've decided that life is for living and I should take a leaf out of Nancy's book…"

They both looked over to an area nearer the stage where Nancy, followed by the ever doting Kieran, had just sat down. Kieran was fussing around her, helping to remove a fluffy little cardigan she was wearing until she shrugged him off and sat looking anxiously around. No prizes for guessing she was hoping that Wayne would appear. This was not really 'Chrissie behaviour' at all and Stella turned to her, her eyes wide and eyebrows reaching her hair-line." Chrissie laughed.

"Well no…not that exactly. But I know she's just taking things as they come, so to speak. I've decided that as Jack and I enjoy each other's company we might as well make the most of this wonderful experience together and not worry about the future."

Stella just had time to smile and give her arm a squeeze before the others started arriving. Jack ensured that he got in first and secured the place next to Chrissie, leaving Jim to cope with Margie. At her own table Freddie sat down next to her followed by Adam, Denise and Sheila with Bernard bringing up the rear and squeezing in on the end.

The dancers were good – a beautiful end to a wonderful day.

CHAPTER TWENTY THREE

Elated...euphoric...full of hope, Stella and Freddie stood on the deck like excited children anticipating a completely unexpected treat. 'The Matisse' was gliding slowly and majestically past some truly beautiful islands – straight out of the travel brochures. This must be it – the paradise for which they were all searching. Palm trees swayed in the breeze, fishermen stood in the surf casting their lines into deeper water; and straw-roofed huts on stilts – only ever previously seen in the magazine sections of the Sunday papers – jutted out into the sea.

It was earlier that morning when Judy's voice had crackled over the loudspeakers; she was delighted to announce that, to try and give everyone something back as compensation for missing the two ports of call, Niue and Rarotonga, the Captain had kindly agreed to make an unscheduled stop at the famous island of Bora Bora. By the time 'Cruisenews' was pushed under cabin doors, the staff had managed to cobble together some information about this island with an area of only fifteen square miles and a population of about five thousand eight hundred people.

Described as 'the Pearl of the Pacific,' even before the advertising men got to it, the history is fascinating, though much of it oral and therefore difficult to verify. Some maintain that it was an isle of exile for Tahitians who broke sacred taboos, but what is known for sure is that the biggest upheaval was caused when the US Navy 'discovered' it in World War Two. An airstrip was built and the GIs sent there had no particular part to play in the war, but were quite happy, surrounded as they were by beautiful girls and lovely beaches. The thriving world market in copra and vanilla ensured that Bora Bora's prosperity continued after the war until tourism took over as the main source of income for the native population.

In 1891 the American historian and traveller, Henry Adams, made the following observation regarding Polynesian morality:

'Man somehow got here, I think about a thousand years ago, and made a society which was, on the whole, the most successful the world ever saw because it rested on the solidest possible foundation of no morals at all!'

But what the Europeans considered lascivious, they gradually stamped out and even the dances seen today are only an approximate reconstruction of those from former times.

Stella waved 'Cruisenews' excitedly under Freddie's nose,

"Look…look, it says here that Pete has managed to book four excursions for us to choose from. Come on, let's go."

They had hurried down to the desk and booked themselves onto one called 'Le Truck' which they were told would give them a good look at the place. They would be visiting Matira Beach, described as 'unquestionably one of the loveliest in the world, its glistening white sand gently sloping into a perfectly transparent lagoon.'

This was it! At last the picture post-card perfection they were all longing to experience.

It was ten o'clock in the morning when they felt the ship tug on its anchor as it came to a halt. There were clouds in the sky and the breeze was a little more brisk than previously, but they were optimistic; surely the clouds would blow away and the sun come out for their trip round this island paradise – of course it would. They sat in The Club ready to go then watched in disbelief as the clouds suddenly dropped their load of rain in an unrelenting deluge that swirled around, completely obliterating the island that only minutes before had beckoned them over to sample its beauty.

"It'll stop, won't it Freddie? Please tell me it'll stop."

Stella stared anxiously out of the window. Freddie said nothing.

But it didn't stop. It howled and clattered ferociously against the ship; then came the announcement that, owing to the weather, the excursions had been cancelled, but the tender boats would still go over as far as the quayside so passengers could visit the stalls there if they wished. What a blow. Stella slumped in her chair then, looking round, her attention was caught by the behaviour of some of the other passengers. They were banging tables, stamping their feet and kicking chairs, stomping about like spoilt children who have been deprived of a treat by their wicked step-mother.

She felt so sorry for Judy who had tried to do something special for them which had been ruined by circumstances way beyond her control. Freddie turned towards her,

"Are you up for it then? A bumpy, wet ride over to the island?"

"Of course."

Stella turned as she left The Club and saw the 'spoilt children' clustering together in small groups, presumably to sulk or complain noisily to each other. Adam and Denise were making their way towards the door, obviously as disgusted by the childish behaviour as she and Freddie were; and she smiled as she watched Adam 'accidentally' bump into and barge as many of the malcontents as he could on his way over.

Puffing and panting, Gracie reached the top of the steps where she paused until Edie, following closely behind, gave her a smart tap on the backside with her stick.

"Keep goin,' chuck. I want to get to me cabin and take off these wet things."

Gracie took a few steps forward and, with a face like a squeezed lemon, addressed the waiting queue,

"I shouldn't bother goin' over. There's nowt there bar about three shops and a few crummy stalls."

Stanley appeared behind Edie followed by Jim then Margie, who added,

"Yeah…Bora Bora? Boring Boring more like!"

Stella and Freddie laughed as they watched the dripping quintet amble off down the corridor. They'd had to be in the first group to go over of course but, as usual, it didn't seem to make them any happier.

"Mmmm…no Chrissie and Jack," mused Stella.

"Probably canoodling in a cabin." Chuckled Freddie. Stella smiled at her husband; 'canoodling?' Honestly what a quaint turn of phrase he had at times.

The tender boat rocked perilously, lashed by the wind and waves. Adam sat down heavily next to them and looked at Stella's flimsy mackintosh which had already let the rain through.

"Here, take this."

In a rare act of chivalry, he reached into Denise's bag and pulled out a spare one she had thoughtfully packed for him.

"Are you sure?"

Stella looked enquiringly past Adam to Denise.

"Yes, take it, Stella. He won't need it."

Stella was convinced when she looked more closely at the industrial strength oil skin that Adam was wearing; and so it was that she arrived at the quayside engulfed in what looked like a marquee. The rain got even heavier, lashing viciously against them as they stepped out of the little boat and ran for cover under the wood and canvas shelter where stall holders were stoically selling their wares. Dripping wet, yet still undeterred, they walked around admiring the jewellery, garments and trinkets for sale.

Stella stopped at one of the stalls and bought a brightly coloured top and a pretty buckle for fastening the bottom of a 'T' shirt. Suddenly her attention was caught by a gurgling noise and she looked over to where, in a central area, some polythene had been cleverly folded to funnel the rain water in onto a large container of plants. It fell like a waterfall on lush, green leaves and, for a few moments, she was mesmerised by the splashing sounds that mingled with the clattering of the rain on the roof in a very satisfying way. Then she became aware of the stall holder, proffering change and smiling,

"You should come yesterday...very hot...very sunny."

The rain continued to lash them as they struggled back onto the tender boat, then into the ship and the calm sanctuary of their cabin where they showered and put on dry clothes. It wasn't until early evening, as they stood on the deck of 'The Matisse' gliding slowly back out past the little islands, that the rain stopped. The sky cleared, fishermen resumed their fishing and a watery sun appeared promising a better day tomorrow – when they would be far away.

CHAPTER TWENTY FOUR

"...and so, ladies and gentlemen, I am delighted to be able to tell you that we are making an unscheduled stop, by kind permission of the Captain, at Rangiroa Atoll where we have managed to negotiate the exclusive use of a privately owned beach for the day. We will provide a bar and a barbecue; you will be able to swim in the sea..."

Undeterred, Judy had pulled another treat out of the bag and sounded delighted to have done so. She was, no doubt, praying that the weather would be more co-operative than it had been in Bora Bora. There followed further instructions about payment of £5.00 sterling for the privilege of setting foot on this beach; the method of travel – this would be either by tender boat, followed by a two mile walk, or local boats, which she had managed to charter to drop people off at the appointed beach with no walking. In this way the halt, lame and elderly were catered for as always, in spite of numerous complaints from them that they weren't. Judy also reminded everyone about the importance of carrying a good supply of water, covering their heads and using sun block. There was no need to carry towels as they would be provided.

A piece about atolls in general, and Rangiroa in particular, appeared in Cruisenews informing everyone that an atoll is a coral ring formed around the top of a submerged volcano, and that Rangiroa is the second largest in the world. The enormous lagoon, measuring 75 by 25 kilometres, could contain the whole island of Tahiti. The population of 3000 are all housed in buildings which are not allowed to be built any higher than palm trees; and historically Rangiroa has had to contend with raids from a neighbouring atoll and devastating cyclones. It was discovered by the Dutchman, Le Marie, in 1616, but only saw the first European settlers in 1851 and is now established as a tourist destination with fishing and pearl production as additional sources of income for the inhabitants.

Like excited children, Freddie and Stella gazed across perfectly blue water at this island paradise – palm trees swaying in the gentle breeze and waves breaking on a shore of golden sand – as they gathered with their fellow passengers and waited to be transported there. This was definitely it! They decided to travel in a tender boat and walk at the other end, a walk that Stella thoroughly enjoyed in spite of the heat, but Freddie questioned as being perhaps a little more than the advertised two miles; he was glad when the appointed beach came into view.

And there together they stood, scarcely able to believe their eyes as they took in the scene before them. The natural beauty of the atoll was impressive with a small beach nestling between trees and the water's edge; the sand looked silky soft, though they had been warned about hidden coral which was prevalent and quite sharp. But what really took their breath away was the amazing spread laid out before them. 'The Matisse' staff had obviously made numerous trips by boat between ship and shore, and the result was a sumptuous banquet, perfect in every detail, exquisitely displayed on tables covered in snow-white cloths and decorated with animals carved from fruit and vegetables. There was a bar with waiters standing quietly by ready to serve them and, in the background, a small army of cooks already throwing large quantities of meat onto a barbecue, laughing and joking all the while. It was a marvellous creation...a fantasy...a film set.

Freddie and Stella were ecstatic and, having been handed beach towels by a smiling waitress, set about finding somewhere to sit. Stella saw that there were numerous logs and large, flat boulders, so plenty of room for everyone, then, glancing around, she saw Bernard and Sheila. They had arrived by local boat, as there was no way Bernard could have managed the walk, and were happily ensconced on a log, big enough to accommodate friends and fairly near the barbecue. Legs stretched out in front of them they were staring out to sea. Stella tapped Sheila on the shoulder,

"May we join you?" she smiled,

"Yes, of course, my dear."

Sheila grabbed the towels off the log and Stella sat down with Freddie next to her, noting that there was enough room left for Adam and Denise. Freddie was still puffing as he wiped the sweat from his forehead.

"Well…that was some walk!" He slapped Bernard on the back,

"You had the right idea, old sport. It's the local boat back for me. Someone's got a rum idea of 'a couple of miles.' Where are Adam and Denise?"

"Oh they went on one of the tender boats like you. Didn't you see them when you were walking?" Sheila replied, "No, come to think of it you wouldn't as they would be slower than you. A little foolish to attempt it if you ask me, with Adam's dodgy hips and, of course…"

She trailed off, though Freddie was sure she was about to refer to his excess weight and was struck, not for the first time, by Sheila's waspishness, thinking that she was more 'headmistressy' than Stella, who had actually been one. He looked back along the path they had travelled, but there was no sign of Adam and Denise and the best spaces for sitting were filling up fast. The blue, sparkling water looked cool and inviting, and he knew Stella would be keen to swim. He turned to Sheila,

"Ok if we dive in?"

"Oh yes, Bernard and I will sit here for a while with our drinks and wait for Adam and Denise. We'll keep all your places."

Stella reminded him to put on old sandals to protect his feet against the coral and together they walked down to the water, glancing back just before they entered it to see Bernard being shuffled along the log by Sheila with towels spread out on either side of him, indicating quite clearly to all comers that these places were taken. She then picked up their empty glasses and made her way to the bar.

"Oh this is heavenly," Stella trod water and gazed out to where 'The Matisse' stood, stark white against a clear blue sky. After a few minutes floating and swimming around Freddie suggested a cool drink, so they turned and made their way lazily back to the shore, promising themselves more swimming later in the day.

"What the hell's going on?" Freddie muttered as they stood dripping on the sand at the water's edge. There were angry, raised voices coming from the direction of 'their log' and they saw that Sheila was standing, hands on hips, shouting at a woman who had planted herself right in the middle of it. Bernard was perched on the end looking confused and, as they got nearer, Sheila moved slightly to the side, enough for them to see that it was Jeannie who had taken possession of the log while Donald hovered uncertainly in the background.

"No you are not sitting here…you are disgusting…you can see perfectly well that we are already established…NOW CLEAR OFF!!"

Sheila – small, silver haired Sheila of the posh voice and genteel manner – was shrieking like a fish wife on speed. Temper had turned her cheeks a livid red and she was shaking with fury from head to toe. Jeannie remained resolutely planted in the centre of the log with legs spread wide, staring defiantly at the figure exploding in front of her. Her head wobbled a bit as she looked up into Sheila's face,

"I'm not moving, hen, so you can do what you like about it. These logs are for anybody. I'm staying"

The words, in a thick, Scottish accent, were slurred and she raised an unsteady index finger, pointing it in Sheila's face. Donald looked embarrassed, but he was also getting angry with her,

"Come on now, Jeannie, we're not staying here…I don't want any more trouble…"

He bent down to take her arm, but she shrugged him off shouting,

"I am staying…I AM SITTING HERE!"

Sheila was beside herself and, apparently unaware of the attention this little scene was attracting from those nearby, shouted,

"NO YOU ARE NOT…!"

With the final word she slapped Jeannie hard on the arm, a blow that caused her to fall off the log onto the sand where she lay sprawling on her side with the contents of her bag, including a couple of bottles, spilling out next to her. There were gasps and a few muffled giggles from a group of other passengers who were witnessing this 'battle' from a safe distance. Moving quickly, Sheila retook possession of the log and motioned to Bernard, Freddie and Stella to sit down and spread along. Adam and Denise, who had arrived in time to see most of this pantomime, also sat down, so that by the time Donald had managed to manoeuvre Jeannie up onto her feet she knew she was beaten.

"Fucking…stuck up…fucking English bitch,"

She screamed, swaying from side to side as she attempted to gather her scattered belongings. Donald bent down and grabbed the last few items then, holding his wife firmly under her arm to try and steady her, pushed her forward and together they staggered away along the sand.

For a few moments no-one on the log said anything. Sheila, breathing heavily, was obviously still quite shaken and Bernard put his arm round her shoulder by way of comfort, but it was shrugged off. Stella guessed, rightly as she discovered later, that he was being blamed for allowing the Scottish woman to push her way onto the log while Sheila was at the bar. Adam, also breathing heavily and sweating profusely as a result of his walk, leaned forward and turned towards Sheila.

"Remind me not to tangle with you! Well done, girl, that was some performance. You saw her off and no mistake. Ha!" he slapped his massive thigh and nudged Denise, "I think we'll call her 'Rocky' from now on – and don't anyone mess with her!"

Sheila looked down at the sand, the ghost of a smile starting to play round her lips. Basking in Adam's obvious respect and admiration, she was beginning to realise that she had indeed triumphed. She had got the better of a woman who had made it clear from the start of the voyage that she would do exactly as she pleased without regard for anyone but herself. Sheila had shown her that she couldn't always get away with that behaviour and, on reflection, was quite proud of herself. Her cheeks were still flushed, but it was a pink glow of pleasure now rather than livid patches of fury. Adam, perceiving that he was indeed helping the situation, warmed to his theme and stood up, moving round until he was facing Sheila then, with exaggerated movements, indicated to the others to shuffle along the log,

"Come on budge up now…let's make sure Rocky's got enough room…don't crowd the lady…now that you've seen what she can do! Freddie…drink for Rocky. Chop, chop…!"

Freddie jumped up and, entering into the spirit of it, quickly wrapped a towel over his arm, waiter style, before making a mock bow in front of Sheila.

"Of course…what would madam like…the world is now your oyster…"

Pink flush deepening on her cheeks, Sheila slapped him playfully on the leg,

"Oh, shut up, do! It had to be done…that was all…"

Adam jumped in again "And you did it, gel. Now come on, drinks all round, what is everyone having…? Rocky first of course. Listen up, Freddie, don't get it wrong or…." He made a fist with one of his massive hands and whacked it into the palm of the other. Freddie made an exaggerated show of 'trembling' and Sheila put her head in her hands, laughing and begging them to stop.

By the time Adam ambled up to the bar with Freddie in tow to help carry the drinks, a good atmosphere had been restored on 'the log,' and the people nearby, who had been thoroughly entertained by the spectacle of Jeannie sent sprawling in the sand by a diminutive, elderly lady, all returned to their chatting and drinking.

The rest of the morning passed pleasantly with everyone swimming as often as they liked in the warm sea and just generally chilling out – they were on holiday. They stared in wonder at two sting rays that arrived near the beach as if checking them out; gathered unusual shells and marvelled at the multi-coloured fish swimming with them in the clear water. Lunch was a real treat – the best barbecue most people had ever experienced and there was plenty for everyone.

With her eyes closed Stella sifted soft, warm sand through her fingers. The afternoon sun was hot on her face and voices nearby had died to a murmur as most people snoozed, replete with good food and wine. She opened her eyes and turned to talk to Freddie, but he wasn't there. She leaned up on her elbows and, shading her eyes, looked out to sea. He wasn't there either, and as the other four were in various stages of slumber, she couldn't ask them where he'd gone. Slipping a silky wrap over her swimming costume, she made her way further up the beach towards a small house that stood behind the barbecue area, just in front of the trees, where a group of people had gathered. As she got nearer she became aware of the sound of music and saw that it was being played by a strange assortment of men on even stranger instruments.

Freddie was standing a little way in from the edge of the group listening intently with his video camera balanced on his shoulder. Stella manoeuvred herself silently in between warm, semi-clad bodies smelling not unpleasantly of salt and sun-cream, until she reached her husband's side. Sensing her presence, he turned and smiled, then looked back at the porch way of the little house and continued to video the scene. He told her afterwards that it was an impromptu 'happening' – the local policeman, the ship's pilot, the immigration officer and a couple of their friends had just sat down and started to play. There were two guitars, a ukulele, spoons and a saucepan and the effect was stunning. The whole scene had a magical quality about it with the smell of char-grilled meat, the hot sun on their backs, chickens scratching in the dust and the rhythmic, joyful playing of this little band – a group of men with tanned, shining faces smiling as they made music on a beach.

Then it rained, in fact it poured, but by that time Freddie and Stella were back in the water again and didn't care. Some people ran for cover while others made for the boats and went back to the ship. After about an hour it stopped and the sun came out giving them more time to enjoy the island experience.

"Oh look, there's Judy," Stella pointed to where the cruise director was sunning herself on the sand in a bikini, actually taking time off for a change. They stopped in front of her and Judy opened her eyes. It was Stella who spoke,

"Sorry to disturb your rare bit of relaxation, Judy, but I must just say how absolutely fantastic this day has been."

Judy smiled,

"Thanks Stella it's good to know that someone appreciates what we've tried to do."

Stella frowned, unable to understand how anyone could fail to enjoy the day, but she and Freddie were dismayed as Judy told them that, in spite of all her extra effort there had still been complaints. '…why hadn't she brought sun beds over to the island…?' '…Why was there only one toilet…?' '…and, by the way, the coral's too sharp…!' Stella shook her head in disbelief and congratulated Judy again, reassuring her that it was their problem not hers; the day had been sensational.

"You'll always find serpents in paradise – and not just among the natural elements," she muttered angrily, as she and Freddie made their way back to 'the log' to pack their things for the return journey to the ship.

Back on 'The Matisse' Edie, Gracie and Margie stared out of the window towards Rangiroa. The Club was unusually quiet and empty; they were alone apart from Central Eating and Two Sticks who snoozed on a sofa nearby. They had been playing cards, but the pack lay abandoned, scattered on the table in front of them.

"I'm right fed up. There's been nothing organised for those of us who are too ill to manage to go over to a 'Hatoll,' whatever that may be." Edie spat out the word 'atoll' to emphasise her disgust with the fact that, as far as she was concerned, her needs had been ignored. "I shall be complaining, that's for sure."

"Oh, I think we should. This would never have happened on 'The Princess Royal.'" Gracie agreed, sitting heavily back in her seat.

"And our tea was late – wouldn't have come at all if we hadn't reminded them," Margie added. She was as miffed as the other two, though she was getting a bit cheesed off with Gracie always going on about the bigger, superior ships she'd been on. And as for Edie's 'disability' – well that seemed to come and go as it pleased. Still they had to stick together over this; it had been a really boring day for anyone not wanting to spend it flopping around on a beach. She looked out of the window again – 'huh, we've got better beaches than that in Cornwall,' she thought, but kept it to herself.

"Yes," she said, turning again to the other two, "We shall definitely be complaining, that's for sure."

CHAPTER TWENTY FIVE

"Actually, love, I'm not feeling too good; I think you'll have to go on your own."

Freddie lay on his bed with his eyes closed while Stella peered anxiously down at him. 'How very strange', she thought, 'this is not like him at all.' She frowned,

"Well we know it's not over-indulgence in alcohol as yesterday was an NA day." They had both decided a while ago that they wouldn't drink alcohol every day, and even when they did their intake, especially Stella's, was moderate.

Freddie chuckled, "Yes, don't tell Adam, you know he'll say that's what's caused it!"

"Do you feel sick?"

"No, just very strange…whacked…lethargic…queasy" Freddie opened his eyes and looked at his wife who was now sitting on the adjacent bed, her face a picture of anxiety.

"I'm so sorry, darling, to be such a drag; you go and enjoy this lovely island. I'm sure a day's rest will sort me out."

His eyes were full of concern for the fact that he was spoiling her day, so Stella decided she had to make the best of it; go over to the island, take lots of photos and tell him all about it when she got back. If she didn't go it would make him feel even worse. She jumped up, putting on the bravest of brave faces.

"OK. I realise this is, of course, just a ploy to get me out of the way so that you can go in pursuit of Margie – or is it Gracie you fancy…?"

Freddie smiled, "Oh there's no fooling you, is there, but actually it's Edie I've got the hots for; trouble is Stanley won't let me get anywhere near her. I don't suppose you would take him with you for the day…you know, give me a chance."

Stella shuddered, "Enough! Now is there anything I can get you before I go?"

"No, love, thank-you. I'll just sleep and be bright-eyed and bushy-tailed when you get back."

Putting a few last things into her bag, Stella tip-toed quietly to the cabin door where she paused and looked back to say goodbye to her husband, but he was already fast asleep.

It was 7.30 in the morning when 'The Matisse' had dropped anchor in the beautiful bay off Taiohae on the island of Nuka Hiva in the Marquesas. No palm trees this time, but volcanic upheavals thrust up from the ocean floor standing out majestically against a bright blue sky, their jagged peaks softened by yellowy-green foliage. There are eleven of these lonely islands off French Polynesia, described in the guide book as 'the remotest pin-points of land in the world, set in the South Pacific 500 miles from their closest neighbours, the Tuamotu Group, and 3,700 miles from the nearest continent, South America.

Stella stepped ashore from the tender boat at around 11.30 and wandered along the coast road, stopping at a small shop to buy cards and then at a covered area with a few stalls selling jewellery and carvings. The weather was very hot but not humid and, as she walked, she had the strangest feeling that time was standing still in this magical place. For a while she saw no-one; the stillness and silence broken only by her own footsteps and the rhythmic crashing of the waves on the shore to her left. She watched as they receded revealing not golden but black sand that it seemed no-one wanted to sit on as the beach was completely deserted.

Thinking of Freddie, who usually recorded their outings with numerous photographs and copious amounts of video footage, she dutifully pointed her camera at the beauties she encountered along the way. There were trees and bushes covered in flowers of flame-red or fuchsia-pink and, near the shore, squat stone carvings of 'tikis' – creatures with wide mouths and huge, bulging eyes. There was an air of neat orderliness about the place: a man picked up litter from the beach and a woman was sweeping a large, stone area covered by an awning. Stella walked past colourful bungalows and a couple of restaurants before turning right and heading up a sloping roadway towards the Cathedral.

She had been told by both Father John and Isobel that the Cathedral was worth a visit, but no recommendation could have prepared her for what she saw. Inside the edifice of warm brick was an abundance of exquisitely worked wood carvings around the wall, fifteen in all, depicting the Passion of Christ in intricate detail and burnished to a finish as smooth as satin. The altar was covered with a bright red cloth and surrounded by more carvings with a large wooden crucifix directly above it. Two thirds of the way up, at the sides, the building was open to the elements, obviously not in too much danger from rain or vandalism.

Stella sat on one of the wooden benches and gazed in awe at these beautiful works of art. She was alone, the stillness and silence pierced only by the occasional song of a bird, its pure notes sharp and clear. She thought about Freddie – dear, good, kind, Freddie; the husband she had almost left when she was young and foolish, wanting…needing…a career, thinking that maybe the grass was greener somewhere else. They were complete opposites, of course, a fact that reinforced her idea that she had made a mistake. Young and in love, they had married and had their beautiful son very quickly afterwards; it all seemed idyllic, but the worm of discontent had crept in. And it was Stella, not Freddie who was eaten away by it. Was he really dynamic enough for her? Was marriage and motherhood what she really wanted? There was a life out there and it was passing her by.

But they had found a pathway through, and she knew now, she acknowledged, that it was Freddie's love, kindness and patience more than anything else that had helped her. He had fully appreciated her need for something more than a domestic life, full of cake-baking and coffee mornings. He had helped with chores when she was busy studying and Stella now knew, beyond all doubt, how much she needed his stability and steadiness in her life and that it was with his help and support she'd had the best of both worlds There was no-one like Freddie. She felt a lump in her throat as she recalled the time when, thinking she was 'doing the right thing,' she had said she thought they ought to part. She was convinced she wasn't being a good wife to him (whatever that is), that she was letting him down and he should have the chance to marry someone else. Looking at her in silence for a long moment he had finally said, very quietly, "Well, go if you must, but I don't want you to – your happiness means more to me than anything else in the world." Stella had known that he meant it from the bottom of his heart and so she knew that she had to stay. If she was that important to him, she had to try again; and over the years she had come to realise that it had been the right decision.

She sighed and looked around. The inside of the Cathedral was cool, the stillness almost tangible, and suddenly she was filled with an overwhelming sense of foreboding. Something clutched at her heart. Was it fear? What had happened? She panicked and gripped the bench, trying to control her breathing that echoed – a jarring, rasping sound – in the otherwise still air around her. Then gradually the panic subsided, giving way to a sense of calm. A feeling of peace spread through her and a voice seemed to be saying something like…'it will be a hard road, but I will be there for you…you will get through…'

She stood up and shook herself. How stupid. It must be thinking about Freddie that brought on that ridiculous fanciful thought; it was Freddie who was always there for her, Freddie who got her through. But supposing he wasn't there? Stella looked towards the altar and raised her eyes to where Christ hung, his feet crossed and nailed, his head to one side. Had he spoken to her? She had faith, a faith that had sustained and guided her over the years; it was her faith that had said, 'think before you act, and then think again. Faith that had made her give her marriage another try. Her twin strengths – God and Freddie – together they had pulled her through difficult times. God would never be missing from her life…but Freddie? '…Till death us do part…'

No, this is too morbid! She started to walk slowly round the cathedral, gently stroking the shining wooden carvings, then made her way out into the sunshine. And there, in the heat of the day, the bird song was accompanied by other notes: 'Silent Night,' picked out on a squeaky recorder, floated through the window of a nearby primary school, reminding her that it was nearly Christmas and evoking memories of Christmas in her own school now so far away.

Strolling back along the dusty path, she passed a group of teenagers speaking French and a woman in a bright red head scarf walking with an old, brown horse following along behind her like a dog. Stella stood and looked at 'The Matisse,' still there, its reassuring bulk solid and stark white against a sky, still as clear and blue as it had been an hour ago. She smiled, her normally buoyant spirits restored. Nothing had changed. Freddie was still there, waiting for her and would soon, she had no doubt, get over whatever ailed him – most likely too much sun. She walked towards the quay, her pace quickening, keen to get back and tell him all about the Cathedral… show him the photos she had taken.

Stella had no way of knowing that in just a few months time this day would come back to her as she sat and listened to the surgeon telling Freddie that by the time cancer was detected it had already been around for quite a while.

"I'm so glad you're feeling better, darling."

"Oh yes. As I told you, I slept for most of the day and that soup at dinner time has filled an empty space. I'm sure normal service will be resumed tomorrow – steak, chips and all the trimmings – that's if Adam doesn't eat it all. By the way, while you were getting ready I had a look at your photos – well done. They are really good."

"Thanks, but I'm not in your league."

"Well…no…but a bit more practise…"

Stella laughed, relieved that her husband was better and ready to enjoy the evening. The decks were crowded as most of the passengers had gathered to watch a dance troupe brought on board to entertain them, and Freddie and Stella were sitting on one of the upper decks with their table companions..

"And still they come," Adam observed, leaning over the rail and looking down to the lower deck where the performance was due to take place and where people were still trying to find spaces to sit, squeezing in wherever they could.

"How does she do it?" he sat back and pointed to where Edie and Stanley were sitting right at the very front of the semi-circular area that had been cleared for the dancers – the prime viewing position, or so it seemed. Freddie laughed,

"Divine intervention perhaps?"

And so it was that all six of them were looking in that direction as intervention of a different kind, in the form of Judy and Stuart, unwittingly provided the warm up to the show. They had obviously realised that there was not enough room left for the dancers so, walking together over to where Edie and Stanley were sitting, they bent down and said something to them. Stella saw Edie's mouth go down at the corners as she planted herself more firmly in her chair. Stuart put a hand gently under her arm, but it was shrugged off. Stanley stood up, shifting uncomfortably from one foot to another, but Edie stayed resolutely where she was until Judy bent down and, taking her firmly by the arm, lifted her just enough to be able to whip the chair deftly out from under her. She turned and made her way across to the other side of the stage with Edie's high heels click-clacking behind her (no stick or wheel-chair this evening!) and put the chair down. Edie immediately grabbed it and hurled it viciously across the deck where it bounced and clattered to a standstill in the centre. This had the effect of silencing the audience for a split second until, recovering from the shock of such a petulant display of temper, they suddenly erupted, filling the air with booing and cries of 'throw her overboard...feed her to the sharks.'

Judy calmly retrieved the fallen chair and Edie and Stanley sat down – with a better view than the one they had left.

The show was excellent and the following day everyone noticed that Edie was, uncharacteristically, rather quiet.

CHAPTER TWENTY SIX

And so began the long haul across to South America – nine days at sea which they all knew were coming and which filled some passengers with dread. What would they do at sea for all that time? Aware of the possibility of chronic boredom setting in and causing untold problems – not to mention multiplying the complaints – the efforts of the staff to provide entertainment reached Olympian heights – literally. The Matisse Olympic Games were introduced: nine days, nine sports: – darts, shuffleboard, quoits, skittles, golf-putting, table-tennis, hoop-shooting, pool-relay and golf-chipping – every day! For the non-sporty there were cribbage, whist and kalooki tournaments – every day! All results were meticulously recorded and published in Cruisenews, but even that didn't prevent a fight breaking out at the table-tennis table.

There was a boat-building competition; guests were urged to use anything they could find around the ship and the effectiveness of their craft would be tested in the swimming pool on 15th December – "…be creative, have fun and don't forget to name your boat."

The shop pulled out all the stops and everything – Baltic amber, hot diamonds, watches, purses, gifts and jewellery boxes – re-appeared as though for the first time preceded by splashy adverts in Cruisenews.

The production company put on some superb shows and the cabaret artistes sang, played instruments and told jokes to the point of exhaustion. Stella was surprised to see Stuart's name slipped in amongst the visiting professionals and wondered what he was like as a performer; both she and Freddie were blown away by the quality of his cabaret act.

"Makes you wonder why they bother with so many visiting acts when they've got someone with his talent on board," was Freddie's verdict, and Stella whole-heartedly agreed.

There was a Gala Buffet: a staggering display of beautifully presented food which passengers were encouraged to photograph before they sampled and this time, learning lessons from the debacle of the Patisserie Buffet, Judy kept control of the event, effectively managing to prevent the greed of some passengers from spoiling it for others.

An engine room visit was organised for those who wanted to go and look at the huge, powerful work horses that kept 'The Matisse' ploughing on through the waves day and night. Freddie took advantage of this opportunity and returned to the cabin with the shining eyes of all 'boys' when they've been in the presence of great, well-maintained machines.

"Whoa...look at this!"

Freddie had picked up the latest Cruisenews from where it lay on the floor, having been pushed under the cabin door, and was waving it towards Stella,

"A Garden Fete! Whatever next? How on earth can that work on a cruise-ship?"

But it did. Rats were splatted, funny hats worn and judged, and many other competitions, with prizes, were organised for what turned out to be a very jolly afternoon. The boat judging was part of these festivities, and Stella saw Bernard shuffling along in the queue round the pool, proudly clutching an object made of drinking straws, string and beer bottles, waiting for his turn to see if it would float and reminding her of her five year old grandson with one of his Lego models.

She was disappointed not to see Sheila round the pool watching; what a shame. There had been many discussions at the dinner table about the construction of this craft, to which Sheila had shown a marked indifference, but Stella and Freddie encouraged as they felt it was something at which Bernard could shine – unlike bridge. She watched anxiously as his turn came, hoping that the weird object would actually stay on the surface of the water – and it did! She cheered loudly, waving to him as he looked round with pink cheeks and a beatific smile on his face. Stella felt even more miffed with Sheila as she watched the little 'boat' bobbing about on the waves and noticed 'The Lovely Sheila' scrawled in black felt tip on its side.

"What the...?!" Freddie and Stella stopped and stared with open mouths. There, just a little way ahead of them, in the short passage leading to the dining room, was a sight that beggared belief. Isobel, the diminutive, elderly port lecturer, was cowering against the wall with tears streaming down her face and towering over her was a large, solidly built man, already known as one of the ship's complainers, pointing and shouting in her face. Freddie didn't hesitate. Walking swiftly over, he put himself between them, giving Stella the opportunity to gently extricate the frail, trembling little woman and lead her, sobbing, to the safety of the ladies' room nearby.

"Oh dear...oh dear..." Hands and lips shaking, she splashed her face with cold water as Stella attempted to calm her, wondering what terrible crime she had committed to warrant such an attack. When she could finally speak, it appeared that the large man, one of her table companions, had objected to the fact that she had reached across him to retrieve her handbag which she had put on the window sill while she ate her dinner.

"....but everyone puts their bags on the window sill...and I did ask if he minded...he said he was fed up with me ruining his dinner by stretching across him...oh dear...oh dear..."

She twisted her handkerchief in still shaking fingers, and it was several minutes before Stella could convince her that she really hadn't done anything wrong – the problem was his. She dried her tears and thanked Stella for her kindness then, still somewhat agitated, made her way out of the cloakroom.

By the time Stella reached her table in the dining room, Freddie had told his side of the story and they were all eagerly waiting to hear what Isobel had done to provoke the man.

"You cannot be serious," Adam exploded when she relayed the 'terrible handbag retrieval' crime. "Of all the …" He brought his massive fist down so hard on the table that all the cutlery leapt into the air, then swivelled in his seat,

"Where is he? The big bully! Freddie, which one is he? I'll show him… picking on that poor little soul…"

"You'll do no such thing," said Denise quietly, re-arranging the cutlery. "It sounds as though Freddie has dealt more than adequately with the situation; I don't think bully-boy will be repeating his performance."

Freddie had indeed seen him off using language best not repeated, but he was still seething when they had finished dinner and muttered something about just going to find him to make sure he was no-where near Isobel and that his 'message' had been clearly understood. So it was Stella's turn to take a firm line with her husband, silently reasoning that the man was physically much bigger than Freddie and the sea very deep. She didn't relish the thought of giving him the opportunity to throw Freddie overboard while no-one was watching; after all if he could bully a little old lady, what else was he capable of? She assured Freddie that, knowing him as well as she did, she was certain he had made his message quite clear and persuaded him that going to watch the show was a much better way of spending the time. She did notice that for the rest of the voyage the man not only had the sense to stay out of Isobel's way, but gave Freddie a very wide berth every time he saw him, always making a point of turning his back on him.

For Stella and the cast, this unbroken time at sea provided the best possible opportunity to break the back of the Christmas show. Most words were learnt, it just remained for them to put it all together and rehearse until it was as good as it could possibly be. Stuart and Stella worked well together, listening to and respecting each other's opinions and complementing each other's strengths. The cast continued to take direction well and Stella was gradually winning the battle to get them to project their voices and not mumble. There were some wonderful moments when certain people showed true star quality and their performances carried the rest along.

A particular joy for Stella was being able to call upon some of the professionals to work with them. She asked Crystal, one of the ship's beautiful young dancers, to choreograph and perform a ballet during a scene with the two youngest cast members. Far from behaving in a superior way, she said she would be honoured to do it and executed an exquisite dance, with apparent ease. The talented Hungarian Trio added their expertise to one of the carols bringing tears to everyone's eyes. Stella was hoping and praying that the performance on Christmas Eve would be a great success, little knowing at that point how near she would come to allowing the evening to be spoilt for her by one of 'The Australians.'

She had heard about 'The Australians,' but had no idea what they looked like or who they were. People would talk about them in exasperated or angry tones:

"You **do** know them, Stella. They're always sunbathing up on deck 8 and **always** moaning...they never join in with anything...you know...there's three of them, two men and a woman travelling together (pause for meaningful looks)..."

"...Yes...you know the ones; they had that blow up sheep with them at the Australian deck party..."

Stifled giggle, "Yeah...their sex toy... do you think we could borrow it for the show? We need a lamb..." Pause for one look at Stella's face, "OK perhaps not. Anyway you do know them. They're horrible!"

No, she didn't know them, but she soon would.

CHAPTER TWENTY SEVEN

Land at last! It was 9.00 o'clock in the morning when 'The Matisse' docked in South America and by 10.00 o'clock Freddie and Stella were part of a group waiting in The Club to be taken on one of the most exciting trips of the whole cruise. They were going to fly from Guayaquil to Quito, the capital of Ecuador, in the Andes basin where they would be able to stand astride the Equator in the Middle of the World. They would be at an altitude of about 9,300 feet and the temperatures were likely to be invigorating, so some warm clothes were essential. Spirits were high and not even Judy's announcement that the flight had been delayed could dampen them; after all there was no way of knowing, at this point, how different the trip was destined to be from anything that had been advertised, or that they could imagine.

They waited and waited, then finally set off for the airport, taking in the sights of Guayaquil on the way. Founded over four hundred years ago in 1542, Guayaquil has grown from an insect infested swamp to become Ecuador's largest city, its main port and thriving business centre with a population of three million. The people are mainly Indian or of mixed – 'mestizo' – stock, the rest being European, Asian or African.

Two hours at the airport and still no plane.

"Don't worry; we'll be airborne by 1.30" Bernice, a particularly level-headed member of the Sailaways staff and one of their guides for the day, smiled reassuringly at the group, some of whom were starting to get a little anxious.

"Look," someone muttered, "The only charter flight on the board doesn't leave until 2.20."

Others noticed this too,

"The day is slipping away from us…"

"It's hardly worth going now…"

"We certainly won't get the trip we paid for…"

The grumbles bubbled up and down the rows of seated travellers who then began to pace about, forming anxious groups.

"…and there won't be time for our **luxury lunch**," snorted one particularly unpleasant member of the party who didn't look as though missing a lunch would cause him any lasting damage.

A decision had to be made. Bernice called everyone together and asked if they wanted to go on or return to the town where they could try and salvage something of the day by visiting the Malecon, a popular new waterside development. Freddie turned to Stella,

"So what's it to be?"

"Go on, of course."

"Even with that cold you've got?"

"Even with this cold." She sneezed loudly and blew her nose, then smiled at her husband,

"It's once in a life time, isn't it? What do you think?"

"Yep. Middle of the World here we come and hang the consequences!"

Mr. 'Luxury Lunch' flicked his fingers at Bernice and raised his voice above the others,

"Oi…you say we'll be brought back at 8 o'clock, but since the weather is obviously causing so many problems how can you guarantee that?"

He had a nasty sneer on his face and Bernice looked uncomfortable, knowing that she couldn't.

"There's no guarantees in life, mate, sometimes you've just got to take a few chances."

It was Adam who spoke and there were a few titters in response. 'Luxury Lunch' turned and glared at him,

"You can if you like, MATE, but I'll make up me own mind!"

"Quite right…"

"Here here…."

"You tell him…"

It was clear that the party was splitting into two camps, so Bernice asked for a show of hands – those in favour of going on and those who would prefer to turn back.

"Oh no..." Stella's heart sank as Bernice counted 35 who wanted to return to the town and 28 who voted to continue with the trip. She felt sure they would have to abide by the will of the majority. She was wrong. A quick call to the ship confirmed that those who wanted to could proceed with the excursion and the rest of the group would be escorted back to Guayaquil.

Feeling quite reckless, they marched out onto the tarmac to board the waiting plane and laughed as they spread themselves around an interior designed to accommodate 70, not just 28, passengers. Stella smiled at Sharon and her husband then noticed Chrissie and Jack take two seats just opposite. Geoffrey, the art lecturer was there with his wife and the craft teachers from the card-making class. Adam ambled past followed by Denise, but Bernard's knees had prevented him and Sheila from even setting out on the trip. Stella silently hoped this didn't mean extra bridge for him. Wayne, the pasty-faced singer, had opted to stay and help Bernice while the other two entertainer/leaders for the day returned with the rest of the party. He minced up the aisle, his small, pert bottom encased in tight, white jeans with Nancy following close behind. Stella turned to look out of the aircraft window where she saw Kieran, glasses dangling between his fingers and his face a picture of misery, watching from the edge of the runway.

Nancy stopped by Chrissie whose eyebrows were raised up to her hair-line.

"...honestly, he's such a wimp. There's no way I'm going back. See you later..."

And she hurried on after Wayne to be sure of bagging the seat next to him.

Freddie turned back from watching Wayne's retreating backside and smiled,

"I'd have had him down as gay, but I don't think Nancy would be so interested if he was."

"You can be sure of that," Stella laughed.

Rattling around with plenty of room to spare, they enjoyed a flight over the Andes, (sadly hidden by cloud but everyone knew they were there) and were given a biscuit and a cup of coffee. Luxury lunch? No, but they didn't care; they were off to the middle of the world.

"Apparently Quito is a beautiful city...the old part protected now as one of UNESCO's World Heritage Preserves. Sadly it has no protection from earthquakes or Guagua Pichincha, a volcano which erupted in 1999 sending showers of volcanic ash on Quito and its neighbouring villages."

Chrissie was studying the guidebook, a look of concentration on her beautiful face and a slight frown creasing her forehead as she picked out just the interesting bits to read to Jack; after all she didn't want to bore him. He was gazing at her and, as far as he was concerned, she could have been reading the telephone directory in Serbo-Croat, he wouldn't have minded. He wanted to go on listening to her forever and couldn't care less if they got back from Quito or not. He was with Chrissie – for how long? Who knew? He just wanted to make the most of every moment. Margie and her cronies hadn't set out on this trip and Jim had opted to return, so they were on their own and he was determined to enjoy it.

The little village in the middle of the world was very exciting with live music and a large number of vibrant pink craft shops selling good quality souvenirs at reasonable prices. Stella and Freddie, along with most of the group, had their photos taken straddling the equator; they were all huddled in jumpers and looked like the Michelin Man in the adverts back home, as the altitude had meant a sudden and significant drop in temperature. They were also warned that strenuous exercise might prove difficult until they got used to the heady atmosphere, but that was OK as all anyone had in mind was a gentle stroll around the village. Everyone's spirits were high and a feeling of being on an exciting adventure still prevailed as they asked Bernice for a few more minutes to enjoy this special place. Stella smiled as she watched Jack and Chrissie dancing to a live band in the middle of a square, obviously designated for that purpose. They were quite alone and oblivious to everything except each other and the crisp, clear notes of music that seemed sharpened, defined, by the heady mountain air. She saw Nancy pull Wayne up to join them, slowly wrapping herself round him until they moved as one to the music. Freddie chuckled,

"Nothing too strenuous there then, no danger of those two collapsing through lack of oxygen…oh maybe I spoke too soon…"

He tailed off as Wayne gave Nancy a long lingering kiss,

"…Blimey…let her come up for air, mate!"

Laughing, Stella dragged him away and they went to collect certificates to prove that they had been to the centre of the world then, without the slightest hint of a grumble, someone tentatively mentioned that they hadn't actually had a meal since breakfast.

"Don't worry, I have a snack ready for you," said Bernice, and sure enough as they boarded the coach to return to Quito there were boxes of food on the front seats. All thoughts of luxury lunches long forgotten, they enjoyed their feast of chicken, salad, sandwiches, cake, fruit and a choice of two sorts of juice.

In Quito, on the way to the airport, they stopped at a Church where everyone except Stella got off to admire what turned out to be a beautiful building.

"My cold's making me feel absolutely wretched, Freddie, do you mind if I stay here? You go and look at the Church. I'll just rest; I'm so bunged up, I'm finding it difficult to breathe."

"No that's fine, love. You might even nod off while we're gone."

Stella curled up on the seat getting as comfortable as she could and was surprised when she heard the engine start. The driver had decided to fill the time by speeding round the streets to show his one remaining passenger the sights of the town. He stopped at a beautiful square and Stella felt it would be churlish not to admire the subtly lit buildings, while all she really wanted to do was try and clear her nose. She dozed, then they were off again, just her and the driver bouncing along through dark streets in a dark, and otherwise empty, coach – a strange feeling. They stopped and the rest of the group returned full of awe and wonder at the magnificence of the Church. They had enjoyed hot drinks and been given chocolates to sustain them for the rest of he journey. If they had known just how long that journey was going to be, they would probably have taken a few extra handfuls.

"I have some good news," the South American guide, who had come with the coach, was smiling, "your plane has been delayed so we are taking you on a tour of Quito."

Stella was, and always had been, a great admirer of anyone who can turn a negative into a positive, and others must have felt the same as no-one even thought of grumbling about the situation. They all sat back and looked around as guide and driver showed them the sights, including the square where Stella had already spent quite a bit of time. They climbed up high above the city and enjoyed breath-taking, panoramic views of Quito at night dominated, in honour of Christmas, by a massive statue of the Virgin Mary.

"I don't know how to tell you this…" It was the guide again at almost nine o'clock when they should already have been airborne, "…but the airport is closed on account of fog."

Nobody said anything. No-one shouted, grumbled or complained. They just sat and continued to admire the sights – Quito, from another angle, all lit up. The guide went to the back of the coach to speak to Bernice and then told the group they were taking them to another airport.

"We will get you back to your ship, don't worry."

And they didn't. The driver put his foot down and they sped through the country-side, only regretting that the darkness hid spectacular views of The Andes that they would have enjoyed in daylight. The journey to Cotopaxi took nearly two hours and still no moans. At one point Stella had to go down the bus to the toilet at the back; Chrissie winked as she passed, a man near the back flashed her a smile and she marvelled at their resilience. She learned later that everyone had the same attitude towards their situation as she and Freddie did – they had made their decision in the full knowledge that this might happen, so they had to take the consequences. Grumbling wasn't an option! The road was bumpy and occasionally they passed little groups of ramshackle houses, poorly lit and ill-kept, some made even more pitiable by a pathetic attempt to acknowledge Christmas with a sparse decoration or two hanging limply outside.

At the military airport in Cotopaxi they were hustled through an empty building and out onto the tarmac to board a jet; then twenty minutes later they landed in Guayaquil where, again, they went straight through the airport with no formalities. Bounding along with spirits still high, they headed for the waiting coach when, crossing a stream just outside the terminal, a few of them became aware of a strange noise.

"Look, it's a frog," someone shouted, and they all stopped to admire the little creature croaking away on a stone at the water's edge.

The coach pulled up alongside the ship at twenty minutes to midnight, five minutes before the appointed sailing time. Stella and Freddie shuffled along the aisle and were aware that the mood was suddenly a little subdued. A lot of people had worked hard to get them safely back and they hadn't caused the ship to delay departure, but how would their fellow passengers view their adventure? Would they see it as foolish – even selfish? They needn't have worried. As they stepped off the coach and started up the rickety steps there were cheers from above and they looked up to see people hanging over the railing to welcome them back.

Still laughing and joking they made their way to the dining room where Judy greeted them and the Maitre d' had hot soup and sandwiches waiting.

"Three cheers for Judy, the Maitre d' and catering staff."

Everyone cheered, as they had already done earlier for the Captain and crew of the jet, and their guide who had insisted on flying all the way back with them – well beyond the call of duty.

Unable to sleep, Stella reflected on their adventure and was struck by how pleasant life is, and what possibilities open up, when everyone is positive and projects…plans…schemes are not weighed down by negative energy, which rarely makes any difference to a situation apart from depressing everyone. She learned later that Pete had had to bribe the military airport to let them through and he had also provisionally booked them into hotels in various places in case they couldn't get back. He was then planning to fly them to the ship at Panama or Barbados.

The group of 28 adventurers thanked him profusely for all his trouble and felt well and truly vindicated when, a day later while crossing the equator, the Captain of 'The Matisse' said he had failed to get permission from Neptune to do this, but it was OK as the brave people who went to Quito had obtained it for him!

But permission alone was not enough. There were two days at sea before the 'The Matisse' was due to traverse the Panama Canal, and a special ceremony to mark the crossing of the equator had to be performed. A paragraph in 'Cruisenews' explained that this was originally an initiation rite in the Navy to commemorate a sailor's first time across this line. It was created by seasoned sailors to test their new ship-mates and ensure that they were hardy enough to endure long periods of time in rough seas. The nick-name for sailors who have already crossed the equator is (Trusty) Shellbacks, sometimes known as Sons of Neptune; while those who have not are called (Slimy) Pollywogs. King Neptune and his court, usually represented by high-ranking seamen, officiate at a ceremony during which the Pollywogs undergo a number of increasingly disgusting ordeals, receiving a certificate at the end to commemorate their new status.

Apparently up to, and including, the nineteenth century the line-crossing ceremony was quite vicious and could include beatings with wet ropes and even throwing the Pollywog overboard then dragging him along in the surf behind the ship. Not surprisingly, this sometimes culminated in the death of the sailors undergoing the trial – a strange and rather extreme way to prove endurance.

Everyone gathered on the pool deck at the appointed time after dinner on the first evening at sea and waited for the ceremony to begin. It was linked with a fancy dress party so a silly mood prevailed from the start. Judy, dressed as a judge, passed sentence on several very game passengers who had obviously agreed to be accused of some 'serious' misdemeanours and to be punished accordingly. The parts of Neptune and Neptuna were played by the glamorous Irma and Antonio, smeared with swirls of lurid green and blue paint, and swathed in chiffon of the same colours. The Captain and two of his crew were there in full uniform while several other members of staff were in costume – Stuart as an astronomer and Amanda as Dr. Blood.

The 'victims' were led forward and ordered to prostrate themselves on the deck in front of Judy as the accusations were read, then all eyes turned towards Neptune to see if his thumb went up or down, thus sealing the victim's fate.

The thumb, of course, went down every time followed by rousing cheers that rang around the decks as the victim was grabbed by Dr. Blood and her assistants to be covered in cold spaghetti or something similar before being dunked in the pool.

Also during these sea days the ship suddenly became decorated with a great deal of glitz and glitter, several Christmas trees and a huge, ceiling-high, blow-up Father Christmas that wobbled about precariously outside the dining room doors.

"You know, Judy and her staff stayed up until after 3 o'clock in the morning to get the ship decorated like this. No wonder they look so tired."

Sheila delivered this piece of information with some authority as she passed the vegetables across the dinner table. Stella had noticed that Sheila always liked to give the impression that she had inside information about what was going on, and she was certainly right about one thing – the staff looked very tired. Stella put this down to the amazing amount of work they all did and the relentless pressure of trying to keep over four hundred passengers happy. No-one, not even Sheila, had any way of knowing, at this point, what the real reason was for their extreme fatigue. They had a major disaster hanging over their heads.

CHAPTER TWENTY EIGHT

PASSAGE THROUGH THE PANAMA CANAL

An exciting and truly fascinating part of the journey! Just about everything had been cancelled for the day so that passengers could take in the ship's progress through this multi-lock canal – an amazing example of early twentieth century engineering. Completed in 1914 (the first ship sailed through on August 15th of that year) the Panama Canal has operated since then without ever breaking down or needing major modernisation. It extends for a distance of fifty miles linking the Atlantic and Pacific Oceans and cutting out the otherwise necessary journey around Cape Horn. The passage through the Canal takes approximately ten hours whereas the trip around the Horn would be weeks, even months.

There are three sets of locks, each of which has two lanes, that work to elevate ships 26 metres above sea level to the level of Gatun Lake, and then lowers them again back to sea level on the opposite side of the Isthmus. During the locking procedures approximately 197 million litres of fresh water are used from Gatun Lake and ultimately flushed out into the sea. There is a Control House on the centre wall in the high chamber of each lock from which the operation is directed. While passing through the locks, vessels are assisted by electric locomotives using cables to align and tow them. They work in pairs and move on rails to keep the ships in position.

People crowded along the ship's rails, cameras held high to try and capture the best pictures of this once-in-a-life-time experience. They stopped chatting at intervals to listen to the commentator who had been brought on board to keep everyone informed about exactly what was happening all the way along. Amongst many other things, he told them that one of the little locomotives had once been de-railed and pulled into the water by a ship though, luckily, the driver had managed to jump clear. They watched in awe as all necessary procedures at each lock were carried out with admirable efficiency and everything ran smoothly. The scenery on each side was ever changing from the shimmering water of Lake Gatun to the jungle-clad hills of the Talamanca and San Blas ranges, interspersed by the intricate machinery of the locks.

As they were travelling from the Pacific Ocean to the Caribbean, they went first through Miraflores Locks then on to Pedro Miguel and finally Gatun locks before sailing out into the Caribbean Sea.

It was as long ago as 1513 that the feasibility of an inter-oceanic canal was debated when Balboa first sighted the Pacific. The United States, Great Britain, Charles V of Spain and Simon Bolivar all considered the problems this would entail, but permission to undertake the task was first sought from Columbia by a French company. An initial survey was carried out by Ferdinand de Lesseps in 1881, although he was 76 years old by this time. Digging began, but was brought to a halt after 18 miles by a combination of problems, including lack of funds, inadequate machinery and a high death toll due to malaria, yellow fever and other tropical diseases. In 1903 Panama declared independence ceding the Canal Zone to the USA and the work was able to continue as the breeding grounds for disease-carrying mosquitoes were destroyed.

Every year, approximately thirteen to fourteen thousand ships make use of this unique waterway, each bringing the Panama Canal Company about fifty thousand US dollars in toll fees. It costs over a hundred and fifty thousand dollars for a hundred thousand tonne cruise ship to pass through and, although this may sound expensive, it is a bargain compared with the cost of a journey round Cape Horn. The fee is calculated mainly by weight and the smallest sum ever paid was 36 cents in 1928 when a man called Richard Halliburton swam from one end to the other taking 10 days – August 14th to the 23rd – to complete the journey. Since the inaugural passage in 1914 more than

190

942,000 vessels have transited the Canal and by the end of the day most of 'The Matisse' passengers felt very privileged to be counted amongst their number.

Jeannie, however, wasn't one of them and neither, for that matter, was Donald. As far as they were concerned they could have been transiting the moon and it would have elicited the same level of excitement. Lying side by side on adjacent beds, smoking and pretending to read, they were each imprisoned in their own cells of abject misery. Donald's eyes slid sideways and, watching a curl of smoke drift lazily from his wife's lips up to the cabin ceiling, he tried to recall the passion for her that had once rocked his world, shaken him to his very core and wrenched him away from Maggie. Maggie, gentle Maggie, his childhood sweetheart and best friend; his beloved Maggie, the girl he had married in that simple ceremony at their home village amongst the heather-clad hills of the Highlands.

Employing what he now realised was deplorable self-deception, he'd consigned, with scarcely a backward glance, the world he'd shared with Maggie to a bin labelled 'things of childhood' and given himself over to the new and exciting world that Jeannie was opening up for him. Church on Sundays, afternoon walks on those familiar hills and then tea with one or other of their parents, even his little son, Rory, none of this mattered any more. Jeannie was the real thing; the clandestine meetings, the excitement of a new body; he was gripped from the start by a passion he had never known before and everything else slid into the background

Then Maggie found out and the web of deception, so strong and tight in his secret world, crumbled to dust as the light of truth shone through it. He sat holding Maggie's hand while she sobbed, her whole body shaking, her world falling apart around her in their sunny little sitting room, and he knew he should give Jeannie up. He knew that Maggie loved him to the very depths of her soul, and so he had fed her a sliver of hope. 'OK, I'll finish it.' She'd looked at him, her gentle grey eyes full to the brim with gratitude, and he could still see her standing at the window watching him go to what she hoped was his last meeting with Jeannie.

But, oh how quickly and easily his wife's gentle face full of love, along with his half-hearted resolution were forgotten when Jeannie threw herself over him in the car, covering his face with kisses, fumbling for the zip in his trousers. Afterwards they had laughed; this was his world now. How stupid he'd been, viewing his wife's dignified forbearance as weakness, and he'd left, left the one person who had truly cared about him, screwed up and thrown away the love of his wife and son – for Jeannie.

He groaned, realising too late that he done so out loud. Jeannie's head jerked round towards him,

"What the hell's the matter with you?"

"Nothing – just a daft bit in this book I'm reading...."

Jeannie grunted and turned back to her own book. Honestly what an idiot Donald was at times. She took a sip from the tumbler of whisky on the bedside table and the words on the page in front of her merged into an indecipherable mass. What exactly had she seen in Donald? She glanced across at the adjacent bunk. Had he always been the lined, grey lifeless person he was now? No, of course not. It took some effort, but she could just recall the tall man with dark wavy hair and a strong laugh that echoed round any room he was in. She saw him again as she had first seen him, striding confidently into the conference room, and she had watched, mesmerised, as, with total command of the situation, he delivered a presentation that had the delegates on their feet, applauding this rising star. She was there to take notes for her boss, but had managed to squeeze in next to Donald at lunch time, smiling and asking him questions about his life. She was disappointed to find that there was a little wife in tow, but made all the right noises when he pulled photographs of her and his son out of his wallet, his face alight with pride. She drew him out, just managing not to laugh at the description of his life in the hills, a miss-match for this dynamic man who could obviously go far – with the right woman by his side.

He must have sensed her amusement and, suddenly seeing himself through the eyes of this sophisticated woman next to him, had assured her that he would soon be moving his family to one of the smarter suburbs of Edinburgh. She had nodded and looked at him in such a way that left her in no doubt there would be a tap on her bedroom door that night. She realised it was probably just that he had to prove something, having appeared so provincial in her eyes – he had even talked about going to Church, for God's sake! It didn't matter. She had him, and she would show him what he was missing. She was still single and had played around enough to know that Donald would suit her just fine.

What she didn't know, until it was too late, was that Maggie and Rory were an essential part of him. He hadn't known it either; but now, in their booze-fuddled reality, he knew only too well that what had sucked the life out of him was Jeannie. And it seemed there was no going back. Oh, he had done well enough, made some money, but his heart ached for Maggie and Rory, his old life of peace and tranquillity in the Highland hills.

Jeannie got up and stretched,

"Will we be going up for a drink?"

Donald rubbed his eyes and sat up,

"Aye. We'll go to the Sky Bar. You go on ahead; I'll just have a pee then follow you up"

He took a couple of steps towards the tiny bathroom but stopped when Jeannie disappeared out of the door. Watching for a moment to be sure she had gone, he drew a piece of paper out of his pocket, carefully unfolded it and sat down on his bed to read it for the fourth time. It was an email from Maggie that he'd printed off earlier in the day and contained two pieces of vital information. He already knew she had married again, several years ago now, a fact which, when he found out, had caused a painful twist somewhere near his heart. Now she was telling him that Jimmy, her second husband, had died; and Rory was getting married. Rory, the son whose childhood he'd missed, as the one shred of decency he had shown in the whole sorry affair was to make a clean break, for the sake of his son – and Maggie. He didn't want to create the situation that was becoming all too familiar these days – a child whose loyalties are torn between warring parents, not that he and Maggie could ever be truly at war – more credit to her than him. So he had never taught Rory to fish, never sailed with him across the loch in an open boat or been there for birthdays and Christmases. Maggie had, over the years, sent the occasional photo, so he knew that Rory had grown into a young man any father would be proud of; and now he was getting married.

Donald folded the piece of paper again and put it deep into his trouser pocket. He stood up. Could it be…? Was Maggie telling him these two things as a sign that she would welcome a visit from him? The thought of seeing her again stirred something inside him – was it hope…joy even? It was a light in this shit-hole of a life he was living and could even make the rest of the voyage on this God-forsaken ship bearable.

CHAPTER TWENTY NINE

The day started in a way that now passed as normal for this group of disparate travellers, thrown together and wrapped in their cocoon of floating steel. Lounging on his bunk, Freddie delighted Stella with the guide book description of Aruba,

"…glorious white sand beaches and water sports galore, this little island, very popular with honeymooners, is also famous for shopping bargains from all over the world, and attractive scenery. In the fifteenth century it had been claimed for Spain, but then in the seventeenth and eighteenth centuries it was taken over by the Dutch and, apart from a brief spell of occupation by the British from 1805 to 1816, it has remained Dutch ever since. Off-shore banking and oil-refining are big business, but tourism is now the main industry of this island which has a population of 71,500."

Still hoping for white sand and crystal blue water, Stella and Freddie had booked themselves onto 'The Beach Express' excursion which promised 'the ultimate Caribbean beach experience.' They would be travelling to the island's best beaches in a colourful open-air bus with steel band music playing in the background. They would enjoy the white sand – sun-loungers and parasols provided – and swim in turquoise waters with restaurants, bars, shopping and water sports nearby.

But they didn't. Halfway through the morning the bombshell dropped. In a clear voice, only occasionally cracking very slightly, Judy delivered her message which sent shock waves around the ship.

"Ladies and gentlemen, it is with regret I have to inform you that, as from midnight last night, the company – Sailaways – is in the hands of the Administrator…"

She went on with the some more official details and finished by saying that the crew and staff would do their best to ensure the holiday would not be affected by this turn of events. Then she repeated the whole message while

Freddie and Stella sat staring at each other, open-mouthed, across the space between their adjacent beds.

"They've gone bust! Sailaways has gone bust...." Freddie gasped as if somehow saying it aloud would help him to absorb and grasp the full meaning of what they had just been told.

Stella wrenched open the cabin door and ran down the passage to the information desk where many of the staff had already gathered. Most were in tears and being comforted by some of the other passengers. She put her arm around Judy whose face mirrored the strain she had been under; she and many of the others must have had this hanging over them for some time,

"I am so sorry..." it was inadequate in the circumstances, but all Stella could think of saying, and she felt a lump in her throat as she looked at the tear-stained faces of the pretty young staff-members, now fairly sure they were out of jobs, but still reassuring passengers they would carry on regardless. They all worked so hard, what a terrible blow this must be. She realised, in that moment, that they had become a family, albeit dysfunctional like pretty well every other family anywhere, and with its share of black sheep. She learned later that 'the Australians,' sun-bathing up on deck 8 as usual, had cheered when they'd heard the news.

At lunchtime the dining room was buzzing and odd words: '...terrible...shame...poor things...shocking...just couldn't take it in...' kept popping out of the general clamour. Sheila carefully dissected her piece of fish,

"...so how does Administrator differ from Receivership – or total bankruptcy...?"

"Not sure. I wonder if we'll have to go straight back to England..."

"Will all the staff be out of jobs?"

"Don't know. I think the crew and catering staff are employed by a different company from the cruise staff – you know, Judy and the entertainers..."

"Oh it's such a shame...."

"Do you think they will carry on, you know, with the same standard of service that we've had so far?"

"Well, to be honest, I have wondered more than once how on earth they can provide a trip like this for the money...probably why they've gone bust."

Conversation ping-ponged around the table and everyone nodded after the last statement, then agreed whole-heartedly with Denise when, carefully replacing her knife and fork in her plate, she sat back and declared,

"Well, even if we do head straight back to England, I for one will not be complaining as I think we will still have had amazing value for money."

"Oh yes..."

"Me too..."

"Quite right."

"Go straight to jail without passing 'go' – or in this case, straight home passing St. Lucia, Barbados and Madeira without stopping."

Adam's lame attempt to lighten the atmosphere failed as Denise gave him a look that said this really isn't a laughing matter.

It was 7.00 pm by the time 'The Matisse' docked in Aruba and Stella and Freddie decided to salvage what they could from the day. Armed with money and cameras, they set off for the town, admiring and photographing the pretty pastel-coloured, ornate gables of the shops and houses, a clear reflection of the Dutch influence. They bought a few souvenirs before returning to the ship which set sail, as planned, at 10.00 pm bound for St. Lucia, with one sea day between the ports – a very special day for them.

CHAPTER THIRTY

Freddie woke on the morning of Saturday 22nd of December 2007 hoping that absolutely nothing would go wrong with his plans, so carefully made, but, of necessity, involving many others who, as far as he could tell, had managed to keep everything from Stella. He looked across at the adjacent bed to where his wife of forty years was still sleeping. Stella, the woman he had loved for every one of those forty years and more. He remembered the first time he had seen her, dancing in the middle of the floor at her college 'freshers' ball; a new student, trying so hard to be cool and sophisticated, but looking very young and self-conscious as she moved to the music, glancing nervously round then smiling at the young woman opposite who mirrored her moves. Freddie had smiled as he watched, at least they hadn't put their handbags on the floor between them! He was there with a few mates from the military base nearby as they'd heard there was a bash on at the college and decided to check it out.

He nudged his friend,

"Do me a favour; you take the one in green, I want to dance with the dark-haired girl in the pink dress."

With the confidence of youth, the two officers split the girls and Freddie was smitten from the first moment he looked across the dimly-lit space between them into Stella's eyes. They went for a drink and he knew he had found 'the one.' Stella was attracted to this confident young officer but, lively, out-going and up for any adventures life would throw her way, she wasn't ready to commit herself to a steady relationship. It sounded rather dull to her; she wanted to experience different things – hitch-hike in a foreign country, cast off and see what life was all about, though she did secretly tell an old school friend during a visit back home that she thought she'd found the man she was going to marry.

Freddie waited and his patience was rewarded as, after an on/off relationship over four years, they married at the Church in Stella's home village.

"Happy Anniversary, darling,"

Stella leaned up on one elbow and tossed a card over onto Freddie's bed, then laughed when she opened his. It was a large piece of blue card with a yellow 4 above a tea bag stuck in the middle with four large ears at the bottom. She read out,

"Four...tea...ears...oh yes...very good – you daft beggar. Thank-you."

She smiled across at her husband and thought, not for the first time that, although she was supposed to be the creative one, he often surprised her with his imaginative gifts. On their twenty-fifth anniversary – twenty five presents, all wrapped in silver paper and every one of them relevant to each year of the twenty five – amazing. Still, she jumped out of bed, no presents this year as they had agreed that the Round-the-World holiday was their present to each other. So a sea day as usual, low key with nothing special happening.

Freddie watched as she dragged a set of casual clothes out of the wardrobe,

"You'd better put on something a bit smart,"

Stella frowned, "Why?"

All these years and she still never does as she's told without question.

"Stella, for once could you just do it."

She looked at Freddie and became suspicious. He's up to something.

He relented.

"Well...OK...I'll tell you now. We have been 'cordially invited by the Captain for pre-lunch drinks in The Sky Bar at 11.15 am.'"

"Really?" She returned the casual clothes and reached for her white trouser suit, "What just us?"

"Yes to celebrate our special day."

"Oh that's lovely…and not too scary. No big party or anything."

Little did she know….

"Oh look…you must have got it wrong, we can't go up there…"

Stella stopped at the door to The Sky Bar and read the notice saying it was closed for a private function.

"That must be left over from yesterday evening. Go on…keep going."

Freddie sounded confident so she pushed open the door, rather tentatively, and wound her way up into a bar they had only ever visited once before, very briefly as, being the only place on the ship where smoking was allowed, the air was usually well and truly polluted.

No smoke today; instead it was transformed and Stella stared in amazement at the small tables set with lemon cloths to match the lemon-coloured chairs facing a large table covered with a white, scrunched up cloth onto which Bernice, the Cruise Administrator, was scattering tiny, ruby-red hearts.

"Oh my goodness….."

Her hand flew to her mouth and Freddie laughed. So far so good, she obviously has no idea what is about to happen.

The door opened and Denise walked in followed by Adam, scrubbed up and shiny, complete with jacket and tie. Oh poor chap. Stella couldn't help feeling sorry for him as she was sure he would rather be in his usual sea-day attire of shorts and 'T' shirt, out on the top deck soaking up the rays. She was touched that he'd made such an effort for them.

'This is definitely not just drinks,' she thought, as the door kept opening to admit more of their new friends. Bernard and Sheila arrived followed by Ray and Vera then Douglas and Jackie, a couple they regularly met for a pre-dinner drink. There was a short pause and Father John arrived, then finally the Captain.

'What on earth is Father John doing here...? Oh my...could it be...?'

A few times in the past Stella had told Freddie she would very much like to renew their wedding vows, but he had made it clear it really wasn't his sort of thing, so she'd forgotten all about it. He couldn't have...surely. But he had.

Bernice told all the guests to sit facing the table then guided Freddie and Stella to the two chairs behind it where they sat, holding hands while they repeated the vows they had made forty years before. It was very moving and, as Stella looked into Freddie's eyes, she was so glad to have this opportunity to reaffirm her vows to the man who had been such a rock in her life. Like every couple, they had encountered problems along the way – some of them huge, some just the irritating niggles of every day life – but they had made it. They had overcome real difficulties and arrived at this point. Oh what joy, and what a blessing that they had this cruise to share together; what a blessing that they were unaware of just how the strength of their love would be tested in the years to come. They were to discover that they could still pull together through unimaginable pain, when both would be stretched to the very limit of their endurance.

But today was about being happy.

"Happy anniversary rang through the air; champagne flowed and canapés were served in a room filled with laughter. A beautiful cake appeared which they pretended to cut, just as they had all those years ago, but on that occasion using Freddie's military sword. There were gifts of champagne, Curacao, chocolates and a framed photograph of 'the six at table 8.' Bernice disappeared and a few minutes later an announcement was made over the PA system telling the entire ship what had just taken place, followed by a loud and prolonged blast on the ship's horn. So much for a low key day.

Back to the cabin and more champagne and chocolates from the family with a message from their son, 'forty years

– it's a miracle!' 'He's right,' thought Stella, 'and I'm so glad that miracles happen.'

For the rest of the day Stella was overwhelmed by the number of cards and verbal congratulations they received – and still Freddie kept telling her it wasn't over until it was over. Very cryptic! Her next instruction was to be ready for pre-dinner drinks in The Mermaid Tavern by 7.45 pm. Well nothing unusual there as they often went up for a drink at that time to listen to the marvellous Hungarian Trio who had joined the ship a while back and were delighting everyone with the quality of their music. What Stella didn't know was that Freddie had arranged for half the bar to be cordoned off for their guests and he had invited the entire cast of the Christmas Show, including the choir – almost 60 people – with their families. He had also included a few other friends: the card makers, Betty and Diane and Geoffrey, the art tutor, and his wife Myrtle. Stuart, the Deputy Cruise Director and Stella's co-producer for the show, also dropped in for a while. It was a wonderful occasion with more cards and gifts, including an hors d'oeuvres tray from the cast along with the message, 'you are both stars in our eyes – just bootiful!'

When dinner time came and they made their way to table 8, Stella was overwhelmed yet again by the huge bouquet of roses waiting for her there.

"How on earth did you manage that? We're at sea with no florists on board as far as I know."

Freddie just laughed and touched side of his nose with his forefinger. (Stella found out later that he'd sent a member of staff ashore in Aruba to buy them.) After dinner the waiters brought another cake and gathered round to sing their customary song: 'Let me Call you Sweetheart,' followed by a lot of 'one more time'…' '…oggie, oggie, oggie…' '…nice to see you...' Then to her utter amazement – and not the usual custom – The Trio arrived at their table and played to them! A real treat in a day full of treats.

On the way to watch the evening's entertainment, Freddie whispered, "just one more thing" and led her up onto the deck where, standing in the moonlight (how did he know there'd be a moon?), he gently placed a beautiful ruby and diamond ring on her finger.

Stella could find no words that would adequately express how she felt about the day. Magical...wonderful...unforgettable – yes, all of those, but they were not enough. She didn't feel bad about the fact that she had kept her side of the 'no present' bargain, as she knew Freddie would have derived immense pleasure from organising the day and that the success of the whole thing, along with her unreserved appreciation of it, was all he needed.

CHAPTER THIRTY ONE

Moving slowly round her tiny cabin, Margie dressed with great care. Today was important; today they would all see what a fun person she really was. Oh yes, Margie from Cornwall, jigging up and down to her beloved line-dancing music; invisible, faceless Margie, just part of the wall paper at the town hall where she worked, taken for granted by Raymond who preferred his boring old model trains to her...today she would show them. The tiny space, described by Edie with a derisory snort as being, '...in t' bowels of t' ship, love...' was the only cabin designed for single occupancy and afforded no window out onto the world, so Margie couldn't see if the sun was shining, she just had to hope it was, and would be for the rest of the day. The juddering of the mighty engines, perilously close to her cabin and the reason she had to keep taking those blessed sleeping tablets, had ceased, so she knew the Matisse had docked in St. Lucia.

A glance at her watch told her it was 9 o'clock. Time for breakfast; time to go up and meet the others at one of the long tables by the window where she knew they would, as usual, swap stories about aches and pains and lack of sleep while chomping vast quantities of food. Then they would drag their way through a morning of cards, crosswords and jig-saw puzzles – or whatever Edie decided they should do – before the afternoon ride along the coast in the catamaran. Edie wouldn't be on that, still going on as she was about 'that dreadful catamoorangue in Australia,' and nothing, absolutely nothing, must be allowed to interfere with her plans for the afternoon. As she squeezed herself out of the cabin door and made her way along the narrow passage towards the stairs, Margie was determined that nothing would.

Sitting around The Club in small groups, people chatted quietly as they waited to be called down to the catamaran. Jack looked out of the huge window across the sunlit bay to the courtyard adjacent to the quay with its array of tempting shops. He and Chrissie had wandered round there that morning in the sunshine and stopped for banana daiquiris at a rum shop overlooking the bay. Gazing out onto the shimmering blue water life had seemed to him to be quite perfect. Was it really only three days before Christmas and was he, Jack, sitting there with the most delightful companion he could ever wish for?

They had wandered on, in and out of the colourful little shops, until Chrissie suddenly stopped, gasping in disbelief at a giant bottle of her absolutely favourite perfume; but she refused to buy it, "...oh no...far too expensive..." though he could tell she really wanted it. He didn't know much about these things, but it seemed to him quite reasonable, and anyway, no price on earth would be too much for Chrissie as far as he was concerned so, unbeknown to her, he'd bought it. It was in a drawer in his cabin where he had carefully placed it between layers of his best cashmere sweaters, and there it would stay until the last day of the voyage when he would give it to Chrissie as a parting gift.

He would love to give it to her straight away, but didn't want to risk her thinking he was trying to buy his way into her affections. By the end of the voyage it wouldn't matter any more as she had made it clear that they were just having fun and their relationship would not extend beyond the duration of the cruise. She had told him all about Maurice, his treatment of her, her subsequent role as his carer, and he silently cursed the man who could treat such a lovely woman in that way. But then he thought of Betty and realised he had no room to judge.

Betty, his wife of forty two years, had been very different from Chrissie. He didn't even know if she had a favourite perfume; exotic fragrances, jewellery and expensive clothes weren't really her style, but they had rubbed along well enough together and he had, for the most part, been faithful to her. He'd strayed only once, tempted into an affair with a work colleague, captivated by

205

her beauty, intelligence and independent spirit. He had been dazzled, mesmerised, and Betty, by contrast, had suddenly seemed very dull; but her distress when she had found out about Julia had pulled him up with a start and made him realise how important his wife was in his life. He had to make a decision. Julia was a delightful treat, but not for every day and he had chosen family life, his wife and two girls, over his mistress. It had been painful, a terrible wrench which left him feeling, for some time, that he was a coward, living a lie, but slowly, very slowly he realised that he had done the right thing as he and Betty had been able to rebuild their marriage.

In fact, they'd both learned lessons from the affair and their relationship became stronger than before, mainly because Betty had been able to forgive. It took a long time but she eventually accepted that, although overtly the innocent victim, her focus on the girls, excluding Jack, marginalising him to the role of provider, had been a contributory factor to his infidelity. A man doesn't usually look for sustenance elsewhere if he's getting fillet steak at home, and she realised that Jack had felt neglected, emotionally undernourished, while she had showered all her love on the girls. At first when he had gently explained this to her, she had been furious, refusing to try and understand, and screamed at him "....they need me, I'm their mother. You're not a child..." until she had to admit, little by little, that he was right. He needed her too.

But still she wouldn't give in. Still the injured party and unwilling (unable?) to relinquish the moral high ground, she continued to wallow in a lot of wound-licking and long, intense talks to friends whose advice, usually based on their own lack of experience, was, for the most part, unhelpful. Unless they had actually been there, pushed down into the dark pit in which she was currently floundering, they couldn't possibly know what she should do or what they would do if it happened to them. "...I'd throw the bastard out..." "...rip up his clothes and walk away with all his money..." were easy things to say from the comfort of a secure relationship. But Jack wasn't a bastard, he was a lonely man who wanted his playmate back and Betty had decided that her marriage was worth saving. His relationship with Julia had been as much about communication as it was about sex, and had made him feel like a man again. Betty, as well as Jack, accepted that she had work to do; and so they had survived until that terrible day when a massive heart attack had ended her life and their years together.

Now he had found Chrissie, a glittering jewel, in a flat, grey world of golf, bowls and the occasional meal with friends, kind enough to invite a lonely widower out for the evening. Sadly it seemed that this added sparkle to his existence was destined to be fleeting – not so much a delightful reward for doing the right thing, as a tempting reminder of what he had missed.

Jim's husky growl brought him back to the present, and he looked across the small round table to where his friend was reading from the guide book while Chrissie, with the perfect manners he had come to know and appreciate as very much part of this lovely woman, listened attentively, her head leaning slightly to one side and a smile on her lips.

"…and the island changed hands between the English and French more than a dozen times during the 18th century, but was then awarded to France in 1802 by the Treaty of Amiens. At the end of the Napoleonic Wars it fell once again into British hands, but The West Indies Act of 1967 finally granted St. Lucia full self-government followed by complete independence since 1979. The island is mainly agricultural with bananas its most important crop, but tourism is developing rapidly."

The growl ceased and Jim peered up at Chrissie through steel-rimmed spectacles that glinted in the light but failed to hide the adoration in his eyes.

"Thank-you for that, Jim," Chrissie patted his hand and he grinned, showing nearly every one of his tiny pointed teeth. Jack smiled at them both, 'Poor Jim, he's as smitten as I am but with even less chance of ever making an impression on Chrissie.' Then he saw her,

"Watch out. Margie alert!" Jack and Jim tried to sink down lower in their chairs but Chrissie, still with a smile on her face, gave them a look which said 'you're both very naughty,' before turning to greet the Cornish woman. It was pointless to do otherwise as she was obviously determined to join them and, pulling up a chair next to Jim, she sat down.

"I'm really looking forward to today…I'm going to have some fun," She said in a voice that was anything but fun-filled.

'Well I was, but now I'm not so sure,' Jim thought as he tried to edge his chair a little way away from the intruder without seeming rude. Jack wondered, not for the first time, how a self-confessed fun girl always managed to sound so lugubrious, and he looked desperately round for Edie, Stanley or Gracie, anyone who would take her away from them for the day. As if reading his thoughts, Margie said mournfully,

"My other friends aren't coming on the catamaran today. Is it alright if I sit with you?"

"Yes, of course it is," Chrissie said quickly with a sharp look that dared the other two to say otherwise.

"It's a special day today," Margie added mysteriously as they were called to make their way down to the quayside.

Once aboard the catamaran they were transported at high speed along the coast past Anse la Raye and Canaries, marvelling at the beautiful scenery and picturesque villages set into the lush green hillsides while they drank rum punch and danced on the deck to Caribbean music. The skipper, a sturdy, jovial man, resplendent in multi-coloured shirt, laughed aloud – all white teeth and shiny brown skin – as he put his foot down, spraying his delighted passengers with droplets of water that leapt up and over the sides of the boat. The catamaran slowed and

Bob Marley's tuneful growl was replaced by the skipper announcing,

"We is here at our first stop, ladies and gentlemen, and there you can see in front of you Soufriere and the Pitons."

With a dramatic flourish, he proudly indicated the island's most famous feature: two cone-shaped, volcanic mountains, now covered in vegetation, with the town of Soufriere nestling beneath.

"'Soufriere and the Pitons,' sounds like a French pop-group," whispered Freddie, standing up in the gently-rocking catamaran to take photographs.

"We go now,"

The skipper, ('you all call me Jimmy') turned the catamaran and headed back along the coast to a bay where again he stopped the engine and, with a flash of white teeth, told his passengers they could swim. Prepared for this with costumes already on under flimsy tops, they shrugged off their outer garments and stood, like excited children, waiting for their turn to descend the few steps at the back of the boat and slide into the water. Stella looked towards the beach, fringed with palm trees – a picture straight out of a travel brochure – where a group of dark-skinned youths were playing football, laughing and rolling into the water like puppies.

Margie stood in line behind Jack, Chrissie and Jim nervously fingering the buttons on her blouse. A dozen butterflies had made themselves at home in her stomach, but she was determined and made her way steadily forward towards the metal steps. Jim glanced round behind him,

"You need to get your costume on, gal," he growled when he saw that Margie was still wearing her blouse and loose slacks.

"It's alright. I know what I'm doing," she muttered and he turned back, frowning and thinking, not for the first time, that their Cornish companion was slightly odd. He didn't know then that a few moments later 'slightly odd' would be fast-tracked to 'totally batty' when Margie reached the top of the steps. And so it was that Stella and Freddie, moving their legs slowly and rhythmically in the clear, warm water both turned just in time to see Margie poised on the end of the catamaran, naked from the waist down, swinging her trousers round her head.

"What the....?"

They continued to stare in disbelief as she flung the trousers backwards into the boat then, quickly removing blouse and bra, jumped stark naked into the sea with a great whoop of joy followed by a resounding splash. She disappeared under the water and came up three times, gasping and spluttering, before someone shouted,

"I don't think she can swim."

Chrissie reached her first and tried to manoeuvre her back towards the steps.

"No...no," she gasped, I'm...going...to...the...beach."

She kicked and struggled in the direction of the palm-fringed sand while Chrissie tried to keep hold of her but was hit several times by Margie's skinny limbs, thrashing in and out of the water. She looked pleadingly at Jack and Jim who were bobbing in the water nearby and, although reluctant to come anywhere near Margie's nakedness, were concerned for Chrissie's safety. They swam over to her and the three of them together managed to support Margie to shallower water.

"Oh Gawd, now she's going to stand up," groaned Jim, already averting his eyes from a spectacle he really didn't want to see.

But she didn't stand. She couldn't. She lolled in the water, her mouth opening and closing like a fish in a keep-net. Jack turned to Stella and shouted,

"Can you go and get us a towel, love. A big one."

Stella turned and swam quickly back towards the boat; she met Bryony, the young dancer in charge of the trip, swimming to the beach and they trod water for a moment,

"They are saying there's a woman in the water with no clothes on...Is there really, Stella...? Is there really a woman in the water with no clothes on...?"

Bryony gasped and Stella nodded, pointing to the scene near the beach.

"But why?…And why is it always on my trip?" Bryony wailed, swimming on towards the shore.

Stella reached the boat,

"Throw me a towel, a big one…quickly," she shouted to the group of elderly passengers who had opted not to swim and were hanging over the rails to watch the drama unfolding a little way off.

Stella managed to keep the towel dry as she swam back and handed it to Chrissie who draped it quickly round Margie's shoulders; then, assisted by Jack and Jim, manoeuvred her up onto the sand and headed towards some sun-loungers a little way along to the right.

"Get this off me…I don't want it," Margie shrugged trying to dislodge the towel, but Chrissie kept it firmly draped round her.

"…and get me some more of that lovely rum punch…"

"I think you've had quite enough," said Jack sternly, then had to pull her back as she turned quickly towards the group of young men, their game temporarily suspended,

"You'll come and drink some rum punch with me, won't you,"

She shouted while Chrissie struggled to keep the towel in place. The lads looked down, circling their toes in the sand, grinning and scratching their heads

Stella and Freddie were still in the water when Jack came striding back and waded in.

"She won't come back until someone has taken a photo of her, so I'm off to fetch my waterproof camera," he sounded understandably exasperated as he plunged into the sea and headed towards the catamaran.

A little later, with the aid of a life-jacket, Margie was manoeuvred back onto the boat and into her clothes where she sat looking demure but unrepentant.

Freddie and Stella clambered back onto the catamaran and dried themselves in the hot sun. Some kindly souls had gathered round Margie, chaffing her hands and offering hot drinks but she shrugged them off,

"Don't fuss round me. I'm perfectly fine; I said I was gonna do it and I done it," she added cryptically, refusing at this point to elaborate further.

The crowd around her melted away, rebuffed by her rudeness, then Chrissie approached and sat down,

"Are you alright, dear?"

Margie didn't push her away,

"Course I'm alright. Tis only a bit of water."

She reached for Chrissie's hand and, staring straight ahead, said,

"I told Raymond...I told him I wanted to have a bit of fun, but he wouldn't come with me...wouldn't come on my last trip."

She stopped speaking and turned to look at Chrissie,

"I got cancer, see. He don't know yet. I daresay I shall have to tell him when I get back cos I've got to have chemotherapy and he's gonna have to look after me. If only he had come away for this last bit of fun. I didn't tell him about the cancer cos I didn't want him coming out of pity; I wanted him to come because he wanted to be with me. But now it's too late... All too late..."

She trailed off, then brightened a little, " But I made up my mind I was going to swim naked off St. Lucia and I've done it."

Chrissie squeezed her hand,

"You certainly have, my dear. I'm so sorry – about the cancer."

"Can't be helped."

"No, it can't be helped," Chrissie echoed, hoping that this information, when she told them, would encourage Jack and Jim to be a little kinder to their Cornish friend.

The trip back along the coast was magical as the sun set gloriously over the water and lights twinkled from the shore. Most of them carried on dancing to Bob Marley and waving at boats that sped past, sometimes drawing alongside to keep pace with them for a while. Tired out,

Margie sat and watched, feeling triumphant...elated even... and sad in equal parts. Why hadn't Raymond been with her? Then she was comforted by the thought that, if he had been there, he would probably have stopped her from doing it. But she had done it – and got the photos to prove it.

That evening they all danced again to a steel band that came on board 'The Matisse' and played far into the night. The story of Margie's escapade travelled round the ship with the speed of a forest fire and people were nudging each other,

"You mean her...?"

"...what the old girl who does the line-dancing...?"

"No...surely not!"

"...she couldn't have..."

But she did.

The Club was almost empty when Chrissie followed Jack towards one of the exits then, looking round, felt tears pricking behind her eyes as she saw Margie, quite alone on the stage in a pool of white light, picking out her strange prancing steps to the last dying notes of music.

CHAPTER THIRTY TWO

CHRISTMAS EVE – RUM PUNCH AND 'THE SPIRIT OF CHRISTMAS'

'The Matisse' left St. Lucia at 10.00 p.m. and arrived in Barbados the following morning where, by 8 o'clock, Stella and Freddie were part of an excited group setting off on an 'Island Safari 4x4 Adventure.' At 2.00 p.m. they would depart for Funchal in Madeira, their last port of call before Southampton, and in the evening they were presenting 'The Spirit of Christmas' in The Club.

The convoy of jeeps bounced along, their occupants full of the Christmas spirit, but Stella didn't know at this point that a different sort of spirit would come close to wrecking her part in the culmination of weeks of hard work. In spite of having been on the ship for nearly three months, she was surprised to find that there were two men and a woman in the jeep she didn't remember seeing before, but they seemed pleasant enough and, like everyone else, were in the mood for some Christmas fun.

Their driver, Junior Johnson, a lively native of the island, was keen to tell his passengers all about Barbados. Looking around, Stella noticed there was a singularly English feel about the place, so she wasn't surprised to learn that it had been claimed for Great Britain in 1625 and remained a British dependency until it achieved full independence within the British Commonwealth, joining The United Nations in 1966.

They sped along the roads before being taken off onto tracks, careering between fields then into a forest of strange trees where they saw exotic plants and even a few monkeys. There was a termite nest and a striped palm tree named, appropriately, a Zebra Palm. There were eucalyptus trees and a prickly palm with spines – huge, dangerous bristles that they were warned not to touch, "...keep your body parts INSIDE the jeep at all times..." was one of Johnson's often repeated mantras during the safari. They passed a sugar factory where molasses is processed – 'rum in the first stage,' according to Junior – and saw hibiscus and okra growing together in a field. There were enormous paintings of animals on rocks at the side of the road at one of the villages they passed through and Junior kept up a running commentary, explaining everything and taking them to see some fine houses before finally reaching the coast.

The beach was stunning with huge waves rolling in on the shingle,

"No-one bathe here. Too dangerous," Johnson told them, but they did see a few surfers venturing out.

They wandered along the pebble-strewn beach and took photographs of some giant rocks, shaped rather like mushrooms, huge at the top and balanced at the water's edge on stubby stalks. They explored the wares that some of the locals had set out on stalls at a grassy area adjacent to the beach. The weather was warm and breezy, reminiscent of an English spring day, and many of the garments for sale – multi-coloured kaftans, tops and scarves – were blowing on lines above the stalls like washing.

Back at the jeep Johnson was distributing generous quantities of rum punch.

"What a lovely idea," Stella thought, taking a plastic cup full and wandering onto the grass where she sipped the pleasant tasting drink while gazing out to sea. She had almost finished when the woman from the jeep who she didn't recognise seemed to spring from no-where and proceeded to fill her cup from a jug she had commandeered.

"No…stop…that's enough."

Stella tried to pull her cup away, but the woman carried on pouring,

"Go on. It'll do you good…"

The cup was full to the brim when the woman took the jug away. She was smiling and, without the influence of the punch she had already drunk, Stella might have noticed that the smile didn't reach the eyes. She smiled back and thought, 'oh well, I had rum punch yesterday in St. Lucia and it seemed fairly innocuous.'

It did indeed taste just like a fruity drink, so she drained the cup before piling, a little unsteadily, back into the jeep with the others where the punch continued to flow, mainly from the hand of the unknown woman, smiling all the while at her two male companions. Stella realised afterwards that she was only saved from complete disaster by the fact that two delightful ladies, both members of the show choir, were sitting between her and the self-appointed bar-maid who was making it her business to ensure that their cups were constantly full to overflowing. The one nearest to Stella lurched unsteadily against her,

"After all your hard work, Shtella, we're going to do yer proud…"

She slurred, as her friend leaned across and, almost falling onto the floor, added,

"That'sh right, Shtella, we're going to shing our heartsh out for yer…"

"Yeah…you'll sing even better after a drop more of this."

The 'bar-maid' filled their cups and managed to get a little more into Stella's.

By the time they arrived back at the cruise terminal Stella was feeling dizzy. The two choir members staggered past her, clinging onto each other, and told her later that they couldn't remember how they got back to their cabin, but when they did one of them was sick and they both had a very long sleep, though they did wake up in time for the show. Stella wobbled and had to lean against Freddie, who was smiling benignly,

"I think I've had too mush punsh,"

She slurred, her mouth feeling strange and her legs refusing to go where she tried to put them. She saw Glenda, one of the principals in the show, and waved, her hand flopping like a rag-doll's at the end of her arm as if someone else was moving it. Freddie steered her up the steps to the cabin where she collapsed onto the bed. An hour and a half later she woke with a furry mouth but otherwise feeling much better. Then, as her head gradually cleared, she remembered: 'Oh no, the back drop...we were supposed to put up the back drop...' She sat up quickly and saw Freddie watching her from the opposite bed.

"The back drop…"

"It's OK, Stuart and I have done it. Nothing to worry about. So how are we feeling then?"

"I'm fine," Stella said, a little stiffly, knowing that Freddie was enjoying every minute of this. How could she? How could she be so stupid as to let someone persuade her to drink too much? It was just not something she ever did – and on such an important day! She got up and smoothed her ruffled clothes then, looking at her watch, was relieved to see there was still plenty of time before the show. She brushed her hair and drank a large glass of water.

"I must go and find Stuart to apologise." She said, making for the cabin door. With a huge grin on is face, Freddie leaned up on one elbow,

"Hey Stella," she turned, "How about a nice glass of rum punch."

"Oh…shut up!"

Stella stood trembling at the side of the stage looking out at the sea of silly antlers waving about in The Club, packed to capacity with a row of people standing squashed in at the back. Edie, planted firmly in her usual front seat, winked at her then Stuart walked forward and raised the microphone to his mouth.

"Good evening, ladies and gentlemen…how are we? Ready for a fantastic evening's entertainment? Because that's what we've got for you tonight. Now before we start, can I ask you please to remove the antlers. I know they're fun and I don't want to be a spoil-sport, but they will prevent the people behind you from seeing the show…" He paused as antlers were removed. "That's better…thank-you very much. Now, some of your fellow passengers and a few of the professional entertainers have got together, worked very hard and produced a terrific show for you, so without more ado, just sit back and enjoy….

THE SPIRIT OF CHRISTMAS!"

A true showman, he raised his arm and voice as he announced the title of the show, then turned and swept off the stage as the audience applauded loudly, obviously ready to be well and truly entertained. Stella said one final prayer before the microphone was put into her hands, the lights went down and, clearing her throat, she began:

> "'Twas the night before Christmas and on The Matisse,
> There wasn't a sound, not even a sneeze.
> Joseph, the barman, and his lovely wife, Dot
> Were serving up drinks and washing the pots."

She sat down as Kevin and Glenda hurried past her onto the stage. Kevin was playing the part of Joe, a grumpy, downbeat character, disillusioned with the world in general and passengers in particular. He had no time for Christmas, seeing it simply as extra work, and the meaning of this annual celebration, assuming he had ever experienced it, had long since escaped him. He was in no mood for his wife's cheeriness as Dot, played by Glenda, in complete contrast to her husband, was poised to enjoy everything, from the tacky to the spiritual, and would reminisce at the drop of a hat, going into reveries about Christmases she had known.

> DOT   Come on, Joe, hurry up. We've got to get cleaned up ready for the passengers' concert.

JOE   Flippin' passengers…flippin' concert. Just means more flippin' work as far as I'm concerned.

DOT   Get on, Joe, and stop your moaning. Put this banner up…and try and get into the spirit of Christmas, for goodness sake!

He puts up a sign advertising the passengers' Christmas Concert.

JOE   Spirit of Christmas? What's that when it's at home, that's what I'd like to know!

STELLA – (from offstage through the microphone)

The spirit of Christmas? Don't worry, Joe, You'll find it right here while you're watching our show.

Joe shrugs and walks off the stage, hustled along by a bustling, impatient Dot.

In the usual Matisse tradition there followed a burst of music and Stuart announced:

"Ladies and Gentlemen…IT'S…SHOW TIME!"

A lovely lady called Dawn danced an exciting fandango, then six women, including Margie, leapt onto the stage in colourful cowgirl outfits, complete with glittery hats, to perform two line dances, painstakingly rehearsed under Stuart's expert guidance. He had struggled to get them to execute the steps with the correct attitude – heavily booted cowgirl, not lightweight tap-dancers – and his hard work paid off as they gave a good performance. The audience applauded loudly as they left the stage, then laughed as Joe ambled back on with a tea-towel on his head and a lamb under his arm. Dot bustled on behind him.

DOT   What on earth are you wearing that for, you daft beggar?

JOE   'Spirit of Christmas' you said, my love, so I'm trying to get into the spirit of Christmas. When I were a lad at infant school they used to shove a tea-towel on yer 'ead, stick a lamb under yer arm and you all 'ad to stand on't stage singing songs. I remember one year I hit Tom Frost on the 'ead with the lamb; he cried and wet hisself and I got a right crack round the 'ead from miss Cartwright. (He smiles and Dot looks exasperated)

DOT   Well you'll get a crack round the 'ead from me if you don't take it off – you look ridiculous! (She folds her arms and gets a dreamy look on her face, reminiscing) Pantos…oooooooo…that's what I used to love! You know with the audience all hissing and booing at the villain…and everyone getting covered with flour and water…and then it always ended with a lovely wedding when the handsome young man (pause for a look at Joe and eyes raised to heaven) marries the beautiful (she preens herself) princess. (She giggles and leaves the stage trilling '…it's behind you…' Joe scuttles after her looking anxiously behind to see if anything's following him.)

At this point Desmond bounded onto the stage with the traditional Pantomime introduction… "Hello boys and girls…" Waits for reply…

"Desmond can't hear you…hello boys and girls…" they reply only louder etc.

Desmond, having returned to the show, had put himself forward for the role of narrator of the panto excerpt, which no-one argued with as he had helped Stella by condensing the original script from two and a half hours down to forty minutes, still retaining some essential elements of pantomime and an easy to follow story line. No mean feat, and one that she and the cast had all appreciated. What they didn't appreciate, and hadn't all the way through rehearsals, was Desmond attracting attention to himself by constantly ad-libbing and throwing some of the rest of the cast who, less confident than him, were struggling with their first ever venture onto a stage.

When picked up for this, his retort was to remind them all that his experience in panto was extensive – (every year with the ex-pat community in Majorca) – and that he should 'play the audience' etc…etc… He also delighted in adding innuendo that went way beyond the usual pantomime vulgarity. Having asked him repeatedly to remove the ad-libbed smut and been ignored, Stella threatened him with a visit in the middle of the night during which she would do something very nasty to him. He still continued to 'do his own thing' and Sharon, (on stage for the first time, playing Aladdin and making a very good job of it), had asked Stella again if she would deal with him as his ad-libbing was really exasperating everyone and confusing her entrances.

Deciding she had also had enough, Stella gathered the cast together before one of the rehearsals and, in front of everyone, asked him to stop drawing attention to himself in this an unacceptable way. She emphasised she was speaking at the request of the whole cast and pulled no punches, feeling sure that her 'lecture' must penetrate even the thickest of skins. He appeared to listen and said, 'point taken,' when she had finished, but his ego was such that he couldn't resist whispering to the prompt, 'wait till she sees what I do on the night,' knowing, of course, that by then she would be powerless to stop him.

She really thought during one rehearsal that the penny had finally dropped when, as he was talking his way towards one particular piece of unnecessary filth that he thought had to be retained as it was so funny (the rest of them didn't!), he suddenly stopped and looked at her. She asked him what was wrong and he indicated Chloe and Ella, the two youngest cast members, who were sitting behind her waiting to rehearse.

"I can't say the next bit…not with them here." (No, Desmond, you can't. That's exactly what we've been trying to tell you!) He looked embarrassed as Stuart and Stella glanced at each other so Stella spelt it out for him,

"They'll be there at the performance, Desmond, and so will Father John. Now take out of the script anything you can't comfortably say in front of **Them** and let's get on with it!"

The pantomime excerpt went well, in spite of Desmond's efforts to hog the limelight; though, in fairness, Stella had to admit that, as an extrovert brimming to overflowing with confidence, he was the right one to hold the show together, never, at any point, needing to be told to project his voice, and his love of being the centre of attention was ultimately an asset. It was a joy for her to see the people she had worked so hard with who had struggled to overcome nerves and the tendency to mutter instead of projecting their voices, giving excellent performances on the night. Every word could be heard and the audience loved it, especially when the Emperor arrived on stage without an essential prop and Stella had to do a mad dash to the dressing room, retrieve it then creep out onto the stage and hand it to her.

Dot and Joe back on stage, Dot first this time with Joe
following behind wearing reindeer horns

DOT   Cor...weren't they lovely, them Pantos?...
        The real spirit of Christmas.

JOE   If you say so, my love, (aside to the
        audience) I 'ated 'em!!

DOT   (turning towards him and noticing the
        head gear) What on earth are you wearing
        them for, you stupid man?

JOE   (exasperated) 'Spirit of Christmas,' you
        said, my love. Well, father Christmas and
        his reindeer.....

DOT   (pushing him aside and going off into
        another reverie) Oooooooo Father
        Christmas! Do you remember that feeling,
        Joe? Going to bed so excited that you
        couldn't sleep and yer mum said 'e
        wouldn't come if yer didn't, so you
        squeezed yer eyes shut, real tight, but you
        still hoped yer might stay awake long
        enough just to get a glimpse of 'im
        without anyone knowing........

Joe and Dot wandered to the back of the stage and there
followed an adaptation of 'Twas the Night before
Christmas,' written around The Matisse and performed by
a small group speaking in unison, with some solo parts.

Then the two girls, Chloe and Ella, came onto the stage
and delighted the audience with a beautiful sketch built
around a child's perception of the magic of Christmas. It
had been an easy one for Stella to write as she had sat with
the two girls and got the basic ideas from them.

CHLOE AND ELLA ON CHRISTMAS EVE

ELLA   Here you are, Chloe, put your stocking up.

CHLOE This isn't mine! You've got mine!

ELLA   No, I don't think so.

CHLOE I think you have. You know mine's bigger than yours 'cos I like bigger presents. And anyway, I should get bigger presents 'cos I'm younger than you.

ELLA   Child! (She throws the stocking at Chloe and grabs the other one from her.)

CHLOE Elle.....do you believe in Father Christmas?

ELLA   (Sarcastically) Yes, of course I do. He rides round on a sleigh, manages to get to every house in the whole world with enough presents for everyone. Goes down chimneys, even though most houses haven't got one...honestly, Chloe, what are you like??
           (They both giggle)

CHLOE When did you first know he wasn't real?

ELLA   It was that year when I got up to go to the loo on Christmas Eve and our stockings had gone from the end of the bed. I was upset and went to find Mum to tell her, and she was in her bedroom trying to fill them up with presents. She was getting all tangled up and looked really embarrassed

224

when I walked in. She just sort of grinned and tried to hide them, but she knew I'd sussed it out. I suppose I sort of half knew already as Sharon-know-it-all-Matthews had been going round in the playground saying that everyone who still believed in Father Christmas was just a silly kid. The funny thing was...I still wanted to believe...it was like I had to let go of something special, and if I said I didn't believe it would be gone for ever.

CHLOE Yeah...I know what you mean. Do you remember that year when I told Dad I could hear bells ringing and the sound of hooves on the roof...the funny thing was, Elle, I did hear them...I'm sure I did. And then I shut my eyes tight so that Father Christmas wouldn't go away without giving us any presents. But the next year I saw Mum creeping into the room and start to fill the stockings. I sat up really quickly and she jumped, then we both burst out laughing.

ELLA Yeah, I remember that because I woke up too and didn't know what you were laughing at.

CHLOE Let's pretend to go to sleep and watch for her to come in.

ELLA (With a sigh, humouring the younger child) OK

They both settle down and Crystal, one of the professional dancers, does the Dance of the sugar Plum Fairy. The audience can see that Chloe is awake; she creeps out of bed and stands watching, a duvet wrapped around her and an expression of awe and wonder on her face. When the dance finishes and Crystal leaves the stage, Chloe goes over to Ella, who is sound asleep, and wakes her.

>CHLOE (In wonder) Elle…I've just seen a beautiful fairy dancing in our bedroom…

>ELLA Chloe, you're too old now to make up these daft stories. Go back to bed.

Shoulders drooping, Chloe goes back to her bed and both girls fall asleep.

Father Christmas comes in and makes a play of putting the largest present in Chloe's stocking then looks benevolently at both girls.

>FATHER CHRISTMAS Sleep well, pretty girls, and remember, you are never too old to see visions and dream dreams; never too old to believe.

After this delightful scene which, like the pantomime excerpt, received rapturous applause, Joe came back onto the stage with a partridge on his head. Dot followed.

>DOT What on earth…??

>JOE (with exaggerated patience) I am trying to get into the spirit of Christmas like you said, my love. I remember a song we used to sing – the one where all them things get given in twelve days…

At this point Sharon and the rest of the cast, still in their Aladdin costumes, leapt onto the stage and led the audience in a special rendering of 'the Twelve Days of Christmas, Matisse style. Freddie and Stella had adapted all the verses to make them relevant to life on board ship and the panto cast had each been designated one of the verses to sing with a particular section of the audience, making them stand as they did so and sit gown when they had finished. Sharon was a brilliant 'master of ceremonies for this and the whole thing was hilarious.

When all was quiet, Dot and Joe came forward again.

DOT   Oooooooo that were a bit of fun

JOE   If you say so, my love.

DOT   But you know, Joe, what I really used to love were the Carols in our Church at midnight. It were so cold walking there and you could see your breath come out like clouds of steam; then in the Church we all huddled together to keep warm. There were a great tree up the front all lit up – lovely it was – and candles glowing all around the walls making shadows. There were ivy…and holly with berries…and, do you know, Joe, when that choir started to sing I used to think I could see Angels looking down. I could see them so clearly as soon as I heard that first Carol…it were something about a city…

She wandered off the stage and Joe followed looking thoughtful.

The substance of Dot's reverie this time was the choir, formally dressed in white tops and black skirts or trousers, processing from the back of The Club as a soloist walked quietly to a microphone in the centre of the stage and sang the first verse of 'Once in Royal David's City.' The rest of the singers joined in with the second verse as they grouped on stage.

As the music died away, Joe came back onto the stage wiping a glass with tea-towel, looking more reflective than previously. Suddenly Dot burst onto the stage, beside herself with excitement.

> DOT   Joe…Joe…you'll never guess what! There's a passenger in a cabin on deck five having a baby!!

> JOE   What on this ship!?! (this was greeted by gales of laughter as all the passengers on The Matisse, with the exception of the two girls, Chloe and Ella, were well past child-bearing age.)

> DOT   Yes, right here on this ship! Honest…I couldn't believe it! I've just heard Judy and Amanda talking about it on them walkie-talkie things…rushing around like headless chickens. I mean…fancy her coming on board in that condition!...I just thought she'd had too many cakes at tea-time!! Well…who'd have thought it?

> JOE   Yeah…a berth on this ship…that is unusual. We normally 'ave to go in on flippin' tender.

Suddenly Antonio's voice was heard on the PA system,

"Code Pink…Code Pink…go to cabin 5994…I repeat, Code Pink…Code Pink…go to cabin 5994. Please take towels and hot water."

This was meaningful to the audience, who were all helpless with laughter, as it was a play on the genuine call

– Code Blue – used in an emergency and delivered over the PA system by the Captain in a heavily accented monotone which Antonio mimicked to perfection. At this point Judy, who had asked to be in the show, ran across the stage, pretending to panic and wearing a pair of bright orange rubber gloves. The audience loved it.

DOT   (nudging Joe) you see. I told you!

JOE   Whatever next! Whatever flippin'next!?!

He and Dot stepped slowly back with astonished looks on their faces as one of the young dancers, dressed in a blue shift and white shawl, walked across the stage, carrying a bundle. She stopped in front of Dot and Joe who peered over her shoulder, smiles spreading across their faces as they gazed at the 'baby.'

The choir sang 'When a Child is Born,' accompanied by The Trio.

JOE   (serious and genuinely moved) By 'eck, I
        think I've found it, my love, The Spirit of
        Christmas.

DOT   Oh Joe…I knew you would.

They stood united in the centre of the stage as the choir sang, 'Joy to the World,' then the whole cast returned for 'We Wish You a Merry Christmas, after which they received well-deserved, rapturous applause. Thanks were given to all concerned, including Stella who was called forward by Stuart.

CHAPTER THIRTY THREE

"It were soooper, real smashin' – and joost what we needed!"

Edie's voice boomed around the deck and her sentiments were echoed by several others, one of them adding,

"I hear it were written and directed by a passenger – fancy her giving up her holiday to do that – it were great weren't it?"

Stella, sitting near the ship's rails and relaxing in the sunshine with no show to worry about, thought she was well hidden until Edie spotted her.

"Aye, it were a passenger – and there she is! Come over 'ere, Stella."

She went and was embarrassed by the praise, but felt pleased on behalf of all the cast that everyone had enjoyed it so much. She was rescued by Freddie and they went down to the dining room for brunch that was being served all day, followed by a Christmas tea, where they would be joined by Father Christmas, then a formal dinner and finally a show by the professionals.

Although redundancies still hung over them like storm clouds, the staff were pulling out all the stops to ensure that everyone had a marvellous Christmas Day which began with them charging along the corridors singing Christmas songs at the tops of their voices. Freddie and Stella were missing the family and attempted to send emails, that they hoped would arrive, then they joined in with the festivities, reasoning that it was the only time they would spend Christmas in the Caribbean.

"Well, I think I should do something; they've been fantastic, setting aside their personal situation and continuing to do everything they can to give us the holiday of a lifetime."

It was during a lull, just before tea in the otherwise full-on, wall to wall, celebrations on Christmas Day that several of the show cast, reluctant to let go of the bonds that had been formed, were gathered together for a different matter. They had all expressed their admiration for the commendable professionalism Judy and her team, as well as the domestic staff, continued to display and it was Kevin, (Joe, the barman) who suggested that they should write a notice clearly stating how highly regarded the staff were and how much their attitude was appreciated. This would be placed in a prominent position for everyone to sign and would then be presented to Judy. They all agreed, and said it would also be useful if 'The Matisse' was greeted by journalists at their last port of call as some passengers had received emails from family and friends telling them that the media had got hold of the fact that Sailaways were in financial difficulties. Glenda agreed with her 'show' husband, adding,

"Yes, and we all know that if there are journalists on the quay, the moaners are bound to get to them first,"

The notice was written and displayed, and an hour before tea time on Boxing Day everyone was thrilled to see that over three hundred people had signed. Kevin was about to take it down when he paused,

"That means there's nearly a hundred and fifty who haven't. We all know there'll be those who don't want to, but there may still be a few who do. Let's leave it and as I come in to tea, I'll get it down and bring it with me."

Everyone agreed. Only he couldn't. He was unable to retrieve the notice as it wasn't there. Someone had taken it down, removed it and no doubt destroyed it so that this gesture, important to the majority of the passengers, couldn't be made. Kevin and the rest of the group were disgusted. How could people be so despicable? The spiteful minority had decided that because they didn't agree with the sentiments expressed on the notice they would prevent it from being presented. There were mutterings about 'the Australians' – everyone was sure it was them but no-one could prove it.

Kevin, unlike the character he had played, was anything but grumpy and rather slow,

"Right! Whoever it was, they're not getting away with it. Tea is almost over. Glenda, you go and fetch Judy and any other prominent staff you can find; I'll keep everyone here, including the waiters who work so hard, and we'll still voice our support and appreciation. Then let's meet afterwards; I've got another idea."

Glenda bustled off in search of Judy as, with much clashing of crockery and clattering of tea-spoons, the staff started to clear away the tea things. Joe stood up and thumped the table,

"Listen up everyone. We want to thank Judy and the staff for giving us such a wonderful Christmas in spite of their job situation," there were nods of agreement, and he continued, "As you know we had a statement to that effect, a notice that most of you signed, well that notice has been stolen…" gasps of amazement and disbelief and mutterings of, 'surely not…!' 'I don't believe it…!' Stella was looking round and, whereas most people were horrified there were a few who obviously thought the whole thing rather silly and couldn't give two hoots. For no apparent reason, she found herself looking to see if the 'rum punch barmaid' and her two companions were there, but she couldn't see them. Kevin continued, taking his cue from those who had obviously supported the notice. "Yes, difficult to credit, isn't it, the depths to which some people will stoop, but we have decided not to let the lunatics take over the asylum. We are going to thank Judy, who I believe is on her way, so please stay – the more the merrier. And watch this space. We'll find a way of getting our feelings down in writing."

At that moment Glenda retuned with Judy, Amanda, Stuart and the Maitre d', and Kevin made an excellent speech, finishing by inviting all those who agreed to stand up and join in three rousing cheers for Judy and the staff. Most people stood immediately and, as she glanced round, Stella was amused to see that even the truculent few, who had stayed out of curiosity rather than as a show of support and obviously didn't want to stand, were shamed into it.

After tea, Stella and Freddie joined the small group who stayed behind and they decided to write another tribute to the staff, get it duplicated in the office, then take the pieces of paper round the dining room in both sittings for people to sign. They had no difficulty getting support and the pieces of paper were filling up steadily when suddenly Stella spotted her for the first time since they had left Barbados. The 'barmaid' – dispenser of liberal quantities of rum punch – was sitting quietly by the window. She would sign, of course she would, they could even have a bit of banter about the drink as Stella didn't imagine it had been done maliciously. She went up to the woman and smiled as she explained about the tribute and put the paper down on the table in front of her. The woman looked up and, for the first time in her life, Stella experienced a truly withering look as she pushed the piece of paper away from her,

"No, I'm not signing that!" She said, her voice hard and cold, then she dismissed Stella, turning her face back towards the window.

Taken aback, but trying not to show it, Stella moved on to a pleasant looking woman further down the table who smiled at her and was only too happy to sign then she scuttled back to where Kevin was standing near the doorway. Trying to suppress a smile, he nodded towards the woman by the window,

"You didn't ask her did you, Stella?"

"Yes, I did."

"I bet she didn't sign."

"Well…no, she didn't. How did you know?"

"She's one of 'the Australians!'"

The sheets of paper were presented to Judy in a crowded Club that evening and The Matisse passengers had the pleasure of seeing this tough, capable woman wiping away tears of gratitude as she told them how much that gesture would mean to all the staff and made all the hard work worthwhile. It was no surprise to anyone that 'the Australians' were nowhere to be seen.

CHAPTER THIRTY FOUR

Five more days at sea to Funchal in Madeira, the final port of call, where 'The Matisse' was due to drop anchor offshore so everyone could enjoy one of the world's best New Year's Eve firework displays. Already there was an end of term atmosphere for most people, a feeling of coasting to the end, though for some it was a time of desperation, a longing to cling to la-la-land rather than face reality. For others it was a time to make life-changing decisions, the feasibility of which would be tested when real life collided with their floating bubble at the quay in Southampton.

Nancy was distraught at the thought of never seeing Wayne again, and Kieran was beside himself with grief as he faced losing Nancy – a notion that seemed strange to her for, as far as she was concerned, he had never had her. Wayne, on the other hand, had, several times in various places about the ship, including a life-boat. Following them up on deck one evening after he had seen them drinking together in the bar, Kieran watched them staggering along, giggling and falling against each other, then scramble into a lifeboat, suspended above the deck, and pull the tarpaulin over them. He had stood alone, polishing his glasses, as the lifeboat rocked from side to side.

Still, even this late in the day, new distractions were provided to help people make the most of the penultimate leg of the journey. One of the last guest lecturers to join the ship was a harmonica player who had worked with the great Larry Adler. His classes proved very popular with those who wanted to learn, but caused much cringing from the rest of the passengers when the door to The Club was accidentally left open during a lesson. Eighty people practising on harmonicas sounded like a torture chamber for cats. The on-board photographer produced a DVD of the cruise which people were invited to purchase; and Geoffrey mounted a final exhibition of art work, declaring that they had all improved. Stella felt she had certainly gained confidence, but improvement? She wasn't sure. There was an American Night and a 'Grease' Night, but the highlight of this sea time was the Guest Talent Night and Stella already knew that Adam would be taking part.

About halfway into the cruise Stuart had asked for volunteers to enter a karaoke competition and in the course of dinner time conversations it had emerged that Adam had some experience of karaoke in Brighton,

"Yeah…I DJ for them quite regularly…"

"And he has a good voice," Denise conceded, obviously speaking from the experience of principal supporter on these occasions. Before the start of the competition, Stella had slipped into the club for a pre-dinner drink and saw Adam there sitting with Ray, which was unusual as he normally drank in The Nautical Bar where there was always a happy hour with half price drinks. She assumed he was there for the competition which was about to start, but just to make sure she slid across the room and leaned her elbows on the back of the banquette where he and Ray were sitting,

"I hope you are entering for this," she whispered.

"Yeah…yeah, Stella I'm gonna have a go,"

Ray turned and laughed,

"Yeah…right. Course you are," obviously thinking it was a wind-up as, not being on table 8, he didn't know about Adam's voice. Stella crept to a seat nearby and waited while Stuart went through the usual, 'It's Showtime,' routine, then introduced the panel of judges. He continued,

"Now, ladies and gentlemen, I would like to invite…" he paused, glancing down at a piece of paper, "…Adam to come up onto the stage. Please give him a huge round of applause as he opens the competition for us this evening."

Ray shot upright in his seat, while Adam ambled over and stood next to Stuart.

"Soooo, Adam, what are you going to sing for us this evening?"

Adam took hold of the microphone and Stella glanced across to where Ray's back was now arched over his knees as he cradled his head in his hands.

"I would like to sing 'Achy Breaky Heart'."

"OK, Adam, take it away."

Ray was still curled down over his knees as the introductory music throbbed round the room where quite a large audience waited expectantly. Adam started to sing and Ray slowly uncurled himself, gaping in disbelief as his friend not only sang in tune, but made a good job of interpreting the song. When he finished everyone applauded enthusiastically and Stella could see Stuart was relieved that the competition had been opened by such a competent singer.

As the applause died away, members of the judging panel were invited to comment and Stella bristled as it immediately became obvious that they had decided beforehand to playact and assume different roles. The first, a female member of the Sailaways staff, made quite reasonable observations, while the second, a young dancer, gushed over everything. The third judge was the singer, Wayne Bradley, who had obviously set himself up as the Simon Cowell of the show and did it very badly. His comments were rude, inaccurate and damming, bad enough in Adam's case but getting worse as he evening progressed.

"…and furthermore I would like to add that for someone to take part in this competition, they actually have to be able to sing in tune!" Wayne leaned back in his seat looking smug and self-satisfied, running his hand slowly through his blond, wavy hair, then turning towards the audience with a sickly smile, 'what a clever boy I am,' written all over his pasty face.

Adam took it in good part, but Stella was furious. How dare he when, as a professional singer, his own voice left a lot to be desired, and she knew that some of the people taking part had had to pluck up a lot of courage to do so. She got even more incensed as he decided to praise the second act, two young women who really couldn't sing at all. By the end of the competition it was obvious to everyone that it was a close call between Adam and a woman with a beautiful voice who had, coincidentally, played the Dame in the pantomime. But who would win? Had Warren's comments scuppered Adam's chances? When Stuart announced that first prize would be shared between Adam and Stella's opera-singing friend, it was already time for dinner and Adam, whose passion for food far out-weighed his passion for singing, was ambling at top speed out of The Club towards the dining room, pursued by Stuart trying to present him with his bottle of champagne.

Well, justice had been done and Stella sat down to dinner at table 8 with the others, congratulating Adam warmly on his achievement; but she couldn't resist sounding off on the subject of Wayne Bradley and his inane comments,

"Honestly what a prat! He just showed himself up as even more of an idiot than I already thought he was; he had no right to set himself up, humiliating people in that way. It would have been a travesty of justice if you hadn't won, Adam."

Although touched by Stella's vehemence and concern, Adam told her to cool it,

"Don't be so competitive, Stella…"

"Well, fair's fair! If they're going to make a competition of it then the right people should win…"

"…and they have…" He raised his bear paws in the air "…and now I'm a Rock God…so I'll sign autographs after dinner…but I need an agent…" he leaned towards Sheila and nudged her, "…Do you want to be my agent Sheila…? Eh…?...Eh?

Sheila giggled and Adam turned to beckon to Miguel for more food.

Out on deck the following day Ray delighted in telling the story to anyone who would listen.

"Honest…I couldn't believe it…I just couldn't believe it! I said to 'im, 'you're not gonna sing, are you?' And 'e kept saying, 'yes,' and I didn't believe 'im. Then when 'e got up, I just couldn't believe it…I was ready to be embarrassed for 'im…I just thought, 'Oh No!' and put me 'ead in me 'ands. Then when 'e started to sing I couldn't believe it; I come up like that (takes hands away from face) and thought, 'Oh…'e's really good!'"

And he was, and that's how Stella knew he would be part of the talent show taking place just before The Matisse reached Funchal, when once again he was the opening act.

CHAPTER THIRTY FIVE

Another island with an interesting history, Madeira was discovered by the Portuguese in 1419 and the early settlers soon established trading links with England, Flanders and Italy. Following an invasion in 1566 by the French pirate, Bertrand de Montluc, Madeira was occupied for sixty years; but even though Portugal came under Spanish rule in 1580, it still retained sovereignty over Madeira. In 1662, after Charles 11 had married Catherine of Braganza, Portugal granted England trading privileges in Madeira and British wine merchants settled there. In 1801 Madeira was defended by the British against possible attacks from the French, and after Napoleon invaded Portugal in 1807, the British returned and remained there for seven years. During the second half of the 19th century the island was ravaged by a series of disasters including blight that wiped out the vines and potato crop in 1852, and a cholera epidemic in 1856 during which thousands of people died.

In 1902 Madeira became self-governing and, although Portugal stayed out of World War Two, the conflict disrupted Madeira's trade. Since 1949 tourism has prospered, mainly on account of the temperate climate of the island. It has been described as 'the island of eternal spring,' as the temperature hovers constantly around 20 degrees centigrade, the sea is clean and clear and there are flowers everywhere – bougainvillaea, mimosa and jacaranda.

For the final excursion on their Round the World Adventure Freddie and Stella had booked a toboggan ride. They would be taken up a hill by coach to a place called Monte, transferred to toboggans – wicker baskets on metal runners – and guided down the hill to Livramento by two men jogging alongside. They would then visit an embroidery factory and sample some Madeira wine. But they didn't. The Matisse was late arriving and didn't drop anchor until 4.30 p.m. by which time all the excursions had been cancelled. They were offered the opportunity to go ashore by tender boat, but decided that the swift turnaround necessary to get back for the Gala New Year dinner would leave very little time for exploration.

"You know, I think we may be near enough to the UK now to be able to make telephone contact with the family."

Freddie's casual comment threw Stella into a state of high excitement,

"Come on then, let's try. Where's best…the most likely place to get a signal?"

And so it was that, consigning Madeira to a possible future pleasure, they stood side by side, leaning over the ship's rail, and enjoyed a long talk with son, daughter-in-law and grandchildren while the sun sank slowly into the sea.

"Goodbye…goodbye…see you very soon…love you lots…"

Stella was finally persuaded to ring off and, choking back a tear, watched the first pin-points of light start to flicker on in the little houses grouped along the bay. Freddie put his arm round her,

"Come on, time to get the glad rags on."

Mesmerised, totally enchanted, by the spectacle before her, Stella was once again leaning against the ship's rail and watching as the sky exploded. Twenty seven tons of fireworks from forty different sites along the shore set the night on fire. The theme was 'Legend of the Ocean,' based on the story of Atlantida, a land which was said to have joined the island of Madeira with the Azores, but apparently fell into the sea. Although this has always been thought to be a myth, recent studies by oceanographers could prove there may be some truth in it. The splashes of vivid fire and colour continued to illuminate the night sky, and Stella could see why the locals had put out into the bay in little boats, bobbing there alongside about a dozen cruise ships, most of them bigger than The Matisse. The whole show was directed towards the sea and, looking round, she realised that the Captain had done them proud by securing a really good spot from which to appreciate this amazing display to the full.

Determined to the last that the passengers would 'have a good time,' Tommy obviously believed that playing loud music and yelling non-stop into the microphone during a spectacle that needed no enhancement would add to the enjoyment of the occasion. It didn't.

"…Isn't it A-M-A-Z-I-N-G, ladies and gentlemen…have you ever seen anything like it…? What a sight…What a display…! Funchal holds the world record for the largest ever firework display on New Year's Eve in 2006 and this must come pretty close. How fantastic is this…?"

Yes, it's wonderful Tommy, now shut up and let us enjoy it! Stella could cheerfully have strangled him, especially when he went on to exhort them all to "…give everyone a BIG, SLOPPY KISS…"

Yes, we will, Tommy – it's New Year's Eve – but after the fireworks. Now shut up and let us enjoy this once-in-a-life-time-experience!

As the last of the fireworks fizzled down into the sea, they did all go round greeting each other with hugs and kisses in traditional fashion and Stella was surprised by how genuinely fond she had become of so many people in such a short time. A stranger, after all, is only a friend you haven't met yet.

CHAPTER THIRTY SIX

Four sea days to Southampton, four days in which to tie up loose ends, settle accounts, say goodbyes and savour the sights and sounds of being surrounded by sea for the last time: To walk the deck, gradually becoming aware of the need for warmer clothes, to pack bags, bulging with souvenirs and to wind down, fondly anticipating home comforts and the pleasure of seeing family and friends again. Telephone numbers and email addresses were exchanged as people vowed to stay in touch, and Stella knew she would never forget the people she had met; the shared experience meant they were now part of each other's lives.

Three more days to go and up on deck eight Jeannie was fuming. Donald, seeing that she was in a really foul mood, had gone to the Sky Bar for a lunch time drink without her,

"Will you be coming for a drink?

"No, I won't!"

She had barked and poured herself a very large glass of gin before slumping down on the bed. Donald had no idea what was wrong with her... until... just about to take the first sip of his third whisky he did something he had done ever since the day he had received it, he felt in his trouser pocket just to touch the note from Maggie. It wasn't there. He felt in the other pocket – nothing. He went hot, then cold. She couldn't have...surely Jeannie couldn't have found the message from Maggie about Jimmy's death and Rory's wedding...a message that would tell her they were still in touch. No. She would have no reason to go through his pockets. It must be in his other trousers...yes, that was it. He felt comforted. Jeannie couldn't possibly have the note; it was in his other trousers and there was obviously a different reason for her bad mood. After all, it was not as if it was a rare occurrence these days; a bout of ill-temper could be sparked by anything – a broken finger nail, running out of gin...anything really. He drained his glass and made up his mind to be especially solicitous towards her, for the rest of the day at least.

Still in their cabin, Jeannie slid off the bed and stood unsteadily beside it, carefully folding the piece of paper and slipping it into her bra. She staggered to the wardrobe and pulled out a dress to wear that evening. They would have dinner…oh yes, that in itself would surprise Donald as they didn't often go and sit in that stuffy dining room with all those boring old farts; it had been better, mind, since they'd been put on the same table as those Australians – good fun they were – but they still preferred to grab a hot dog in one of the bars. No, tonight they would be in the dining room as tonight she wanted an audience.

Donald spent longer than usual in the bar then, realising he was well on the way to being drunk, snoozed for a while in the quiet lounge before climbing up to the cabin on deck eight. Not sure whether his prolonged absence would have improved or exacerbated Jeannie's mood, he opened the door quietly and took a couple of tentative steps inside. He was totally unprepared for the greeting he received.

"Hello, darling, have you had a nice afternoon?"

Jeannie said with a smile and, walking up to him, put her arms round his neck as she kissed him on the lips.

"Aye…I have…have you?"

"Oh yes. I thought I'd freshen up a bit; in fact I'd like to go and have some dinner tonight. Is that alright?"

She was asking him? Actually asking him if it was alright, instead of telling him what they would be doing? He'd noticed the minty smell on her breath as she'd kissed him – obviously to cover the smell of alcohol (she didn't usually bother to do that) – and she was a little unsteady on her feet, but she was wearing a smart blue dress and had put on some make up. What was going on? Still, why question; she hadn't found the note and she was in a good mood. Everything was OK. Of course they could go in to dinner, it would be good to have a laugh with the

Australians, though it had to be said Jeannie liked them better than he did. They were a bit too crude for him. Still, it was a small price to pay for domestic harmony – and she hadn't found the note! Whistling, he showered and dressed for dinner.

The sixth bottle of wine was put on the table at the same time as the waiter attempted to serve desserts.

"What the hell's that? It looks like someone's boob! A boob's fallen off onto my plate. It's not yours, is it, Jeannie? Can I just have a look to see if you've lost a boob?"

One of he Australian men, who insisted he really was called Bruce, lurched towards Jeannie and tried to look down the front of her dress. Everyone at the table, with the exception of Donald, was falling about, helpless with laughter while the waiter stood looking embarrassed holding a tray full of pink cream desserts topped with cherries. Bruce looked up and, playing to the gallery, pointed and shouted,

"Look there's more…we've all got boobs for pud."

Swaying dangerously on his chair, he swerved round and waved an unsteady arm at the nearby tables, first to one side and then the other, shouting all the while,

"Hey…have you all got boobs for puds? Who's lost their boobs? We've got them on our plates…SERVED UP AS PUDS."

People turned away in disgust and attempted to ignore him, but the raucous behaviour at that table made compulsive viewing and it was impossible not to keep turning round just to see what would happen next. What did happen next was that Jeannie used this unexpected, unscripted bit of horse-play to begin putting her plan into action.

"Oh, Bruce, yes, it must be me…look…my boobs have fallen out…no, wait a minute…I didn'y have any in the first place. 'Tiny tits,' that's what they call me. But …what have I got here?" She pulled the piece of paper out of her bra with a flourish and held it up, waving it about as the Australians laughed even more heartily and Donald became increasingly ill at ease. He shifted uncomfortably in his chair as Jeannie continued,

"Donald likes tits…his little ex-wifey – Maggie – now she's got tits…comfy big tits, hasn't she, Donald? Tits to sink your face into… and I think our Donald wants to go back to those comfy big tits, don't you Donald?"

Donald stood up, and tried to take hold of Jeannie's arm,

"Come on, we've had enough…"

She shook him off,

"Had enough…? Had enough…? I've only just started." She screamed then lowered her voice to a hiss and stuck the note in his face, "Look what I found while I was going through your trouser pockets for a lighter."

She scrambled unsteadily up onto the table where she wobbled, waving the note about and screeching,

"Our Donald here has had a wee note from his wee wifey… 'Oh dearie me, my husband has died and our Rory is getting married…wouldn't you like to come…?' 'Come and see us…perhaps we can be family again…'was what she meant, wasn't it, Donald? Silly wee cow!"

As she spat out the last three words, Jeannie leaned forward towards Donald and lost her balance. She toppled off the table and Bruce caught her just before she was sick on the floor. Donald turned and walked out of the dining room. Yes, he would go to his son's wedding; he would go and see Maggie and he would do whatever it took to get her back, to try and find some peace and decency in his life before it was too late.

Two more days, only two days and then I'll never see her again. Jack sat alone in the bow of the ship staring straight ahead, watching 'The Matisse' split the grey water, turning it to a white foaming spray as they ploughed steadily on towards home. Tiny droplets touched his cheeks and he hugged his jacket round him, fervently wishing they could stay on the ship for ever if it was the only way he could be with Chrissie. What was he going home to? Yes, his house was beautiful and he was lucky to have it, but it was empty, his whole life meaningless, rattling around there on his own. He had pictured Chrissie in every room, laughing and bringing the place to life; he had seen her in the garden, redesigning it to her own taste. He'd had playful arguments in his head as they tussled over colour schemes and she proposed digging up his vegetables so that she could plant roses. He would pretend to resist her changes, but would always give in, happy to let her do anything she wanted. Happy to make her happy. He saw them laughing as he drove her to shops and garden centres where he would delight in pretending to think something was too expensive, then buy it for her. He could see the smile light up her beautiful face and his pleasure would be complete. They would find somewhere lovely and quiet for lunch then drive slowly home, enjoying the afternoon sun, sitting out on the terrace to watch it set while sipping champagne. Then he would go in and appear a few minutes later with some dainty food – the sort of thing she loved – giant prawns, thinly cut, soft brown bread and a tiny, very rich, truffle dessert, or some strawberries.

But it was no use. He knew this was all fantasy – a lovely dream that would never come true. He winced as he remembered the night he had proposed to her, sitting on the deck watching the sun sink into the sea. It was just after that catamaran ride along the coast in St. Lucia where Margie had decided to go skinny dipping. He and Jim had made jokes about it during dinner, but they had stopped when Chrissie told them about the cancer. It reminded him that life is short and full of terrible shocks as well as the occasional lovely surprise. How could he possibly have known that he would fall so deeply in love at this time of his life? What a surprise that was; so he had to ask her, had to try and see if she would consider spending whatever time they had left with him. He recalled the way Chrissie's face had clouded when he had told her how he felt and asked her to marry him. Firmly, but kindly, she had said no, and somehow he knew she was thinking of Maurice. Thanks to Maurice she was finding it difficult, maybe impossible, ever to trust another man. She had made vows which had compelled her to look after him, even after he had deserted her, and Jack sensed that she never wanted to get trapped like that again. No, he would give her the perfume he had bought for her then turn and walk away.

Lost in his reverie, he didn't hear the approaching footsteps and was only aware of someone sitting down next to him as the chair scraped against the wood of the deck. Instinctively he turned his head.

"No don't look round."

Chrissie reached out and took hold of his hand. She continued speaking, very quietly,

"I've been thinking, I'd better come and have a look at that house of yours. No…don't look round!"

Jack stared straight ahead,

"You mean for a visit?"

"Something like that." She paused, "But how would it be if the visit lasted for a very long time? Don't look round!!"

Keeping his eyes fixed firmly on the foaming sea ahead, Jack swallowed hard.

"Chrissie, the visit can last for as long as you like, and I am now going to look round."

He turned and she was smiling. He hardly dared to hope,

"Does this mean you've changed your mind and you will marry me?"

Chrissie laughed; he reminded her of a very excited little boy. She stopped laughing and looked into his eyes,

"No, Jack, I won't marry you; but if you'll have me I will come and live with you. I've been a wife, but I've never lived with a man, just as myself – women didn't do that in our day. I'd like to give it a try and we'll see what happens. What do you say?"

He leaned over and kissed her,

"I say yes."

One more day then home. Adam sat in the quiet lounge looking at the sea, not blue anymore, but grey and choppy now as England came ever nearer. He was holding a newspaper, but not reading it, preferring instead to mull over the pleasures of the cruise he had enjoyed so much, especially the food. He was just beginning to ponder on the possibility of persuading Denise that they could afford to treat themselves to another one, if they were careful with money and if she carried on working in the solicitor's office – after all she was happy enough there – when his thoughts were interrupted by a loud voice very close by.

"Eeee, I thought it were lovely…" he turned to see Edie looking down at him with an expression on her face like a proud mother whose child has just won a cup on sports day,

"…your, singing, love, at the Talent Night, I thought it were lovely. Me and Gracie both did, didn't we, chuck?"

Gracie nodded and they sat down. Adam groaned inwardly as they proceeded to yak, non-stop, about the cruise, the ship and what they were planning to do now that it was nearly over.

"I've got three more booked for this year," boomed Edie, "Three more crewses on bigger and better ships than this. It's like you're always saying, Gracie love, this one in't really mooch cop. Eeee, it'll be grand. Oh here's Stanley with me chariot. Got to go. See you later Gracie. Bye Adam."

She climbed awkwardly into her wheelchair and was pushed away through the quiet lounge by the ever-patient Stanley.

"Three more cruises…just like that," Adam mused and was surprised when Gracie declared, quite vehemently,

"That's what she thinks!"

Adam looked at her, frowning and Gracie, a little embarrassed, realised she had said too much but, oh, what the heck.

"Well, I shouldn't really tell you this, and whatever you do keep it under your hat, but I work for Social Services and I get sent on these cruises to winkle out the benefit cheats. We've got her number in more ways than one. It's amazing what they tell you when they think you're one of them"

Adam noticed that she spoke with almost no trace of the harsh, northern accent she had obviously adopted for the role and, as she stood up, she winked and smiled at him. He watched her walk across the lounge and laughed – Stella should have had her in the play! And yes, he'd keep it quiet, but only after he'd told the others on table 8 at their last dinner that evening.

Slowly, and without the razzamatazz that had attended their departure, 'The Matisse' slid quietly up to the quay and the ropes were tied for the last time. As Stella and Freddie boarded their coach they waved to Stuart, walking towards one of the others to begin his long journey back to New Zealand where he had his own TV show. He smiled and waved back, and Stella felt so glad to have had the opportunity to work with such a lovely and genuinely talented man. She thought it doubtful that their paths would ever cross again.

As they sat down, she looked out of the window and caught sight of Wayne weaving his way quickly through the crowd then, glancing up for one last time at 'The Matisse', she saw Nancy leaning over the rail looking anxiously down at the sea of people all milling around. Kieran was standing a few feet away from her, staring at the back of her head, polishing his glasses and looking miserable. Stella nudged Freddie and pointed,

"It's like that play…'In Camera,' I think it's called, by Sartre, where three people are stuck in a room and they each want the one who doesn't want them…mind you, in that case Wayne would have to fancy Kieran and I don't think that's going to happen!"

"If you say so my love," Freddie replied, in perfect imitation of Joe, the barman.

Stella's heart sank as she saw Edie, helped by Stanley, struggling up the steps of their coach. She didn't remember seeing her on the outward journey, but there would have been no reason to notice her then. Her selfishness prevailed to the very end. Their coach was crowded and many people, including Freddie and Stella, had purchased an extra bag in which to put all the treasures picked up along the way. These had to be put somewhere and the driver chose a few of the seats near the emergency exit at the back where Freddie and Stella had decided to sit as there was plenty of extra leg room.

They felt fortunate in gaining this space, even though the pile of bags grew alarmingly as more and more people boarded the coach. Several of the other passengers became concerned and wanted them to move as they were afraid the bags would fall on them. But there were no spare seats. One of the men approached Edie who had sat down in a seat by herself, relegating Stanley to the one behind, obviously deciding that, for her comfort, she needed the whole seat to herself. They exchanged a few words and the man, not someone Stella and Freddie knew well, but pleasant enough, approached them with a face like thunder.

"She won't budge, selfish cow!"

"It's really OK," Stella reassured him, hoping they could hang on to their seats as they were able to stretch their legs out almost completely straight in front of them. She also hoped the fuss wouldn't suddenly alert the driver to the health and safety aspect of their position. The man frowned,

"But we're concerned for you, Stella love, if the bus stops sudden like, you'll get crushed under all those bags...."

He turned back towards Edie and shouted,

"You're a selfish woman...you've been selfish the whole trip!"

Ignoring him, Edie looked out of the window and Freddie and Stella stayed where they were.

They didn't get crushed by an avalanche of bags and at nine o'clock that night, Freddie and Stella stood on the pavement outside their locked electric gate surrounded by ten pieces of luggage. It had been raining on and off all day and Stella looked up to see the drops reflected in the lamplight before bouncing onto the glistening pavement; the road shone like polished leather and the Church stood silent and still on the other side of the river. The holiday let next door had been occupied over Christmas and some wet rubbish swirled in the driveway making the gate difficult to open. But it did open and Stella grabbed some of the bags then followed Freddie down to their front door.

They'd done it; they'd been around the world.

Lightning Source UK Ltd.
Milton Keynes UK
UKHW011819170220
358865UK00001B/154

9 781785 077814